PRAISE FOR SARIAH WILSON

The Seat Filler

"Wilson (*Roommaid*) balances the quirky with the heartfelt in this adorable rom-com."

—*Publishers Weekly*

The Friend Zone

"Wilson scores a touchdown with this engaging contemporary romance that delivers plenty of electric sexual chemistry and zingy banter while still being romantically sweet at its core."

—*Booklist*

"Snappy banter, palpable sexual tension, and a lively sense of fun combine with deeply felt emotional issues in a sweet, upbeat romance that will appeal to both the YA and new adult markets."

—*Library Journal*

The #Lovestruck Novels

"Wilson has mastered the art of creating a romance that manages to be both sexy and sweet, and her novel's skillfully drawn characters, deliciously snarky sense of humor, and vividly evoked music-business settings add up to a supremely satisfying love story that will be music to romance readers' ears."

—*Booklist* (starred review), *#Moonstruck*

"Making excellent use of sassy banter, hilarious texts, and a breezy style, Wilson's energetic story brims with sexual tension and takes readers on a musical road trip that will leave them smiling. Perfect as well for YA and new adult collections."

—Library Journal, #Moonstruck

"*#Starstruck* is oh so funny! Sariah Wilson created an entertaining story with great banter that I didn't want to put down. Ms. Wilson provided a diverse cast of characters in their friends and family. Fans of *Sweet Cheeks* by K. Bromberg and Ruthie Knox will enjoy *#Starstruck*."

—Harlequin Junkie (4.5 stars), *#Starstruck*

The
Paid
Bridesmaid

The Paid Bridesmaid

a Novel

SARIAH WILSON

Text copyright © 2022 by Sariah Wilson
All rights reserved.

Published by Montlake, Seattle

www.apub.com

Amazon, the Amazon logo, and Montlake are trademarks of Amazon.com, Inc., or its affiliates.

ISBN-13: 9781542030564
ISBN-10: 1542030560

Cover design by Philip Pascuzzo

Printed in the United States of America

For my sister Rachel—
Until we meet again

CHAPTER ONE

"Bride or groom?" I asked the top of a man's head, plastering on my "hi, I'm sociable" smile.

He sat in a chair, texting on his phone. He was young and tall, had dirty-blond hair, and was this side of rude if he couldn't be bothered to make small talk at this event.

The man also didn't have on a name tag. Why couldn't people follow simple directions and make life easier for everyone?

"Bride or groom?" I repeated.

"I'm neither one," was his wry response and I only just refrained from injuring myself with an eye roll so massive it could be seen from space.

"I know you're not the bride or groom. I was asking if you're here with the bride's family or the groom's family." Wasn't that obvious? Was I losing my touch for making small talk at weddings? This welcome brunch was the first event of many and I was supposed to be making nice with everyone. Instead I was trying to reel in my sarcasm.

Then he glanced up at me and it was like the time when I was eleven years old on a school field trip to a petting zoo and a goat had headbutted me in the stomach.

He was fantastically attractive. Dark-green eyes, a jawline that could have cut glass, shoulders that seemed to span miles. He wore his obviously expensive suit like it was a second skin. Wow.

I drew in a shaky breath, willing my heart rate to return to normal.

That he was giving me an appreciative once-over did not help out with my current pulse problem. Especially since it felt so strange. It had been a long time since a man had looked at me that way because I put out such strong "do not disturb" vibes.

I wondered if he was imperceptive or just didn't care. He said, "I'm here with the groom. I'm the best man. Camden Lewis." He slid his phone into his pocket and offered me his hand. I hesitated a moment before taking it. I was already having an inappropriate physical reaction just to the way he looked; I couldn't imagine touching him would make things better.

Camden Lewis. I knew that name because I'd done my research. He was the groom's best friend, and the CEO of their tech company. They'd been friends since childhood, and although Sadie had shown me a picture of him, I suppose I'd been more focused on the job ahead than how attractive Camden would turn out to be.

His large hand wrapped around my palm and I nearly sighed from the tingly pleasure of his skin on mine.

Then I realized an embarrassingly long amount of time had passed and that I was still holding his strong, firm hand and hadn't told him my name yet. I was making it weird. I quickly let go and said, "Rachel Vinson. Maid of honor."

"Rachel?" he repeated, looking puzzled. "I've never heard Sadie mention you before."

That was because until a month ago the bride, Sadie Snyder, and I had never met. I told him the backstory I'd prepared for this wedding. "We're old friends. We went to summer camp together in New York when we were kids and have stayed in touch all these years."

His "hey, you're cute" look disappeared when he asked, "Really? Which one?"

"Which one what?" What was he asking me to specify? People never followed up once I'd offered my false explanation of how I knew the bride. I reached up to make sure my modified french twist was in place. It was like a piece of my armor, a way to feel professional without drawing attention to myself, but something about talking to this man made me feel a bit undone. As if a bit of that armor were slipping.

"Which summer camp?" he clarified.

"Oh. Camp, um . . ." Krista, my friend, employee, and fellow bridesmaid, had chosen a camp name that at the moment I was totally blanking on. Or maybe my brain was just distracted by the magnetism he seemed to be emitting. As he stood there staring at me politely, clearly expecting a response, I thought back to the airplane ride where Krista and I had been discussing the poor state of airline snacks and how she had mentioned the name, and the answer came back in a rush. "Oheneya. Camp Oheneya."

"I've never heard of it."

Given that it was made up, I didn't expect that he would. "It's a tiny family-run place. I think it closed down a few years ago."

That puzzled look was back. "And Sadie went there? To a sleepaway camp? Aren't those usually expensive? Dan mentioned that she didn't have any money growing up."

That would be Dan Zielinski, the groom. Who presumably knew Sadie better than anyone in the world. I fixed my fake smile back on my face. She should have mentioned her upbringing to me when we were coming up with our backstory. I'd told her there couldn't be any surprises.

Surprise!

Instead of answering I said, "Speaking of Dan, there he is." I'd always found distraction to work best when nearly being caught in a lie. I expected to see Sadie with her groom-to-be, but he had an older woman on his arm who was wearing a colorful scarf on her head.

"Is that Dan's mother?" I asked. Sadie had definitely mentioned Irene. She was being treated for breast cancer and had recently gone through a round of chemo. The doctor was uncertain of her future prospects. They had hope, but there was a possibility that this might be her last family event. It was important to both Sadie and Dan that everything go off without a hitch.

Which meant I was going to have to find a way to manage Camden Lewis and his pesky questions.

"It is. I should join them." He stood up, started to walk away, and then stopped. "You and I should get together later and talk about our mutual responsibilities. Maybe tonight at the cocktail party?"

"Sure," was what I actually said. What I wanted to say was, *I plan on spending this entire week avoiding you, thank you very much.* He seemed the naturally suspicious type and I did not need that in my life right now.

Sadie was a huge client, not only because she had five million followers on Instagram, but because she had an impressive network of fellow influencers just like her, young women who were on the cusp of getting married in the near future and might need professional bridesmaids and maids of honor. It was a fantastic opportunity for my business.

"Nice to meet you," he said.

I nodded, not quite able to say the same. I'd developed a good instinct for people at weddings who would be an issue for me, and this guy was trouble with a capital *T*.

In no small part because for the first time in forever, I wanted to bend my no-mixing-business-and-pleasure rule. It was the most important rule that I had for myself, and while I wouldn't do anything to jeopardize my company or the women who worked for me, I felt a bit tempted.

Especially once I saw the smile of delight on Dan's mother's face at seeing Camden. Their entire interaction was so sweet. I thought of what she had gone through and resolved to do my best to ensure that she had a good time during this week. There was a bridal shower scheduled for tomorrow, and I made a mental note to sit next to Irene and do whatever I could to help her have fun.

As a camera operator nearly slammed into me, I reminded myself that Dan's mom wasn't the only parent I was going to need to concern myself with. Sadie's mother and stepfather had gone through a nasty divorce and hated one another. Sadie had made a throwaway comment that her mom, Brandy, tended to get drunk and make scenes. I needed to keep an eye out.

Especially since every moment of this wedding was being broadcast live to Sadie's Instagram account. She was a lifestyle, fashion, and travel influencer. She was giving her fans full access to all of the activities, and I heard the director sending two of the camera crew in opposite directions to prepare for Sadie's arrival. The director wanted her to make a grand entrance at every event, wearing a different couture gown from her fashion designer sponsor.

My gaze traveled back to Camden. My brain told me he was a threat, but the rest of me had other ideas about what it'd like to do both to and with him. I figured this was obviously a sign that I needed to get out there and be dating more. I'd been so focused on building up my company that I hadn't had time for relationships.

Maybe it was time to correct that. After this destination wedding came to an end. I averted my gaze to look out the floor-to-ceiling windows at the white sand beach, palm trees, and turquoise water in the bay just outside the hotel. I brushed my fingers against the pink-and-white floral lei around my neck. I'd always wanted to go to Hawaii, and it was living up to all of my expectations. If I closed my eyes, I could almost smell the salt air of the ocean beckoning me outside.

Despite the gorgeous scenery just a few steps from this room, I couldn't help but look back at Camden, who was laughing, again. Somehow the joy on his face made him more attractive.

"Who is that?" Krista asked as she sidled up next to me and handed me a mimosa. I took it but didn't drink it. I'd never been much of a drinker and so I tried to steer clear of it while I was working. Falling down drunk at a reception would have ruined my reputation.

My initial instinct was to pretend like I had no idea who she was talking about. I chided myself for being so obvious in paying attention to him. "Camden Lewis. He's the best man."

"I agree. He is definitely the best man here," she said with a wink. "They should serve him up as a dish at this fancy welcome brunch." She reached out to grab one of the sandwiches. "Seriously, look at this thing. Have you ever seen anything more perfectly cut?"

I nodded in agreement. The hotel was another one of Sadie's sponsors. Every single aspect of her wedding had a corporate sponsor—from her shoes to the travel to the alcohol—and the camera crew was here to capture every moment for all her fans, who wanted to be just like her and would go to the same hotel and buy the same jewelry and order from the same bakery that did her wedding cake.

As far as I knew, she and Dan weren't spending any of their own money on this wedding.

Other than what she was paying me.

"The food is fancy," I agreed.

"All of this is over the top. I mean, the party I had after I got engaged was my wedding."

Krista surprised me. She never mentioned her ex-husband, and certainly not in a joking way like this. "This is the gig. And speaking of abusive jerks from your past, are you staying away from the cameras?"

"Yes, Mother Hen." She gave me a slightly impatient smile. "I've told you, you don't have to protect me. I'm fine. Even if I'm on camera,

I don't worry about him anymore. Things have been changing for me recently. Did I tell you I went out on a date last week?"

That made me almost giddy with joy. Krista deserved the absolute best. "You did?"

"I did." She looked very pleased with herself. "But when I tried to describe to him what we do—I wish you could have seen his face. I said women pay us to pretend to be their bridesmaids so that when they get married it looks like they have more friends than they do. He didn't get why that mattered."

It mattered because every woman who hired us was looking for help. Either she didn't have close friends or the groom had more groomsmen than she had bridesmaids and she wanted to balance it out or she was looking for a professional to handle all the small but important details. For someone who would support her emotionally and physically (I had become a true expert at holding a bride's gown while she peed). It was not uncommon for women of this generation not to have any true friends. Or like in Sadie's case, to have one really close friend who had screwed them over. Her former best friend had exploited Sadie's fame and used it to get her own following. Sadie had a hard time letting people in since then.

More often than not, the brides who hired us wanted a grown-up in their party to keep an eye on unruly family members (Sadie's mom) or to manage rowdy bridesmaids. Unlike them, we would not be trying to hook up with a groomsman or going on a bender.

Sort of like Sadie's third bridesmaid, her cousin Mary-Ellen, who I'd noted was currently on her third mimosa. I was going to have to remind her to eat something and/or escort her from the brunch if she didn't slow down.

"Is that Camden guy single?" Krista asked and I arched a single eyebrow at her. She sighed. "I know, I know, no messing around with guests at weddings. It just seems like a shame."

It was a sentiment my mother wholeheartedly shared. She'd been devastated when I'd left my cushy finance job and started working as a bridesmaid for hire. Until she decided that weddings were the perfect place for me to meet Mr. Right, despite me telling her it wasn't going to happen.

She was fervent in her belief that I would catch the bouquet and everything would magically fall into place. I let her live in her fantasy world because it just wasn't worth the argument.

Krista kept talking. "Your rule doesn't mean that I can't appreciate that delicious man. And you can deny it, but I saw you checking him out, too. If this was any other situation, I would tell you to leap on him like a cheetah on a sickly gazelle."

"That's a lovely image," I said and, without thinking, took a sip of my mimosa. I immediately spit it back into my glass.

"People are going to think you're pregnant. Or Mormon," she told me with a laugh.

"I don't care what other people think." And I wasn't about to start now. "We're here to do a job, and that's all that matters."

She put on her serious face. "Right. Sorry. It's just so beautiful here that it's easy to get caught up in the fantasy. Should we even be talking to each other? Since we're trying to be undercover?"

"We're both bridesmaids." I was technically the maid of honor, but she knew what I meant. "Which would mean we're both friends of Sadie's, so it would make sense that we're friendly. Although we should probably be mingling with the other guests."

"Sure thing, boss."

It was such a plum assignment—a week in Hawaii for the wedding festivities—that I'd chosen Krista to come with me. She'd been my first employee when I'd started my business. Escaping a terrible marriage, she'd sought refuge in the relative anonymity of what we did, as we moved from one wedding to another. Most of my employees had similar stories. I made it a point to hire women who needed second chances.

Just like I'd needed one.

These days Krista did most of the administrative work, but she still stepped in as a bridesmaid from time to time. She was also my research guru, and while she excelled at coming up with believable backstories, she wasn't so great at remembering them.

Which is why I told her, "Don't forget that your last name is Richter." I had asked her to use an alias so that her ex-husband wouldn't be able to locate her.

"Yep. Off to lie to everybody," she said cheerfully.

"It's not a lie . . ." I let my voice trail off and didn't finish with my usual "we're protecting people" because she was busy mumbling "Richter, Richter, Richter" to herself.

I sighed. That wasn't at all suspicious. I hoped Camden didn't notice.

Because I'd signed a non-disclosure agreement as thick as my wrist. My company couldn't take the financial hit if Krista or I revealed that we didn't actually know Sadie. Not to mention how Sadie's former friend had betrayed her—there was no way I would do the same thing. I'd keep her secrets safe.

Speaking of the bride-to-be, there was a commotion at the door and Sadie strolled in. She wore a lace crop top and a matching long white skirt. She looked breezy and effortless even though I knew she'd just spent hours getting her hair and makeup done and that the outfit she was currently wearing had been custom tailored for her by Stefan, the representative from the designer label.

She seemed to be glowing, and that only intensified when she saw her groom. I'd liked Sadie as soon as I met her, and I considered myself a pretty good judge of character. She was sweet and caring, and one of the most single-minded and determined people I'd ever met (a trait I admired and shared).

Plus, she was actually in love with Dan. It probably seemed like a foregone conclusion, but when you were in my line of work you saw everything. From the couples who were madly in love that you knew would stay together until they died, to the people who openly hated each other yet still got married. I'd also helped more than one bride flee.

It made my job more enjoyable when the couple were blissfully happy like Sadie and Dan. It apparently had been an extremely short courtship and engagement—she'd confided in me that they'd both known the first night they met that they were meant to be together.

As he leaned her back and kissed her to the crowd's delight, I tried not to let out a little sigh of jealousy. Despite what I said to my mom, I did want that for myself.

I'd add that to my master to-do list. *Find a soul mate.*

Easy enough.

I turned around and dished up a small plate of food for Sadie. In my experience so many brides forgot to eat at events like this one—I'd had several faint on me. It was my job to look after her when she was too busy to look after herself.

With my plate in hand, I approached her group, saying hello. Sadie hugged me and then quickly introduced me to Dan and Irene. When she got to Camden, he had a weird look on his face and announced, "We've met."

"Here." I gave Sadie the food. "I wanted you to eat something."

"Thank you! That's so thoughtful!"

Although I wasn't making eye contact with him, I could feel Camden's gaze on me. It wasn't in a sexy way, like he found me attractive and couldn't stop himself from looking at me. More like he was a highly skeptical person and I'd accidentally tripped his danger alarms. I again resolved to spend the rest of this week ignoring him. Starting with right now.

"You're welcome!" I told her. "Can I steal you away for a minute?"

Dan said, "Only for one minute. I can't stand to be away from her for much longer than that."

He was so sincere in his adoration that I didn't even feel the urge to roll my eyes. It was sweet. Sadie and Dan kissed quickly before she and I moved over to a corner of the room. I wondered if she knew how fortunate she was to have a guy like Dan, who clearly worshipped her.

"I'm the luckiest girl in the world!" she said with a sigh, as if she'd known exactly what I was thinking. "And everything is almost perfect, except . . ."

She dipped a celery stick in ranch sauce and I was super impressed when she ate it without spilling a drop. If I'd been wearing a white outfit I guarantee I'd have decorated the front of it with ranch dressing.

I wondered what Camden Lewis would think of me then. I glanced at him again, and he was still studying me. I forced myself to focus all of my attention on Sadie and what she was trying to say.

I prompted her, "Except?"

"My mom. She took a Xanax on the plane because she doesn't like flying. She's sleeping it off in her hotel room." She was striving for a light tone, but I could see from the way the corners of her mouth tugged down how upset she was. I didn't know if that was from her mother not being at this event, or from her taking too much prescription medication.

"Don't worry about it. I've got you and I'm on Brandy-watch. Everything will be fine."

She smiled at me, but it didn't quite reach her eyes. "You know you don't have to do that, right? I brought you here to be in my pictures and videos. You don't have to be my mom's babysitter."

I nodded. I could be in pictures and help keep an eye on her mother. "I know."

"Good. I want this to be a magical experience for everyone that attends. Including you. Maybe you'll meet someone."

I would not look at Camden again. "Doubtful."

"Sorry, but I'm that annoying bride that is so happy I'm determined to make sure everyone else is happy, too."

"I'm happy."

Are you, though? my mother's voice said inside my head and the sound of it weakened my resolve, having me glancing over at Camden again. Sadie seemed to notice and said, "Maybe you could be happier. I don't know how much I told you about Camden before but he is so smart and nice and I think the two of you would really hit it off."

Unless by *hit it off* she meant a mini-interrogation and suspicion, she was going to be disappointed. I recognized that matchmaking tone in her voice. I'd heard it nonstop for the last three years from my mom.

I settled on "Who knows?" That was neutral enough and noncommittal. "He asks a lot of questions." Invasive, personal questions.

"Oh," she said with a wave of her free hand, "that's just Camden. He treats life like it's some big puzzle that he's going to solve. Seriously, though, you should give it a shot. I think you might like him."

Instead of telling her how wrong she was, I did what I do best. I nodded and smiled. She was the bride and it was my job to do whatever she wanted and needed, even if I thought it was stupid.

Because nothing was going to happen between me and Camden Lewis, no matter how much Sadie wanted it to.

CHAPTER TWO

After the brunch ended I went back to my hotel room to get ready for the cocktail party that evening, or the "Booze and Board Games Extravaganza," as it was listed on my schedule. Apparently a game manufacturer was sponsoring the event, along with Sadie's top-shelf liquor sponsor.

The schedule was conveniently located in the welcome bag provided to all the guests. It reminded me a bit of my bridesmaid emergency pack that I took with me everywhere. Their bag had an intertwined *D* and *S* embroidered on one side. Along with the schedule, the bag also had a bottle of wine, bags of macadamia nuts, dried pineapple chips, aspirin, a few Band-Aids, a coconut and lime–scented candle, sunscreen, bottled water, lip balm, and breath mints, all of it elegantly matching and sporting the wedding's two hashtags—#DanAndSadie and #SadieMarriedLady, which was apparently in reference to a song from a musical I'd never heard of before.

I threw out the paper schedule and grabbed my laminated copy from my purse. Sadie had given it to me two weeks ago and I'd laminated it immediately, as every good outline should be.

Then I reached for my cell phone. I texted Sadie to see if she needed anything. She responded quickly, saying she was happily spending time with her future husband. I dropped the phone on my bed. Some jobs I was busy every minute of every day during the festivities and then there were other ones like this, where I was obviously going to have a lot of downtime to do what I wanted.

Letting myself out onto my balcony, which overlooked the ocean, I figured there were worse places to be stuck with my own thoughts.

After appreciating the view for a few minutes, I went back in and decided to take a shower. It might have been paradise, but this island had a humidity level I was unaccustomed to. The cool water helped.

Wrapped up in my fluffy white robe, I went back out to the balcony with my laptop. It had occurred to me while showering that I needed a bit more information on Camden. Knowledge was power, right?

I sent texts to Krista and to our IT manager, Taimani. I asked them to find out what they could about him. Krista sent me several suggestive emojis, but I replied that it was work-related.

Within a few minutes I had links to articles about him. Things I already knew. He was the CEO of the company he and Dan had started. He'd grown up in California, like me. I was an LA girl, and he had lived in a little town north of San Francisco.

But nothing else. He had no social media at all, which seemed strange.

I didn't, either, but I had a good reason for it.

There were several images of him at charity events with Dan that I may or may not have examined very thoroughly.

For professional reasons.

And as I sat there and thought of him, I wondered if he was thinking about me. The idea that he might be made my skin inexplicably goose-bumpy.

Why had he asked so many questions about how I knew Sadie? Maybe he was just a curious person, as she'd suggested. Or maybe he was trying to look out for Dan and Sadie. Thinking I might be someone from her past wanting to take advantage of her, as so many of her family members seemed intent on doing.

That made some sense, but as far as he knew I was one of her best friends and wanted only good things for her. So why the third degree?

I supposed it didn't matter. I had no intention of talking to him again, just nodding at him politely across the aisle as Dan and Sadie said their "I dos."

Glancing at my laptop's clock, I realized it was time to get ready. I pinned up my dark hair and headed over to the closet to grab my sparkly burgundy cocktail dress. Over the years I'd amassed quite a collection of dresses—everything from informal to ball gowns. I'd packed several cocktail dresses for this trip, along with some sundresses. It was funny, but as a little girl I'd loathed being put in a dress. I had wanted jeans or nothing. But as I'd grown older, I'd come to love the way dresses made me feel, like the femininity of a skirt swirling around my legs.

I put on some matching lipstick, a little bit of mascara, and grabbed my purse. I double-checked to see that the keycard was in my purse pocket before heading to the door. I'd locked myself out of my own room more than once and didn't want to repeat that particular experience. I went into the hallway and tugged on my door, making sure it was shut.

The door right next to mine swung open, and I jumped slightly when Camden walked out.

And despite the fact that I'd just spent a good amount of time drooling over pictures of him, seeing him in person again sent little jolts of awareness through me.

He grinned at me and the sight of his smile nearly bowled me off my feet. His hair was slightly damp, as if he'd just gotten out of the shower. He smelled amazing, all clean and yummy.

"Looks like we're neighbors," he said.

"Yep." Well, that was just perfect and what I absolutely needed. To go to sleep at night knowing that a man who I'd marked as off limits was right next door.

I tried holding my breath so that I wouldn't draw any more of his scent into my rebellious nose.

It didn't work.

He took a step toward me and my treacherous body leaned toward him in response. "Are you headed to the party?" he asked.

"Yep," I said again. He was going to think I was so brilliant and witty with my inability to form complete sentences and the way I kept repeating the same one-syllable sound.

None of this seemed to be a deterrent to him and he flashed that should-be-illegal grin at me again. "Should we go down together?"

"Oh. No. I can't. I have to go, um . . ." Where was I heading and what was I going to do when I got there? His eyes were like grass fields in spring in Ireland. How was I supposed to think? "Upstairs. I've got to go check on . . . someone first." I'd nearly told him I was going to see how Brandy was doing. Sadie's mother's drunkenness was something Sadie wanted to keep quiet and I'd nearly hinted to him that something was amiss.

I expected him to pounce all over it and ask me a bunch of follow-up questions. Instead he leaned against the wall in this . . . lounge-y way and for some inexplicable reason I found it extremely attractive.

His voice had gone soft and low. "Then I guess I'll have to catch up with you later."

Without waiting for an answer, he reached out to take a piece of lint from my sleeve. Even though he didn't make any skin-to-skin contact, my skeleton nearly jumped out of my body.

Where had this flirtatious creature come from?

Then he *winked* at me. I'd never been winked at before.

When I didn't respond, too caught up in my openmouthed shock, he added, "Save me a dance?"

He walked off toward the elevators and now I was the one leaning hard against the wall, my hand over my fluttering stomach.

What the what? Where had that come from? I'd been ready for him to grill me and instead he winked at me?

My ovaries just did not know how to take that.

I waited for a minute or two until I was certain he was gone. When I reached the elevator bank, I let out a sigh of relief that he wasn't waiting for me. I was supposed to be shutting this guy down and it was like he'd completely changed his entire approach toward me and I didn't understand any of it. He was giving me a serious case of whiplash.

As I got onto the elevator, I wondered if this was Sadie's doing. She'd been not so subtly encouraging me to go out with him . . . maybe she'd done the same thing to him?

Even if she did interfere, isn't it a good thing when a handsome man flirts with you? my inner-Mom Voice asked me and I did my best to ignore it.

Besides, it didn't really make sense. Most men, when they discovered they were being set up, tended to run in the opposite direction. Was I supposed to believe that Camden was the one guy in the universe who said, "Yes, my best friend's fiancée, I would like you to arrange for me to date that woman I've never met and maybe fall in love with her and have a wedding just like yours."

Ridiculous.

If Camden Lewis enjoyed solving puzzles as Sadie had said, maybe he enjoyed being one, too. I just didn't have the time to try to figure him out.

Brandy's room was two floors above mine. I knocked on her door and heard a heavy thud and a muttering voice. A few seconds later her door was thrown open in a dramatic fashion.

"Can I help you?" Sadie's mom asked, slurring her words. She had her robe loosely tied and her face felt familiar. She had the same delicate features as Sadie, the same honey-blonde hair that I'd assumed was from a bottle.

The similarities ended there. Currently the stench of booze oozing out of Brandy's pores was overpowering. I could see dozens of tiny, empty alcohol bottles on the floor. I wondered if, when the hotel had agreed to comp these rooms as part of their sponsorship, they'd factored in the thousands of dollars Brandy was going to run up from her mini-bar in her apparent quest to drown her liver.

"We met earlier. I'm Rachel. Sadie's maid of honor? I told her I'd walk down with you to the party."

"I'm tired. I'm going to bed."

She shut the door on me and I heard it lock. Then there was another loud thump, some cursing, and another thump. I knocked again.

"Are you sure you don't need anything?" I asked loudly.

But Brandy didn't come back to the door. For a moment I wasn't sure what to do, but figured it was better to let her sleep this off than drag her to a party where she most definitely would not be on her best behavior.

I headed to the cocktail party, which was on the south lawn. Music was playing and several tables had been set up, covered in white linen tablecloths. Tiki torches outlined the area and a DJ was playing easy-listening music in the corner. An employee offered me a lei and I ducked my head to let her put it on and thanked her.

Right away I noticed Dan and Sadie talking to Camden. First I wondered why she was here already without making an entrance. But considering how annoyed the filming director looked, I assumed she'd blown that off. Camden ran his fingers through his hair and then laughed and that heavy fluttering was back in my stomach.

Wrenching my gaze away, I spotted Krista, who was deep in conversation with an older couple. Her face was animated and lively as she told a story. It made my heart happy; when I'd first known her she'd tried so hard to make herself small, to not be noticed. Now that she felt safe and secure, she was a freaking delight.

I couldn't put her and her employment / my business in jeopardy for someone like Camden.

Troy breezed past me and called out, "Find your name, the games are about to begin!"

At every table a different board game was set up for four people, and there were name cards at each chair. I started looking for my name, figuring I would be seated close to the front with the bridal party.

Sure enough, I was at Table 2. I was about to sit down when I noticed that Camden's name card was set up right next to mine.

So was this a "you're the maid of honor and he's the best man" kind of situation, or was Sadie taking this matchmaking thing too far?

Either way, it wasn't conducive to my plans. I grabbed his name card, planning on finding Krista's and switching them so that I'd at least get to spend the evening with her by my side.

"What are you doing with my name card?"

Obviously, I was going to get caught. Because this was how things worked for me. I placed the name card back down, sighed, and closed my eyes, asking the universe for strength, before turning around to face Camden.

He looked amused. "In case you didn't hear me, what were you doing with my name card?"

Moving you to another table. "Looking for you to make sure you knew where you were sitting."

"That was thoughtful of you." His words sounded nice, but his tone let me know that he did not believe me. As well he shouldn't. He gestured toward the set-up board game on the table, one I'd loved as a kid and had sometimes even played by myself because I was an only child. He tacked on, "I thought maybe you were afraid of a little competition."

"Ha." I actually said *ha*. "If I run into any, I'll let you know."

He gave me a wolfish grin and sat in his chair. "In that case, let's play. And please know that I'm going to destroy you."

"Not in this lifetime. I'm a gaming master."

"I can't wait to see how well that works for you in a game based on chance."

"Be prepared to be blown away," I told him.

"So long as you get ready to be blown away by how badly I'm going to beat you," was his sardonic response.

My blood pumped hard at the idea of him challenging me. I had been overly competitive my entire life. Like, it had cost me friendships and relationships. I was better as an adult, but I could not resist a gauntlet being thrown down.

Not good. I needed a distraction. Maybe we'd have engaging game partners in the two other chairs and my hormones could stop jumping up and down at the idea of sitting next to Camden. Especially once he scooted his chair closer to mine so that our knees brushed. I couldn't help it, I reflexively jerked my knee straight up at the electric sensation, ramming into the table and nearly knocking all of the board game pieces over.

"Are you okay?" he asked and I just pretended like I didn't hear him.

My hopes that I'd have a good distraction and some conversation were dashed a moment later when we were joined by Dan's aunt and uncle. After introducing themselves, they started murmuring things to each other under their breath, like they were having an argument that had been going on for twenty years. They were far more interested in the custom drinks that had been named after Dan and Sadie.

I was distracted from their silent disdain when Troy grabbed the DJ's microphone and announced, "Now that everyone's in their seats, let's play!"

The unspoken fight between the couple across from us apparently escalated as the wife stood up suddenly, knocking over her chair in the process. She stomped off, her husband trailing behind her and calling her name.

Leaving us alone.

"What color would you like to be?" Camden asked me.

"Red." I was always red.

"I'll be blue. You can go first. Also, in case I didn't tell you earlier, you look very pretty."

I was in the middle of reaching for a card when he said that and I paused. It had been so long since a man had said anything like that to me that I didn't know how to respond.

I went with, "Um, thank you?" My mom had always taught me to accept a compliment, but at the same time, I didn't want to encourage whatever he was doing. Mostly because I didn't have a handle on myself when it came to him. I was far too intrigued.

One of the hotel employees stopped at our table, offering Camden a shell-and-bead lei. After she'd put it around his neck he turned to me with a huge smile on his face.

"If you make a joke about getting lei'd, this conversation is over," I warned him.

"I wouldn't dream of it," he said but his grin told me he'd at least considered it. He wore the gleeful expression of a naughty boy who had plotted a scheme but called it off at the last minute. And I found that endearing when I shouldn't have.

Turning over my card, I moved my red token five spots on the board. "I already have a dad for those kinds of jokes."

"You're lucky." His tone made me want to question what he meant, but I reminded myself that I wasn't interested in him or his life and was just trying to make it through this week. Before I could say anything in response he went on. "I tried looking up that camp of yours. Where is it again?"

Were we really back to this? "Upstate New York."

Camden took his turn and moved three spots. He asked, "Where specifically?"

We were playing more than one kind of game here. Was this what he was up to? Trying to lure me into a false sense of security and then springing questions on me? To his credit, it felt a little like it might work. But I was stronger than that. "I don't give out that kind of background detail. It might be one of my security questions for a website where I've forgotten the login."

"Is it a security question?" he asked as I skipped my token ahead six spaces. "Do you think I'm going to hack into your bank accounts?"

"I don't because I'm not going to give out personal information like that."

This seemed to amuse him as I again tried to figure out what he was up to. His arm brushed against mine as he moved his token, and it sent tiny shock waves of electricity dancing along my nerves.

I pulled my arm away, feeling ridiculous. That know-it-all grin was on his face, like he knew exactly what had just happened. Now I was irritated. Maybe it was time for me to go on the offensive instead of passively waiting for his next question or a further attempt to make my knees go weak.

"What is it that you do?" I asked. I knew, but he didn't know that I did.

A strange expression crossed his face. "Why do you want to know what I do?"

"Um, it's a common question that people ask one another. It's also your chance to brag if you've got a great job and you're that kind of guy."

"I work at a tech company."

Well, that was underselling what he did. It made me like him more—that he hadn't tried to impress me when he could have.

"What about you?" he asked. "What do you do?"

"Event coordinator." It was my standard response.

"Are you working at this event?" His question was pointed, calculated sounding. Did he suspect what I really did?

"No, I'm just here for Sadie and to celebrate her special day. I think Troy's doing an amazing job. It's nice to not have to be the one in charge." That was a package we offered brides—we would plan their entire event and be by their side for every decision they had to make and then ensure the day went smoothly. I had, from time to time, been an event coordinator. So, not a lie. Technically.

Camden's expression made me feel like a big old fibber, though. His phone buzzed and he pulled it out of his pocket, glancing at it. "Excuse me a second."

He had an actual flip phone. Why would a tech CEO have a relic older than my mom?

As he stood up I said, "Okay, but I hope you tell whoever's on your call from the ancient past that I'm definitely winning."

He grinned at me, seeming to enjoy both my joke about his phone and how I was going to beat him. "We'll see about that."

I watched as he walked into the darkness, past the lighted torches, and wondered who was on the other line.

I also wondered why I was spending so much time interacting with and thinking about a man that I was never going to see again after this week ended.

Instead of watching him pace back and forth while he talked, I decided to check my own phone.

Where there were thirteen missed text messages from my mother.

I let out a groan. This was not going to be pleasant.

CHAPTER THREE

I didn't bother reading her texts; I didn't need to. They would all be some variety of Call me right away! If I didn't respond to her soon, she'd start calling me. Nonstop. I was about two more texts away from that happening.

If I'd been able to, I would have just turned off my phone. I couldn't, though, because we had two of our staff working as bridesmaids at an event in New Jersey with a bride who was, shall we say, very enthusiastic about perfection. I took pride in coaching them through her drama because I was something of a bridezilla whisperer.

But it meant I was available to my mom, as well.

I dialed her number and she somehow picked up before it even rang on my end.

"Rachel! Where have you been? I've been trying to reach you!"

"I'm working," I told her, glancing around to make sure that no one could overhear me.

"Oh! Right. In Hawaii. How is it?"

"It's beautiful here. You and Dad should come visit."

She let out a sigh of disgust. "I didn't mean the scenery. I meant the men. Are there any attractive, eligible men there?"

I couldn't help it. My gaze was drawn to Camden, still engrossed in his own conversation.

Unfortunately, my mother correctly interpreted my momentary silence. "There is! What is his name?"

I sighed. It truly wasn't worth the fight. "His name is Camden. He works in tech."

"So he's smart. That's good. Then my grandchildren will be smart."

I'd been a late-in-life baby. My parents had suffered from infertility and then my mother miraculously got pregnant with me when she was thirty-nine years old. I was apparently their reason for existing, and there had never been such helicopter parenting as I had growing up. They thought every fever meant I had meningitis and every bruise must mean internal organ failure. I was pretty sure they were the reason my pediatrician had been able to buy a second home in Aspen.

"Mom, I just met Camden. No one is giving you grandchildren."

"I know! That's the problem!" she said in an exasperated tone.

Because she'd been older when she had me, that meant all of her peers not only had grandchildren, but some of them even had teenage grandkids. For some reason this made my mom desperate and she'd been pushing me since my twenty-first birthday four years ago to fall in love and have babies as soon as possible.

I pointed out to her once that even if I did find a guy, I might have the same fertility issues she'd had. That conversation had not gone over well.

When I didn't respond she added on, "I'm not getting any younger and neither are you."

I was only twenty-five but she acted like I was close to retirement age. "So, Mom, other than me depriving you of babies, how are things going?"

"Oh no, you don't get to change the subject on me. I want a picture of this Camden. I need to see what we're working with here."

Closing my eyes, I counted silently to ten. No wonder I was so good with demanding brides—my mom could be the worst. "I'm not taking a picture of him."

"Please send your poor, deprived mother just one picture. I spent thirty-seven hours in labor with you."

I could feel the guilt trip coming on, and I wasn't interested in booking passage. I didn't need the laundry list of all the ways I'd made her suffer before I was even born.

"Fine," I grumbled. "Hold on." Better to give in to this small bit of madness than for her to escalate things. I looked up to see where Camden had gone, but he wasn't on his phone.

I had one heart-stopping moment where I was terrified he'd returned to the table and was standing behind my chair listening to every word, but when I turned around he was talking to Dan's mom, Irene, at the next table over. I let out a sigh of relief and then got up to walk past him, turning my phone at the last second to catch him laughing. I checked the photo, seeing that his face was mostly visible if a bit blurry, and sent it off to my mom.

"Done," I told her as I headed to the outskirts of the party, not wanting anyone to overhear. I'd lost track of Camden once; I didn't need it to happen again. One of the camera crew had pointed his camera at me, and I put my hand up in front of my face so they'd stop filming me.

"How do I find it again?" she asked. I had to walk her through how to put me on speaker and then scroll to her messages to find the photo.

"Well, he's handsome!" she declared. "I approve."

Just what I'm living for. Your approval of a relationship that's not happening. I smiled, even though she couldn't see me. I'd read once that your tone changed when you smiled. "It was so great catching up with you but I need to go and get something for the bride to eat."

"It feels like you're trying to get off the phone with me."

I am, I wanted to say, trying to ignore the hurt in her voice. It was a lot of pressure being a long-waited-for child. I headed to the dessert table, piled a plate with chocolate-covered strawberries, and then brought it to Sadie. There. Not a lie.

She smiled up at me, saw I was on my phone, and said softly, "Come find me later. There's something I need to tell you."

I nodded to show that I'd heard, and was about to ask her what was going on when the director came over, wanting to set up some shots of Dan and Sadie playing the games.

So instead I told my mother, "I really do need to get back to this party."

"Are you taking fish oil? You need those omega-3s for fertility. And you should probably be taking folic acid, too. Just in case."

If they gave out medals for patience, I should have been awarded the Purple Heart. "I haven't even kissed him."

"I have faith in you! Use your wit and beauty. Go get him!"

"Bye, Mom." I hung up my phone. That woman had no boundaries whatsoever. I looked at my calendar and realized it was the night for my dad's weekly poker game with his buddies. He was usually the voice of semi-reason and had the effect of helping to dial back most of my mom's obsessiveness.

I went back to my table and saw Camden seated there, shuffling the deck of cards.

"What are you doing?" I asked. He set the cards back in their spot on the board.

"Nothing." He gave me a sheepish look and I sat down next to him, not able to hide my grin. I grabbed the cards and started tabbing through them. Every other one was a large number.

"You're cheating," I said. This should have upset me, but it tickled me. That he was so desperate to beat me that he'd resort to cheating. And doing it so openly and badly was just icing on the cake.

"I'm not cheating," he responded in a tone that was both indignant and teasing. "I'm just . . . giving myself a strategic advantage."

"You were literally stacking the deck in your favor. Do you know what this means? It means you know I'm better at this game than you. I don't even need to actually win at this point because I've already beaten you."

He grinned at me, his green eyes dancing with delight. That surprised me. I'd dated a guy in college who was competitive, too, but in an ugly way. If I'd accused him of cheating, he would have thrown the cards to cover up what he'd done or gotten up and sulked for two hours while I tried to make things better. I'd told myself that I'd never date another competitive guy again, but I appreciated that Camden was willing to own his competitive streak and somehow managed to make his cheating seem playful. That he seemed to thoroughly enjoy that I challenged him. I probably shouldn't have thought that was cute, but I did.

I could date a guy like him.

No, you cannot, I told whatever inside me had come to that conclusion.

It was hard to remember that as he leaned in toward me, and I got a whiff of that delicious clean smell. I swallowed hard as he said flirtatiously, "You caught me. I hate to lose. But the game's not over. Nobody's beaten anyone yet."

"Semantics," I replied, with a wave of my hand, willing him to not come any closer. "Potato, tomato."

He looked amused. "What? That's not how the saying goes."

"It should be because do you know anyone who says poe-*tah*-toe? No. Everyone I've ever met pronounces it exactly the same. So, *potato, tomato* has always made more sense to me. Two different items that sound alike."

"You surprise me. You seem like the type to be a stickler for saying things correctly. I like that."

I shrugged, inwardly delighted at the idea that he liked something about me.

"It's the third time tonight you surprised me. The first was when you brought Sadie some food. It's very cool of you to look after her that way."

"It's my job." The words fell out of my mouth before I could stop them, as I felt all warm and fuzzy inside that he'd been paying attention to me. I pressed my lips together. What was it about this man that made my tongue so loose? I was usually the best at hiding this stuff and watching my words and it was like he exuded some kind of truth serum that made me want to tell him things. Things I wasn't legally allowed to tell him. "As her maid of honor. It's my job to look after her."

"You did that earlier today, too. It made me think you were a kind person."

The warm fuzzies intensified, preening at his praise. Feeling a tad embarrassed about my reaction, I said, "I might have my moments."

"I get the feeling you have a lot of moments."

"So what was the second moment?" I asked. "When I surprised you?"

"That would be when you took a picture of me."

Those warm fuzzies fled as icy shock gripped my spine. I instantly felt both foolish and like I'd been exposed. I thought I'd been so nonchalant and careful. How in the world had he seen me?

There was no way I could admit to it. I would look so, so stupid if I did and I didn't have an explanation that would make sense as far as my mother was concerned.

"Vain much?" I countered.

"I saw you," he said in a low voice that made my skin flush.

"You have a great imagination."

"Let me see your phone, then."

I grabbed my phone tightly. "No."

He had a self-satisfied look on his face. "That means you did take a picture of me."

"You coming to a conclusion doesn't mean you're right."

Camden shrugged. "You could easily disprove it right now."

"Not going to happen."

"You seem like the kind of woman who enjoys being right."

This had nothing to do with being right because I obviously wasn't. "I like my privacy."

"Me too," he agreed. "I noticed you don't have any social media."

I had two immediate reactions to this information. The first was a giddy, "Yay! He looked me up!" and the other was its polar opposite—a sinking sensation in my stomach of "Oh no, he looked me up."

Camden's phone rang again. He glanced at the screen. "I'm sorry. I've got to take this."

He again excused himself and walked away from our table, despite the fact that we'd been in a pretty intense back-and-forth. If some girlish part of me had hoped he was interested, he'd just laid out where I stood in priority to his phone. My mom had told me to win him over with my wit and beauty and it looked like that wasn't happening.

Wit and beauty—zero; technology—one.

You don't care, I reminded myself. It didn't matter.

Except it did.

Which was annoying.

Sadie had just finished filming a segment and I remembered that she'd said she needed to talk to me. I walked over to her to see if she had a minute.

"Rachel!" she exclaimed, hugging me again. I wasn't really a hug type of person, but with Sadie I never minded.

"How are you?" I asked. "You probably have so much to deal with. There's a ton of people here."

She grimaced. "Dan and I would have preferred something small and intimate. Just us and our immediate families. But the sponsors wanted a bigger gathering. And not everyone's even here yet. There's some people who are coming just for the wedding and reception."

"Speaking of immediate families," I said, "I checked on your mom and she was a little . . ."

"Drunker than a frat boy on New Year's Eve? Not surprising." She let out a big sigh. "Part of me wishes she hadn't come. That's awful, isn't it?"

I didn't have a parent who, if not a full-blown alcoholic, was at least an understudy for the role, so I didn't know. "I have often wished that my own mom would disappear for a little while. Not permanently, but I'd love it if she could go to the magical land of Don't Bug Your Daughter About Grandkids and have a long, extended vacation there."

This seemed to reassure her, as her smile was only slightly still sad. "I know I've probably made her sound horrible, but once you get to know her she's . . . even worse. I mean, she's in Hawaii for her only daughter's wedding, and she's drunk in her hotel room instead of being here to support me. I've never asked her for anything and she can't even do this?"

"I'm sorry." I didn't know what else to say. I'd have to talk to Krista about redoubling our efforts to make sure that Brandy was relatively sober and started coming to the events.

"No, don't listen to my whining. I'm marrying the man of my dreams in paradise. Everything else is just a nuisance."

"That's a good attitude. Focus on what matters."

"Or . . . I could distract myself. By asking how things are going with Camden. Are you two hitting it off? I told Troy to seat you two together tonight."

I did not sigh. Even though I really, really wanted to. "It's fine. But you need to be careful what you say about me to him."

"Why?"

"You forgot to tell me that you were poor growing up."

She visibly swallowed, her lower lip trembling for a moment. "It's not something I like to think about. Why does it matter?"

"Because our backstory is that we met at summer camp. Something that's typically expensive and in a different state than the one you grew up in."

"Oh." She blinked slowly, her mouth twisting to one side. "Don't they have like, scholarships or something?"

"I mean, we can say that if we're specifically asked, but the more we elaborate, the more unbelievable the lie becomes. Especially with someone like Camden, who seems to notice everything."

"Yes, he's very attentive." Her cheesy grin told me exactly what she meant by that and this time I did sigh.

"Speaking of, did you tell Camden to flirt with me?"

Sadie frowned. "I didn't. But he's the reason why I wanted to talk to you. Camden decided to flirt with you all on his own."

I found myself literally holding my breath. As if we were in high school and she was about to tell me that Camden had told Dan, who told her, that he thought I was, like, so cute and totally wanted to take me to homecoming. I forced myself to breathe out and pay attention.

"Why?"

"Because he thinks you're a spy."

CHAPTER FOUR

"I'm sorry . . . what?"

For a second I thought I was having an auditory hallucination, but it was such a weird thing to say that I knew I hadn't made it up.

"A spy," she repeated.

"Like . . . he thinks I'm in the CIA?"

"No." She took me by the hand and led me away from the party and the cameras. "I told you about how he and Dan run that tech company. Dan's designed this doohickey thing that makes computers go faster. The company's going public next week and they're going to make a lot of money. So apparently other companies are engaging in corporate espionage and trying to steal information."

"Can't they just patent their device? Doesn't that protect it?"

"Not in some foreign countries, where the companies there will ignore patents and make stuff anyway. Plus, a patent is only good for like, twenty years, and then anybody can take your design. Dan says he's thinking long-term, so they are keeping it secret."

"Have people already tried to steal it?"

Her eyes lit up, like she was enjoying telling me this. "Definitely. It's happened like, three different times. One guy went into a cubicle of an employee that was on vacation and tried to use his computer. Another got hired as an executive assistant and wasn't aware that their keystrokes were being logged. The last one dated their lead engineer. She was the one who came the closest to getting what they were looking for."

This had all taken a hard turn from what I'd thought she might say. Finance had so many rules and regulations we had to be careful to follow so that we didn't end up in prison. I couldn't imagine trying to steal something from another company. "This is all so ridiculous. That he would think that about me."

"If anybody new comes into their circle, Camden's suspicious. He even doubted me for a while, but my whole life is online and available for public consumption."

None of mine was. Taimani had made sure to scrub every image and every reference about me off the internet. I wonder if that had set off alarm bells for him. "So, why would he flirt with me then?"

"To find out whether or not you are a corporate spy and get information from you."

"What, like I'm a German soldier and he's a hot French girl?"

She elegantly shrugged one shoulder. "I don't pretend to understand everything that Camden is thinking. I'm sure it made sense to him."

"That makes one of us."

"You know, I set him up with my friend Sharlene and they dated for a hot minute, and according to her, Camden's an amazing kisser. I mean, as long as he's trying to woo you into admitting something that's not even true, you should enjoy yourself."

There was absolutely zero chance of that happening, and she could tell that from the expression on my face.

"Oh no, I've ruined things, haven't I?"

"There was nothing to ruin," I told her. "Nothing was going to happen, anyway. I'm here for you, and nothing else."

"Okay." Sadie looked unsure, so I put on my bridesmaid smile.

"Don't worry about me. It's my job to worry about you."

She hugged me tightly. "Sometimes I forget that we're not really friends."

"We're really friends," I said as we released one another. That wasn't always true; there were plenty of brides I was happy to put in my rear-view mirror. But Sadie? I liked her and could see myself staying friends with her. Especially since we both lived in New York.

"I better go check in with Troy and my husband-to-be to see if there's anything else I need to do. You are officially off duty for the rest of the night. We can catch up tomorrow at the fitting."

I said I'd be there and watched her walk away to rejoin her fiancé. Even though she'd been gone for only a few minutes, Dan picked her up and swirled her around like she'd just returned from active duty.

Well, now I knew how to explain Camden's treatment of me. He had been suspicious and the full-court press had come about because he thought he could romance me into telling him all of my secrets.

Of course he wasn't really interested in me because, hello, my life.

"There you are." Camden's voice was low and warm against my ear, making me shiver slightly in response.

How could I still get tingly feelings when I knew that he was trying to trick me?

He thinks you're keeping a secret. And you are.

I told my Mom Voice to shut up. I wasn't interested in her opinion on this subject.

"Here I am," I said tightly. How could I be both pissed off and wanting his lips on mine? Now all I could hear was Sadie's words, that he was a great kisser, and I desperately wanted to test that out myself.

Which was pathetic.

"So, Rachel Vinson, what do you say to taking a stroll on the beach?"

Yes.

But that wasn't what I said. "I have to get back to my room and send some work emails. I have had some fascinating conversations tonight. I gathered up some great intel. Good night!"

His face fell, but I didn't stay to see what he thought about my blatant attempt to bug him. Since he'd already jumped to a stupid conclusion, he could twist in the wind and spend the rest of the night worrying about what I might have "discovered."

I hurried across the lawn, wanting to get back to my bed and put this night behind me. To think that I'd actually considered letting my walls down with him, maybe getting to know him better.

How had I gone from being wary of him to thinking he was cute to being crushed that he was only being nice to me because he thought I was trying to steal from him?

My gut had been right. I needed to steer clear of Camden. He had been playing with my emotions because he was paranoid. Before Sadie had told me the truth, I would probably have been excited to go on a midnight stroll with him. Now? His offer felt completely hollow.

If this was the game he wanted, two could play.

~

I woke up in a mood and was grateful that today had been designated as a free day. Sadie and Dan were leaving it up to their guests to fill their day themselves. They had left a sheet of information listing local tourist attractions, restaurants, the number for the spa downstairs, things like that. I ended up depending on room service for the day, not wanting to venture out and accidentally run into Camden. I wasn't interested in his false overtures.

There were two things scheduled that I had to attend—the final dress fitting and the bridal shower later in the afternoon.

Trying not to think about how much the Camden situation still annoyed me (a spy? Seriously?), I focused on work for the day. We had some inquiries about hiring our services and I spent my morning responding to emails and checking in with my girls in New Jersey to make sure they hadn't ritually murdered their bridezilla yet. She'd chosen our company because all of her friends had refused to be her bridesmaids, a fact that didn't surprise me in the least given what my employees were going through.

Thinking about my own unpleasant situation with Sadie's mom, I got in touch with the hotel concierge and requested that they not refill the mini-bar in Brandy's room. Maybe that was overstepping my bounds, but I was going to do what I could to protect Sadie. I also asked him to speak to the bartenders about not serving her. He gave me his phone number and requested a picture of Brandy. I found one on social media and sent it to him. He promised that he would do his best to take care of it and that, if Brandy did get out of control, the hotel had security.

But that was all we needed. Brandy being escorted out of an event by security because she had made some kind of drunken scene while Sadie's camera crews captured every humiliating moment.

I didn't know how I was going to prevent that from happening, but getting the bartenders and housekeeping service on board felt like a good place to start.

In the afternoon, just before the fitting, I called Krista and asked her to join me to go over our game plan.

She arrived quickly, looking fresh-faced and dewy. She'd spent the morning in the spa and I was glad she'd gotten the chance to relax. I should make sure that Sadie had the same chance. I reached for my big organizer, where I kept my to-do lists, and for today's list I wrote *suggest to Sadie she spend some time in the spa.*

The women at my company often teased me about my lists, about how I would add things that hadn't initially been on my daily checklist just to have the satisfaction of crossing them off. I loved lists. They made me feel in control of my life.

My master to-do list was kind of like a more practical bucket list. It was filled with things I wanted to accomplish, some of which I'd already been able to cross off. Like *start my own company* and *help someone else start over*.

Before I could talk myself out of it, I added *find a soul mate* to the list. It seemed important to include it. Not because I was giving in to my mother's siege attacks, but because the first man I'd been attracted to in like, a year was only flirting with me because he thought I was trying to steal information about his company.

I needed to put myself out there more.

After I wrote it down, I added three stars to it. I rated all my entries from one to three, three being most important. I was going to focus on this next when I got back home.

I was usually surrounded by happy brides and grooms, but there was something about Sadie and Dan that seemed special. Something that made me really want that in my own life.

My internal Mom Voice said, *Maybe it has nothing to do with them and everything to do with the best man.*

Someday, in the far distant future, when my mom died, I wouldn't need to worry about missing her because I was pretty sure I was forever going to have her voice in my head.

I flipped my pages over to today's list. "Okay, so Sadie's stepdad, Geoff, arrives today with his fiancée, Maybelle. Our mission is going to be twofold. We've got to keep Brandy sober and showing up for events and we also have to keep her away from Geoff and Maybelle and those livestream cameras."

Krista nodded. "I have potentially good news on that front. The director, Hank? I think he might like me. He keeps making googly eyes at me. Like the ones you make at Camden."

"I do not—" I cut myself off before I started protesting too much. "I have never made googly eyes at anyone in my entire life."

"I know! That's why it's so exciting because now you are."

"You shouldn't be excited," I said, setting down my planner. "You don't have all the information."

Her eyes lit up with interest as I started telling her the entire Camden saga, leaving out the parts where I'd been intrigued by him. After I'd given her most of the details, she laughed for longer than she should have and when she finally calmed down I asked, "What do you think I should do going forward? I'm planning on avoiding him completely. He's already trying to uncover my background; we can't let him find out about us."

There were still tears of laughter in her eyes as she responded, "What should you do going forward? I think you should have a good time!"

"What?"

"Girl, if he wants to woo you, go get your luxury car!"

"Why would I get a luxury car?"

"Because he's rich and the way to a woman's heart is with a luxury car. At least that's the way to my heart." She went into my mini-fridge and grabbed herself a bottled water, twisting off the lid. "Usually you're an undercover bridesmaid, but Camden thinks you're undercover as a spy. That's pretty fun."

"Or not fun," I retorted. This could be a huge issue if we didn't come up with a way to handle him.

There was a loud crashing noise from next door. I raised both of my eyebrows at Krista and whispered, "That's his room."

She excitedly whispered back, "Do you think he has someone in there? Like of the female persuasion and they're knocking over furniture?"

My heartbeat increased rapidly. "What? No!"

Why did that bother me so much?

"That would definitely solve your problem. If he was interested in someone else."

But I didn't want him to be interested in someone else.

What was wrong with me?

Krista tiptoed over to the wall and put her ear against it. "I can't hear anything," she reported. "Hand me one of those glasses."

"This isn't a cartoon. That doesn't actually work."

"Come on, we're supposed to be spies, remember? Have some fun with me!"

One of the reasons my working and personal relationship with Krista had been so great was because of situations like this one—where I was caught up in my own inner drama and she was reminding me to have fun. Because our job was fun. Even when it was stressful, we still got to get our hair and makeup done and get free dresses and eat excellent food and dance the night away.

We could spy on a boy for a moment.

I tiptoed over and put my ear against the wall but couldn't hear anything, either.

"We need to get going to the fitting," I told her. "Down at Sadie's villa." The hotel had provided her with a private villa that sat right on the beach.

"Fine," Krista said with an exaggerated sigh. "Let's go."

I checked to make sure I had both of my keycards on me as we left our room. Some small part of me hoped Camden would come out when he heard my door shut, but he didn't.

And I was disappointed.

As we walked down the hallway Krista said, "Just tell him you're not a spy."

"I'm sure he'll believe that. Because he seems like the trusting type."

"I don't know what else you can do. There's no way he can find us online."

That was true. Taimani made sure of it, and her ability to scrub our names was one of the reasons I'd hired her in the first place. She made certain that our real names were never connected with any pictures of us that were online. I had stopped using aliases because Taimani was just that good.

"Or," Krista said, "you could just play along and flirt back."

"I don't think I want to do that." Because so far my body couldn't tell the difference between real and fake, so even if my brain knew it didn't mean anything, I didn't think I'd be able to convince my heart.

"It will be fine," she told me. "Just grab that bull by the horns and see where things go. We're in Hawaii. Let's do our job, but let's also keep having a good time."

She pushed the button for the elevator and we waited in silence for it to arrive while I considered her advice.

Grabbing a bull by its horns wasn't a great analogy because I wasn't up for being gored if things went sideways.

And working at weddings had taught me that stuff always seemed to go sideways.

CHAPTER FIVE

Stefan quickly finished with the dresses for me, Krista, and Mary-Ellen. This was our first time meeting with him, but we'd already sent in our measurements. I hadn't known what to expect when we arrived, but Sadie had selected some beautiful gray silk dresses that draped like they'd been made for us.

Which, I supposed, they had. It was just nice to get a dress that was so pretty. I actually could wear it again, unlike most bridesmaid dresses.

As Stefan circled around me, moving the fabric this way and that, he tutted and sighed loudly. He made me feel like I should apologize for having hips.

Then he started muttering to himself about things he had to change and I tried to be helpful.

"I think it looks great just the way it is."

His imperious glare let me know that I was wrong. Technically his company was paying for the dresses, so I decided to keep my mouth shut and just go with the flow. So often the bridesmaids' dresses selected for us were hideous, even though the brides repeatedly assured us that they were "like, so pretty!" and we could "totally wear them again." Unless I planned on going to the future marriage of Big Bird and Barbie, the hot-pink dress with yellow feathers from the Hemmings' wedding was definitely not something I was ever going to put on my body again.

I took off my dress and handed it to Stefan's assistant. Who was also shooting me dirty looks. I changed into my regular clothes, smoothing my hair in its french twist so that I didn't look too messy.

Sadie said, "I'm coming out!" I stepped around the screen to see her, and her dress was stunning. It was fitted with a lace overlay on the bodice and was open in the back. The bottom half of her dress surprised me—she'd gone for a poofy skirt with a tulle overlay.

"Does it not look good?" she asked me.

"No, you look gorgeous! It just surprised me that your dress has such a princess feel to it."

"I considered a lot of different styles, but in the future, I'm going to wear formal, more traditional dresses. When will I ever get the chance to wear a Cinderella-esque ball gown like this again?"

She was right. Her designer, Stefan, walked around her making more noises.

"It looks like it's all finished," I offered, not wanting him to stress out Sadie, and he brushed me aside with another icy stare.

"Of course it's finished. I'm making sure that we don't need any last-second alterations. You don't know how many brides put on five pounds the week of their wedding because of all the stress eating," he replied.

Oh, trust me. I did.

A camera operator panned up and down Sadie's dress, but I knew this wasn't being broadcast live. They wanted the footage for later, and for the wedding itself to be the big reveal of the dress.

Sadie teared up and I was right there with a tissue, to make sure she didn't get any mascara on her dress.

"Happy or sad?" I asked her while Stefan ordered his two assistants to get the dress off right away as he fretted aloud about possible tearstains.

"Sad," she said, moving her arms out of the sleeves and stepping out of the dress. She grabbed her white robe that had *bride* emblazoned across the back and sat down in an armchair.

"What are you sad about?"

She let out a shaky breath, like she was trying to hold off big sobs. "When I imagined this moment, I thought my mom would be here. But she's off somewhere with my aunt."

I immediately felt guilty for not anticipating this. "You didn't tell me you wanted her here." If she had, I would have personally poured coffee down Brandy's throat and then made sure she'd behaved.

"I know. I just thought she'd want to see me in my dress, and she said, 'I'll see it when you get married.'"

I pressed my lips into a thin line. Her mother was so selfish.

"But," Sadie continued, "I think she was afraid Maybelle would be here today. I hate that my mom's making me choose. Geoff is the only father I've ever known and I want both of them to be here and to just be happy for me."

"I understand that. And I'm going to do my best to help that happen." Her mentioning Geoff as a father made me realize this was another part of her life she'd glossed over and that I needed more information in case Camden went digging around again. "He married your mom when you were thirteen, right?"

She used the tissue to wipe away some tears. "Yes. Life was so hard before they got married. We were poor. Like, living in a mobile home with aluminum over the windows and gaping holes in the floor kind of poor. My mom always went from one man to the next, trying to find someone to take care of us instead because her drinking made it so she couldn't hold down a job. Then she met Geoff, and she was on her best behavior for a few years. Our lives were so much better. But then she started drinking again and he couldn't deal with it. So he left her and moved on."

"That's rough," I told her.

She nodded, blowing her nose before continuing. "I decided that I was going to make my own money and never depend on someone else for survival. So I'm paying for this wedding through sponsorship and it means I'm giving up a lot of say-so, but it's worth it to me to have this. I love Dan, and I don't ever want him to think I'm after him for his money. Or that I can't take care of myself."

I one hundred percent understood this, but for different reasons. "He knows that. It's easy to see how much the two of you love each other."

"Sadie! Where are you?" Stefan stuck his head around the dressing screen. "Shoe time. Let's get your dress back on and make sure the length is right!"

Sadie smiled at me and headed off to do as she was told, again, for the sake of her sponsors. To be honest, I'd thought her decision to use sponsors for her wedding had been self-aggrandizing, but it turned out that she'd done it to prove something sweet to her groom.

She was a bit different than what I'd first initially imagined her to be.

What if the same was true for Camden? Maybe there was something beyond the spy stuff.

I straightened my back, lifting my head. It didn't matter if he was the world's greatest guy and this was all a misunderstanding. I didn't date men I'd met at weddings. A rule I'd set for the whole company.

I couldn't ask the women who worked for me to follow one important rule that I was ready to ignore because of a pair of pretty eyes. As president, I needed to lead.

When I went looking for a soul mate, I'd have to find him somewhere else.

～

Later that afternoon Krista and I walked down to the bridal shower together, gifts in hand. We hadn't picked them out; they'd been provided to us by event sponsors. I hoped Sadie was going to be excited about getting a bunch of alcohol and lingerie.

The first thing I noticed on the south lawn was the decorations. There were massive balloon arches of pale-pink and gray balloons, banners with Sadie's name and their hashtags, a dessert table laid out with treats in various shades of pink, white couches with pink and gray pillows. It was like walking into somebody's Pinterest board.

The next thing I realized was that there were men here.

"This is coed," I said to Krista as an employee put a lei of pale-pink flowers around my neck.

"So?" she asked.

"So . . . it would have been nice if someone had brought that to my attention before right now."

"Why? Oh," she said in a serious tone. "Because of your boyfriend."

"Seriously? I'm going to get more of this from you?"

"I can't help myself. It's hilarious. From my perspective, anyway. Plus, I never have things to tease you about and this is too much fun."

Her calling Camden my "boyfriend" made me question whether he was seeing someone. If he was flirting with me solely to seduce information out of me, that meant he wasn't interested in really pursuing me. He might have someone back home waiting for him.

The thought made me uneasy.

This party was listed as being "casual." Not sure what that meant in wedding planner Troy's world, I'd opted for my favorite lavender sundress. Most of the women were in skirts or dresses and a bunch of the men were wearing linen shirts and cargo shorts. Like some kind of uniform.

Knowing Sadie's sponsors, it might actually be a uniform.

"There's Dan's mom. I'm off to socialize," I told her. Krista said goodbye as I approached Irene. Dan's mother looked peaceful, her headscarf a pink and gray mixture, just like the wedding colors. I thought it was a particularly sweet touch.

"Irene, right? I'm Rachel. The maid of honor. May I join you?"

"Please do." I sat down next to her on the couch, putting my purse by my feet. "So you're Rachel! You're the one Camden's been going on and on about."

My heart did flips at her words. Until I realized that it might not have been positive. "Good things, I hope."

She patted my hand. "Nothing but good things!"

It would be wrong for me to accuse someone who had cancer of being a liar, right? Because this was something I'd dealt with a lot before—weddings did tend to bring out the matchmakers in people. All that love and happiness. They wanted to spread it around, like Sadie had been doing. Apparently Irene was on board.

I settled on, "I find that a little hard to believe." I had no idea how far he'd spread his corporate-espionage theory.

Irene gave me a motherly smile. "He said he thought you were beautiful."

Whoa, that sent my stomach into free fall. "Did he? Well . . . I'm sure his girlfriend wouldn't appreciate that."

I couldn't help myself. Even if I couldn't date him, even if he suspected me of trying to ruin his company, I wanted to know if, under different circumstances, there might have been a chance for us.

"Camden doesn't have a girlfriend. He hasn't seriously dated anyone in . . . well, it's been quite some time."

"Oh." I didn't have a better response because I was far too happy about her statement and knew I shouldn't be. What if she was just guessing? How could she have any real insider information into Camden's love life?

While I was wrestling internally with trying to figure out if I could trust what she said, Irene asked where I was from and our conversation grew from there. I genuinely enjoyed getting to know people and talking to them. It was one of the things that made my job so enjoyable. I'd been defensive and on edge at this particular wedding only because of Camden's shenanigans.

She had just finished telling me an adorable story about her knitting club and how they made hats for infants at the local hospital when she tacked on, "If you'll excuse me, I'm going to find a restroom."

I'd noted earlier that she'd either been sitting or on Dan's arm whenever I saw her and so I said, "Do you need any help?"

"You're a dear, but no thank you. People fuss over me all the time. I can manage."

She scooted carefully to the end of the sofa and had a bit of a struggle standing up. I wanted to assist her but didn't interfere because it seemed important to her to do it on her own.

My phone dinged with a notification and I flipped it on to see the final score of the Michigan game. Yes! They'd won! That meant they were moving on in the March Madness tournament.

"Is this seat taken?" a man asked, and I looked up to see that it was Camden.

I had this strange mixture of emotions—I was internally celebrating over the Michigan win, annoyed that Camden had found me and was looking too handsome for his own good in a green linen shirt that matched his eyes, and . . . excited to see him again. Like I'd spent so much time thinking about him that I was happy he was here and I got to see his face.

Weird.

I should have told him to go. Instead I said, "I was saving it for Ben Barnes, but he looks like a no-show."

Camden sat next to me on the sofa, closer than was necessary. I could feel warmth radiating from him and smell that delicious clean scent of his. I was tempted to get up and walk away but Irene would be coming back and I didn't want her to think I'd abandoned her.

"What are you up to?" he asked.

I held up my phone. "Checking the scores."

"For?"

"The game."

"Which one?"

His constant, persistent questions made me briefly wonder how many years I'd get for assault. "Michigan."

"Please tell me you're not a Michigan fan."

The disdain in his voice was obvious. "Let me guess, Ohio State fan?"

"My dad ran track at Ohio State," he said.

"My dad went to Michigan." We sounded like little kids on a playground comparing whose father was better.

He nodded, looking far too amused. "I think this means we can't be friends anymore. Our houses are at war. Like Romeo and Juliet."

"Well, if it makes you feel any better, we weren't friends to begin with."

Camden put his arm across the back of the sofa and I could feel the heat of it next to my shoulders. "Are you really a fan or are you one of those girls who pretends to like sports?"

I narrowed my eyes at him. "Are you one of those guys who thinks it's his job to gatekeep fandoms?"

At that he grimaced. "I'm sorry. My friend Vance is huge into fantasy football and he dated a girl who said she was into it and it was all a ruse and she was using him."

I briefly wondered if Vance was the lead engineer that Sadie had mentioned, the one who a spy had used to try to get info about Camden's company. "So now you're worried that every girl who says she likes something is a liar?"

"It's probably more sports specific."

"If you need me to rattle off rebounds or steals or assists for the Michigan team, I can do that."

He raised his eyebrows. "That would be impressive." But his tone indicated that it was more than just impressive. Like he would find that . . . attractive. "Again, I'm sorry. I didn't mean to be that guy."

"That's good, because you were basically in the running to be the CEO of That Guy Incorporated."

I wondered if me saying *CEO* would be a red flag for him, but he barely seemed to notice. Maybe I shouldn't be trying to mess with him. He had apologized, after all.

That impressed me. In the regular sense of the word and in the I-found-it-attractive sense of the word.

Then, like he was trying to change the subject away from the uncomfortableness of supporting rival schools, he said, "You know, we never did get to talk about our mutual maid of honor and best man responsibilities last night."

"That's because one of us was busy cheating at a board game and taking multiple phone calls on his antique from the Civil War."

He grinned at me. "You say cheating, I say ensuring victory." Then he added, "Potato, tomato," with a wink and I admit it, I melted a little.

I knew he was flirting with me because he was trying to get me to reveal that I wanted to steal from his company. I knew this, and I was still falling for his act. I wondered what that said about me.

Or maybe it said more about him. That he was very charming and good at making women fall in love with him. I found myself wanting him to drop his arm around me and pull me in close.

Determined to go back to my original course of action and ignore him instead of engaging with him in his game, I pointedly looked at my phone. I started scrolling mindlessly through the scores of other games but I wasn't paying attention.

"I like college basketball, too," he said. "In case I didn't make that clear earlier. I've got tickets to the National Championship."

I was torn between wanting to tell him to be quiet and asking him about those tickets. Like exactly how many he had and what he wanted in return for one of them. Whether he might accept a firstborn child as payment. I continued my silence, thumbing across the screen of my phone.

"So . . . I'm getting the feeling you don't want to talk to me." He said this with a hint of disbelief, as if such a thing were impossible. That he was irresistible.

Which I got, because trust me, it wasn't easy. "Thanks for picking up on my blatant social cues."

My sarcasm might have chased a less determined man away, but Camden stayed put and smiled at me.

And I liked that he did.

Ugh.

Now I felt bad for being snarky when he was at least pretending to be polite. "Do you have a question for me?"

"What?"

"Whenever you see me you have a million questions." I wanted him to know that he wasn't being nearly as smooth as he thought he was, and I'd noticed his pointed questions from the beginning, even before I knew that he suspected me of planning some nefarious scheme.

He looked slightly uncomfortable. "I don't mean to pry."

"Don't you, though?"

He didn't refute my statement. He couldn't, because it was true.

Part of me wondered if I should tell him that I knew exactly what he was up to and bring all of this to a screeching halt.

Or if I should keep letting him dangle on this hook.

CHAPTER SIX

I didn't confront him because I didn't know if it was the right thing to do. Sadie hadn't said one way or another if she was okay with me telling him what she had shared with me. It was my job at weddings to avoid scenes, not create them.

Instead I stayed quiet and he seemed to take this as some sort of permission to forge ahead and ask those questions I knew he had rattling around inside his brain.

"Okay then . . . how old are you?" he asked, and I didn't know if it was because it was the first question that occurred to him or if it was part of the background check he was trying to conduct on me.

Sadie was a couple of years younger than me, which made our "we're friends from camp" story a little more unbelievable.

I'd learned early on in my job that one of the best ways to deflect questions you didn't want to answer was to ask a question in return. "How old do I look?"

"Oh no, Dan's dad taught me that when a woman asks you that, it's always a trap."

Dan's dad? I wondered why not his own father. Would he tell me what that meant if I asked? I got the feeling he wouldn't. Maybe I could skirt around the subject and get him to reveal more. "You said your dad ran track?"

If he noticed my change of subject, he didn't acknowledge it. "Yes, he did. That's why I used to run."

Camden certainly had an athlete's build. "Used to?"

"Long story short, I was training for the Olympics and stopped when I hurt my knee."

He tugged the hem of his shorts up slightly, and he had multiple scars across the surface. It looked like he'd taken shrapnel in a war zone or something. I found myself wanting to ask about it. He had been training for the Olympics? That took some serious talent and dedication. How had he hurt himself?

I couldn't stop my curiosity, the desire I had to know more about him. I wondered whether under different circumstances his feigned interest in me might have been real.

Irene exited the bathroom and for a moment my heart lifted, like she was going to come back and save me from Camden.

But not in the "I need to get away from this guy because he's annoying me" kind of way. More of a "I'm liking him more than I should and want to know things about him and this obviously spells eternal doom so please, Irene, save me from the madness before I do something really stupid" way.

Camden followed my gaze and announced, "Irene likes you. I can tell."

I tried not to preen under the approval in his voice. "Still watching me, Mr. Stalker?"

His lazy grin told me he could hear how my question lacked conviction. "It was sweet. The way you wanted to help her stand up."

"How would you even know that?"

"From the way you were sitting, perched on the edge of your seat, leaning toward her, your hands folded tightly in your lap." Now he was the one leaning in, and every single cell in my body tingled in response to his closeness. "I happen to be fluent in body language."

"I just bet you are." I sighed, the words escaping before I could stop them. There was a fiery intensity that looked like desire in his eyes, as if he wanted something more. Something real.

It died out quickly and he angled himself away, trying not to be obvious about it. Which was a good thing. Because he was trying to trick me.

A pang of regret did hit me hard, though.

Which was probably what prompted me to blurt out, "You told Irene I'm beautiful."

Even if I hadn't meant to say it, I did want to see his reaction. Would he deny it? Brush it off? Try to use it to his advantage?

"It's the truth. I'm not one for lying."

I should have won an award for not laughing. Wasn't he technically lying to me right now? Smoldering and smiling at me in turns, trying to melt all my defenses so that he could look into my soul?

"Seriously?" was all I could ask.

He seemed a bit miffed. "Yes, seriously. The last time somebody lied to me it cost me my future." His hand drifted to his hurt knee and I wondered if he meant the corporate spies. But they hadn't really lied to him. Just near him. They were lie adjacent.

Or maybe he was talking about something else.

I would not ask him about it. I would not.

"So," he said, in a sexy, low voice, "how about we get together after this and go over those duties of ours?"

What duties? I was the one with all the responsibility. His job was to wear a tux, arrange the bachelor party, and bring the ring to the wedding. Even though I thought his suggestion was stupid, I still wanted to say yes. Instead I settled on, "After this? That's much too soon for something that's never going to happen."

A lock of my hair sprang forward, escaping the clip keeping my knot in place, like it was trying to disagree with the rest of my body's decision to blow off Camden.

And he took it as an invitation. He reached out with his long fingers and softly brushed the hair behind my ear, lingering. The sensation sent heated tingles coursing through my veins and I drew in a sharp breath.

He smiled at me seductively and it irritated me that he knew exactly the effect he was having on me.

"I know what you're trying to do," I told him.

Camden lowered his hand and I found myself aching to have him touch me again.

"Well, I'm not being subtle," he said.

At that I backed myself against the sofa, like a cornered animal. I couldn't let him touch me. He set me on fire with just a glance or that smile of his, and when his skin connected with mine? It threatened to overwhelm me.

Camden retreated to his corner, further proving his ability to properly read my signals. Which was good that somebody knew what was going on, because everything happening inside me was completely confusing.

"Don't worry," he said. "I'll grow on you. Like mildew."

That broke the tension and made me smile, and I could see from his expression that it had been his intent.

The comfortable silence that settled between us was interrupted by a new couple arriving at the party.

"Hey," Camden said, "that's Sadie's stepdad and his fiancée."

Geoff looked like he was in his fifties but was the kind of man who hadn't heard that frosted tips didn't look good on anybody and did not, in fact, make him look younger.

And the woman with him? "That's her? That's Maybelle?" I asked in shock. She looked like she was sixteen. "She's a fetus."

"She is younger than Sadie," he offered and I nearly gasped again. She was obviously legal, but they looked like a dad and his daughter out for a day of fun. Sadie had never shown me a picture and I was kind of regretting that now. Mostly because Camden seemed to be enjoying my reaction far too much.

"I just . . . There's nothing I can . . . wow," I said. "She's *so* young."

He nodded. "Geoff couldn't date much younger without having to notify the proper authorities. Maybe she has something other women don't."

"A curfew?" I asked, and that made Camden laugh.

And oh, that sound. It was glorious. I grinned in response.

"I'm sure what he lacks in youth and appearance she more than makes up for by not having a personality," he teased and now it was my turn to giggle.

His eyes lit up, like he enjoyed making me laugh just as much as I had.

As if on cue, Sadie arrived with her mother in tow. Now that I knew how important it was to Sadie to have her mom show up, I'd offered to walk Brandy down to the party. Sadie had insisted on doing it herself. Maybe she was trying to show her mom some support, knowing that Geoff and Maybelle were here.

I noted that Brandy looked bright eyed and rested, which made me feel relieved. Now it was my job to keep her that way. Geoff and Maybelle moved to the opposite end of the party and I hoped they were smart enough to keep doing that for the rest of the events.

Sadie and her mother came over to us.

"Our maid of honor and best man together! So cute!" Sadie exclaimed and I brushed it off. Whatever she hoped for was not going to happen. "Mom, have you met Rachel yet?"

I was about to say that we'd already met when Brandy interjected, "I haven't. Pleasure to meet you." I didn't know if it was intentional, or if she'd just been so drunk she didn't remember.

"You too," I said.

Then Brandy asked, "Rachel, was it? You're the friend Sadie's never mentioned before."

Camden straightened up next to me and my heart froze. Brandy could easily upset everything. She knew that Sadie had never gone to summer camp.

I was at a loss here. Mothers of the bride weren't usually this hostile. I mean, sometimes they were but never toward me, because I devoted my time to keeping their daughters happy.

When I didn't answer, Brandy pressed on. "Are you enjoying your free vacation?"

Her words were angry, menacing. And a bit hypocritical. As if she herself were not enjoying the same free vacation while simultaneously drinking all of the alcohol contained in the state of Hawaii.

But it was not my place to say anything critical. "I'm having a wonderful time, thank you."

She compressed her lips into a flat line, as if she'd been itching for a fight and I'd just denied her.

"Rachel is sacrificing to be here with me," Sadie said and it was easy to see that she wasn't very good at lying.

"How is she doing that?" Camden asked and I wanted to tell him to be quiet and mind his own business, but right now Brandy and Sadie were pouring all of our business into his lap.

Sadie floundered for a second and I was no help. I had no idea what to say. The cameras were pointed at us and I ducked my head down slightly, willing them to not zero in on my face. Hopefully they remembered that Sadie was the main attraction here.

While I was worrying over how this might show up on video, Sadie's eyes flashed brightly, like the proverbial light bulb had gone off over her head. "Because it's her birthday tomorrow. And she came out here to be my maid of honor."

"Birthday, huh?" Camden asked. "We should celebrate."

"Yes!" Sadie glommed on to his suggestion. "We should! We don't have anything scheduled tonight and we can just invite the entire wedding party and celebrate a day early. I'll find you later, Rachel, and we can go over the details. Come on, Mom. We've got lots of people to talk to."

When they walked away Camden immediately said, "Now I know why you couldn't tell me how old you are. Because it's changing tomorrow."

"Yep." I wanted to add, *That must be the reason why. You figured it all out with your brilliant sleuthing*, but I refrained.

"Is there anything you want for your birthday?"

You.

My pulse was frantic, my head buzzing, all staticky, because I did not know if I'd said that word out loud or in my head. When his expression didn't change, I sighed, relieved that I'd managed to at least hold on to my dignity. "How about a break from your interrogations?"

"I'm not interrogating you."

I let out a smothered sound of disbelief. "Yes, you are. There's been a couple of times where I felt like I should be asking you to adhere to the Geneva Conventions."

He laughed and it was just as thrilling the second time. "I think I can do that."

Out of the corner of my eye I saw that Brandy had ditched Sadie and was headed for the bar. Time to intervene.

"It was great talking to you"—*not*—"but I have some stuff I need to do." I stood up.

"Of course." He stood up, too, and took a step forward so that he was totally encroaching on my personal space, but my body did not care. It was far too delighted at our proximity.

I swayed toward him but then forced myself to turn and walk away. This was getting to be too much. None of my plans where Camden was concerned seemed to be working out. I was getting sucked in even though I knew better.

You have a job to do, I reminded myself.

Brandy was getting angry at the bartender, who was offering her one of their many soft drinks. "That's not what I want!"

"He's been told not to serve you," I said, keeping my voice low and calm.

She sneered at me. "By who?"

"Me. I'm here to make sure you don't ruin Sadie's wedding."

There was a fleeting expression, one that almost looked like guilt or regret, but then the anger returned. "You can't tell me what to do."

"Right. But I'm still going to keep an eye on you." Sadie would have her perfect day.

"I'm not some kind of alcoholic!" she declared before marching off. I probably shouldn't have been so harsh with her, but she reminded me so much of my mother's sister, who had repeatedly declared she wasn't an alcoholic, either, before she died from liver failure. I tried to shake off my own memories, telling myself this wasn't about me and my family issues. This was about protecting Sadie. I noted that Brandy was keeping clear of her ex-husband, so I was two for two so far.

"You must have drawn the short straw." A woman had appeared at my side and smiled at me sympathetically. She seemed vaguely familiar.

"Excuse me?"

"I'm Mary-Ellen's mom, Brandy's sister. My name is Mandy."

I introduced myself and then started to ask, "Are you two—"

She cut me off. "No, we're not twins. My mother was just unimaginative. And my sister's a handful, so thank you for helping to keep an eye on her."

I nodded. "It's too bad she can't keep from drinking for a few days."

"It is too bad. We had a rough childhood. Our mom was an alcoholic, too. Brandy is suffering from the delusion that she's not nearly as bad. That she has her drinking under control. I've tried talking to her, Sadie's tried, Geoff tried, but nothing seems to get through. She doesn't believe us."

I wished I could do something more to help. "I'm sorry. That can't be easy."

She cleared her throat. "Thanks. We keep trying and hoping."

"I know Sadie really wants her here and to be sober."

"That's part of growing up with an alcoholic parent. You're angry with them and resent their choices, but at the same time you want their love. You want them to choose you, to be more important than getting drunk."

That struck me as unbelievably heartbreaking. "I'm here to help. Let me know if I can do anything."

"Same here. I've been dealing with this for a very long time and I'm kind of an expert." Her voice sounded bleak, at total odds with her peaceful expression. "Let me give you my number. In case you need it." I put it into my phone and then texted her, so she'd have my number, too. When I was finished, Mandy smiled at me and said, "It was good to meet you." She walked away.

It made me so sad for Sadie, but I didn't want to be distracted by my sympathy for her. So instead I found a spot to keep an eye on all the players I had to worry about in this game—Camden was talking to a man with black hair I hadn't met yet, Mandy was sitting with Brandy, and Geoff and Maybelle stayed as far away as they could.

Everything was calmer than I'd anticipated. From what Sadie had told me and what I'd witnessed, I'd half expected a drunken *Real Housewives*-type brawl. But they all seemed to be on their best behavior. I was thankful for it.

Troy announced that it was time for Sadie to start opening her gifts. Krista and I had already decided that she would take point on this part so that I could continue to watch Brandy. Krista grabbed a seat next to Sadie, holding a pad of paper and a pen to write down the names and presents.

Sadie somehow managed to look surprised and delighted with each and every prearranged gift. As if she didn't know exactly what she was getting.

I was so caught up in the fun atmosphere of Sadie enjoying her presents that it surprised me when Camden appeared next to me.

My body knew he was there before he even spoke, as if I'd somehow become attuned to him. His hand brushed gently against my arm and I shivered under his touch.

"I'm headed out," he said.

Why did it give me a thrill that he was making sure to say goodbye to me? "You're leaving before Sadie finishes opening the gifts?"

He held up his sad little flip phone. "I have a phone call I have to take."

"I understand. Tell Abraham Lincoln I said hi."

He grinned at me and said, "I'll see you at your *birthday.*"

As he walked away I realized that he didn't believe it was my birthday. I mean, it wasn't, but he was always so paranoid. He was going to give himself a stress-related heart attack.

I might not have been what he suspected, but he obviously knew something was going on.

I just had to keep him from finding out exactly what that was.

CHAPTER SEVEN

After Sadie had finished with the presents and the party started to wind down, she came over to join me. I was seated at a table, keeping a close eye on Brandy. I had expected she might try to leave and score a drink somewhere else, but whatever Mandy had said to her earlier was keeping Brandy in line.

"Everything has gone so well!" I said, trying for a light and cheery mood. Sadie seemed a bit worn down, and I couldn't blame her. Most brides had enough to deal with when it came to events and obnoxious relatives without Sadie's added difficulty of her Instagram livestreaming. "You must be really happy."

"Things are going well," Sadie said, letting out a sigh as she sat. "Sometimes that worries me. Like the calm before the storm."

"I get that."

"So let's talk about happier things. Like how glad I am that you and Camden have been hanging out."

This is not the time to roll your eyes and make a gagging noise, I reminded myself. "The guy who thinks I'm a spy. Yeah, that's going really well."

She ignored my sarcasm. "You guys were laughing. I was waiting to come in with my mom and I saw you two."

We had been laughing about her stepdad and his soon-to-be child bride. I certainly couldn't tell Sadie that. "Just because we shared a laugh doesn't mean anything. I have a really strict personal policy about not dating guys from weddings. I'm a big believer in the separation of work and date."

Krista chose this moment to join us, sighing happily as she sat down and kicked off her heels. I'd hoped the presence of a new person might deter Sadie, but no such luck.

"I would consider it a huge favor if you could bend your policy just a little bit this time. You're here to make me happy, right? Knowing that Camden had someone to hang out with would make Dan happy, which would make me happy."

"Why would Dan care?"

Sadie smiled sadly. "Dan worries about his best friend. He thinks Camden is lonely and a workaholic."

"So you decided to foist him off on me?"

"Oh come on," Krista said. "You're a workaholic, too. You literally picked a job that you could do twenty-four hours a day."

Sadie tried to make it better. "If you could just help him have fun and not focus so much on work, that would mean a lot to me. Dan and Camden are basically like brothers. They were raised together."

I couldn't help myself. "They were?"

"You should ask him about it. Get to know him better. You don't have to date him. Just be friendly, please." I knew Sadie meant well and she seemed so sincere.

As if she sensed me wavering, Krista chimed in. "You don't really have a choice now. Customer satisfaction is our number-one priority."

This was how they wanted to play it? "The two of you planned this. You guys are setting me up." I should have known better than to let them talk as Sadie opened her presents.

"Us?" Krista said in exaggerated shock. "Never!"

"It's my fake birthday," I grumbled, knowing I would do as she asked. "Shouldn't I get to choose who I want to hang out with?"

"Sadie's wedding trumps your fake birthday," Krista said with a sorry-not-sorry expression. "And it must be oh-so-hard to have to spend time with a charming and extremely handsome man."

Feeling obstinate I muttered, "He's not that good-looking."

That caused a heavy silence to descend over the table as both Sadie and Krista stared at me like I was stupid.

Krista was the first to speak. "If the world was about to be destroyed and I had to pick one man to repopulate the planet, he's the one I would choose."

Then you hang out with him was the reply that sprang to the tip of my tongue, but I swallowed it. Mostly because I'd been trying harder lately to not be rude or snappish, but also because of the inexplicable jealousy that had bubbled up inside me at the idea of Krista flirting with him.

Sadie had her phone out and was texting. "Speaking of your celebration, I've got it all planned out. There's a club in Honolulu who wanted to sponsor an event for the wedding but because of my exclusive contract, I couldn't be in my stories drinking any other brand of liquor. Since this is your birthday and technically not part of my wedding, we can go. My social media agent is setting up the whole thing. This will be so fun. And I could really use a night off."

I stifled a groan. It was my job to give her as many nights off as she wanted. "Fine. I'll do it." I would go to my pretend birthday party and I would be nice to Camden.

Sadie squealed and got up to throw her arms around me. "That is so great! Trust me, you won't regret it!"

Too late.

Krista and I shared a cab to the club. Sadie wanted to go over a bit earlier to make sure everything was set up and ready. I offered to take care of the details for her, but she insisted that since it was my "birthday," I should let her do it.

"I still can't believe you brought a present," I said to my friend. "You know it's not my actual birthday."

Krista looked highly offended. "Of course I brought a gift. I'm not rude. Now let's get inside, you international woman of mystery."

I never should have told her about the spy thing. A bouncer at the front door asked for our names and then told us to follow his associate, another large and burly man. The front door was opened for us and the EDM sound waves hit me square in the chest. The thumping techno beat was so loud.

The second bouncer led us into a private room where you could see the dance floor, but it was soundproofed enough that you could hear yourself think. It was then that I realized Krista and I were the last to arrive, a feeling I did not enjoy. Five minutes early was ten minutes late in my world.

The room had been decorated with red balloons and streamers, my favorite color. There was a cake with red icing roses on a table. It wasn't much, almost like a last-minute kid's party, but I was touched by the effort.

Camden was sitting on a couch by himself, in a darkened corner of the room. He had his phone out and was pushing a lot of buttons. Again I had that thrill of excitement at seeing him, glad that I got to be near him.

I had to stop doing that.

Sadie ran over to hug both Krista and me.

"No camera crew?" I asked.

"Not tonight," Sadie said. "I promised the club to take some footage with my phone and to mention them in a post, but we don't need to do anything more than that. Come on, let me make introductions."

She took us by the hands and led us over to where the other men had congregated. "You know my incredibly handsome groom, Dan, obviously. This is Rick, his cousin and one of the groomsmen. And here's Vance, the other groomsman. He's also a programmer at Dan's company."

I said hello and nodded as the men waved back. They were all huddled around Dan's phone, and I wondered if they were looking at college basketball scores. Sadie sat next to Dan, linking her arm through his and resting her head on his shoulder.

Before I could ask the men what they were doing, Mary-Ellen joined us. "You already know me. In case you forgot, I'm Sadie's cousin. The other bridesmaid. My name's Mary-Ellen. Although some of my friends back home call me Melon."

My eyes flicked between her head and her breasts, which both seemed average, and I wondered why she had been given such an unfortunate nickname.

At my apparent confusion she added, "It's because they squish Mary and Ellen together. Melon. Isn't it the cutest?"

I was pretty sure I was never going to call her that. "It's definitely something."

She noticed Krista laying her present down next to two others and announced, "When Sadie told me this was a birthday celebration, I briefly considered getting you a gift but . . ."

After I realized Mary-Ellen wasn't going to finish her sentence I said, "Don't worry about it. It's the almost thought that counts."

Rick left the group and approached Krista, offering her his hand, to properly say hello. They started chatting and I realized that she and Sadie had left me alone with someone who wanted to use the same nickname as a cantaloupe.

"Hey." Mary-Ellen scooted closer to me and I took a step back at her invading my personal space. "You're friends with that Camden guy, right?"

"*Friends* is a generous word."

She blinked, as if she didn't get my meaning. "Right. You have to help me out. Be my wing woman. I've been trying to talk to him for the last couple of days and he keeps blowing me off."

"Did you tell him people call you Melon?" I shouldn't be snarky right now, but it was like it was just pouring out of me. More jealousy? I refused to self-reflect.

She didn't seem to pick up on my sarcasm. "That's exactly what I'm going to tell him. I bet he'll think it's cute. Us bridesmaids are such a great squad. We should have our own motto. Like 'in squad we trust.'"

The desire to say mean things threatened to overwhelm me, so I let her grab my hand and pull me over to where Camden was seated.

She said, "Hi!" brightly to him and sat down on his right. There was no room for me to sit next to her, and I was forced to sit down on his left side.

The look on his face when he saw me . . . I was trying to forget it. How he looked genuinely glad to see me, excited even. I willed the tropical butterflies in my stomach to calm down and to stop flapping their massive wings so freaking hard.

"What are you up to?" Mary-Ellen asked, leaning over to play with one of the buttons on his shirt. It took all of my willpower not to slap her hand away.

"Responding to a text."

That made me smile. "Does it take you like, ten years to reply?"

His mouth twisted to one side, as if he were trying not to be amused. "You get pretty fast at getting the right letter from each button."

"Yeah, I mean at least the person getting a text from you can appreciate how much you have to work at it. You want to use the letter *Z*? You're going to have to press the 9 button four times. That's commitment."

"Then it's a good thing I'm not texting about grizzly buzzards who like pizza."

My breath hitched for a second as my pulse thumped. I so liked how his brain worked. To distract myself from my wrong impulses and reaction, I asked, "So what happened? Did your carrier pigeon get lost and you had to use this instead?"

He put his left arm along the back of the couch and physically turned his body toward me. I wondered if Mary-Ellen noticed.

"If you knew anything about how tech works, you'd get rid of your smartphone right now," he told me. "It's listening to you, tracking you."

"I know it listens to me. That's a convenience. Whenever I want to buy something, I talk really loudly about what I'm looking for and just wait for the ads to show up in my social media feeds."

He could tell that I was teasing him and he responded to it by leaning even closer. "I think I liked it better in the olden days when phones were dumb and people were smart."

"Good times," I agreed, realizing that I was moving toward him, too. I straightened out my back, inching away slowly.

He totally noticed and that lazy smile of his gave me actual goose bumps. He slipped his phone into his pocket, apparently ready to focus his attention on me.

But not for the reasons I wanted him to.

We were interrupted then by a waitress. "Good evening! My name is Carol and I'll be taking care of you. Are you guys celebrating something tonight?"

Mary-Ellen spoke up. "We're sort of celebrating a birthday, but the real reason we're all here is to pregame for my cousin Sadie's wedding!"

While I wondered how someone "sort of" celebrated a birthday Carol said, "Congratulations! Can I get you a bottle of complimentary champagne?"

"Yes, please!" Mary-Ellen said, and then added in a really bad British accent, "I just love champers."

Be nice, be nice, be nice.

"I'll take a gin and tonic," Camden told Carol.

"Can I get a strawberry-banana virgin daiquiri?" I asked and Carol said, "Of course!" They could lead this horse to a nightclub, but they could not make me drink. Although tonight wasn't technically a wedding event, I wanted to stay on this side of sober. I did not need my inhibitions lowered around Camden.

As Carol went to take everyone else's orders Camden asked, "Virgin fruit daiquiri, huh? Isn't that basically a smoothie?"

"Maybe I'm on a health kick. Or trying to cut calories."

"You don't need to." I drew in a sharp breath. How did he do that? How did he say something so simple and utterly meaningless and turn it into a molten stab of liquid heat that I felt in my stomach?

Mary-Ellen, apparently tired of being left out, put her hand on Camden's shoulder. "So, Mr. Gin and Tonic, what is it you do?"

"I work at a tech company," was his answer. I noticed that he didn't pepper her with questions. Although to be fair, I don't think anybody would ever suspect Melon of being a spy.

Carol was standing next to Dan and Sadie and I heard Sadie order a club soda. Carol seemed confused. "You're the bride, right? Are you sure I can't get you something a little stronger?"

"No, thanks. My mom's an alcoholic and I usually try to steer clear."

That broke my heart a little. Carol seemed uncomfortable by Sadie's proclamation, but she covered it up with a smile and promised she'd return quickly. Sadie turned and caught me looking at her. She pointed at Camden and at me, then gave me two thumbs up. I smiled back weakly. At least I was making the customer happy.

My nerve endings were also pretty excited, sparking with delight at being so close to him again.

Since I was sitting right next to them, I couldn't help but eavesdrop on Mary-Ellen and Camden's conversation. Or more accurately, Mary-Ellen's monologue. She was talking about a British reality show she loved called *The Only Way Is Essex*, and while she was describing the premise of it she had somehow lapsed back into that mangled English accent.

Camden briefly turned toward me and mouthed the words, "Help me."

I tried not to laugh and had to put my hand over my mouth. Personally, I thought he deserved to be a little bit tortured after jumping to such an outlandish conclusion about me.

Carol returned with the drinks and passed them out, taking care to pour Mary-Ellen her "champers." Camden looked like he was ready to knock back his entire drink in one gulp. I took a big swig of my drink and made a face—both because the strawberry taste was a little overwhelming and from the brain freeze. Carol told us she'd be back to check on us and left some extra champagne glasses.

Having the drink gave me something to do. Mary-Ellen was downing her champagne like her liver was on fire. I wondered how responsible I should be for her. She was still a bridesmaid and Sadie's cousin. Why wasn't she as concerned as Sadie about becoming an alcoholic? They came from the same gene pool.

Camden took this opportunity to try to talk to me again. I couldn't blame him for attempting to disengage with Mary-Ellen. "Look at them."

He had nodded toward Sadie and Dan, who were still intertwined with one another. "They are adorable," I said.

"Yeah . . . I think they go into convulsions if they're farther than six feet apart." It was a sarcastic remark, which I always appreciated, but I could hear the affection underneath it. He liked that they were so in love. Most guys I'd dated, when they were around a committed couple, freaked out about it and ran in the opposite direction. Like they were going to catch it.

It was refreshing to be sitting with a man who sounded like he was longing for it in his own life.

Upset that Camden had stopped paying attention to her, Mary-Ellen poured a bit of her champagne on his lap.

"I'm so sorry!" she said. "Let me get that!"

She reached for a cocktail napkin and started blotting the liquid in a way that might have gotten her arrested in a Bible Belt state.

Camden quickly stopped her, taking the napkins. "I've got it. Thanks."

"Now where were we?" she said and then launched back into explaining the TV show to him. Camden raised his eyebrows at me, like he expected me to save him, but I was enjoying my frozen fruit. He was a big boy. He could handle himself just fine.

Mary-Ellen had started describing the second episode of the first season when Vance came over and asked her if she'd like to dance. I caught a glimpse of the sneaky look on Sadie's face and knew that she'd put him up to it. But why? Did it matter who Camden was hanging out with as long as he was having fun? Did it have to be me?

Although, to be fair, he had looked like he wanted to gnaw off his own leg to get away from Mary-Ellen.

After Vance and Mary-Ellen left, Camden moved in closer so that his words were hot against my neck, sending tingling shivers dancing across my skin. "Alone at last."

CHAPTER EIGHT

Technically we weren't alone. Sadie, Dan, Rick, and Krista were all still in the room.

But I found myself wanting us to be.

I sucked up the last bit of my drink as I saw Carol walking by. I waved her in and asked for another. "You got it," she said.

Then I made the mistake of looking over at Sadie, who waggled her eyebrows at me, silently cheering us on like we were her favorite couple on a dating reality show.

"It seems like Sadie is trying to send you not-so-secret signals," Camden remarked. Of course he'd seen.

"She wants me to be nice to you. Like I'm your wedding geisha or something, here to entertain you during the festivities." The words slipped out of me and while they were a tad bit tinged with resentment at being put in this position when I'd told everyone I didn't want to be, the truth was I did enjoy being around Camden. No matter what I said to everybody else.

"Or she just thought we'd hit it off."

"She's very delusional that way," I said.

"If there's one thing I'll say about Sadie, she's definitely not delusional."

Carol returned with another frozen daiquiri and I thanked her while I tried not to think about what Camden had just said. Because what was that supposed to mean? Was he just appreciating her realism or was he hinting that there might be something between him and me?

I hated trying to figure out men. Especially ridiculous men who thought ridiculous things.

"Girls do this. Especially when they're brides. They want to set everybody up and have them all pair off like we're about to board Noah's Marriage Ark. Do your friends do that?" I asked.

"Nope. My friends are guys."

That made me laugh without meaning to, and now it was my turn to accidentally spray Camden with pink liquid.

"I'm sorry!" I said, still giggling.

"Just don't try to grope me and we'll call it even," he said with a wink. "It's good to see you laughing, though. For a bit there you were looking like the before picture for Prozac."

"Clubs aren't as much fun when you're not drinking." Maybe Camden wasn't as fluent in body language as he thought. I wasn't depressed. I felt . . . unmoored. Like I was drifting through a situation I had no clue how to handle and I didn't enjoy that feeling. I was used to things going my way and I liked being in charge of my life.

Now Camden was upending all of that and I didn't know what to do about it. The first issue was that all of this was happening solely because he wanted to get information from me. Which definitely put a huge damper on things, but only when I remembered. And he made it oh so easy to forget.

The main issue was my rule: no dating men at work. I couldn't go against a rule that I had set.

You made the rule, you can unmake it. You're the boss, my mom's voice said.

Yes, so I have to be the example.

From Camden's questioning expression I realized that I'd said the words out loud. Arguing with my inner-mother voice as if she were here in the room with us.

Pretty humiliating.

I tried to direct him a different way. "You've been awfully quiet tonight. You didn't want to ask me what city I was born in or the name of my childhood pet?"

"I'm not allowed to ask you any questions. It was what you said you wanted for your birthday."

That was seriously the sweetest thing ever. He was being not annoying as a present for me. I could feel my heart doing little happy flips in my chest.

Before I could respond he added, "But I'm not really sure how to have a conversation without asking questions."

"It is difficult," I said, staying quiet to make it a bit harder.

"You could ask me questions," he offered.

"I could. But I don't think I will."

"That's not fair."

I took another sip of my drink as I shrugged. "I'm not trying to be."

Camden took that challenge with a little half smile. "Okay. So, you should tell me what sort of things you do in your free time."

"What do you mean?" I asked, being deliberately obtuse.

"A hobby, perhaps." He was choosing his words so carefully, trying to skirt around the "no questions" situation.

"I do have hobbies. There are things I do in my free time that I definitely enjoy."

"It would be helpful if you could be maybe seventy-four percent less vague."

"It would also be helpful if you could be like, seventy-four percent more honest," I told him.

"What am I not being honest about?" He finally caved and asked a question, either forgetting that he wasn't supposed to be doing that or he was truly perplexed by my statement.

I reminded myself that this was not the time to confront him about his misplaced suspicions. This was about Sadie and her wedding. It wasn't my chance to pretend like I was on one of those daytime talk shows where I'd strap him to a lie detector to prove "that was a lie!"

"You know," I told him, "I said I didn't want you to interrogate me. I didn't say anything about not asking me questions. Those two things are different. I know a conversation is supposed to be give-and-take."

His hand drifted up, like he meant to touch my face, and my cheek tingled in anticipation. Then there was the sinking disappointment when I realized he wasn't going to follow through.

But he made up for it when he said in a low, rough voice, "I think I'd like giving and taking with you."

That had me swallowing hard, made my breathing shallow. My body apparently didn't care that none of this was real. I cleared my throat, trying to relieve the tightness. "I know that asking questions about another person is important. The last man I went on a date with didn't ask me any questions at all. Well, that's not strictly true. He did say, 'What else do you want to know about me?'"

He studied me for a moment, like I was a mystery he didn't understand. "I find it hard to believe that anyone lucky enough to date you wouldn't want to know everything about you."

He's playing us, I tried to tell my lady bits, but they were not listening. I needed to get all of us off this track. "You asked how I spend my free time. Um, I read. I watch TV. I volunteer on weekends when I'm not working. Boring stuff like that."

Camden nodded slightly, as if agreeing to the change in subject. "Where do you volunteer?" he asked.

"There's this shelter downtown that's associated with the humane society."

"Do you mean the Herbert and Wanda Leibowitz Center?"

That made me raise my eyebrows. "You know it?"

"Yes. That's one of my charities. We give them a large donation every year. Why haven't I ever seen you around?"

"Um, probably because I go to the local shelter and you hobnob with bigwigs at galas."

He seemed a bit confused, and it suddenly occurred to me that I probably wasn't supposed to know that he had money. I could easily explain it away by the quality of his clothes or his expensive watch, but to my surprise he didn't ask a follow-up question.

"I adopted my cat, Belle, from there. She's part Maine coon. A silver tabby."

Wow, that "I was just headbutted" feeling was back. Why was it incredibly hot that he owned a cat? So many guys hated cats and considered them to be "woman pets" that it immediately told me three things about Camden that I hadn't known so far—that he was secure in himself and his masculinity; that he might be a little unconventional; and given the affection in his voice as he talked about his kitty, that he had a big and loving heart.

All three of those things were incredibly attractive.

Camden, not knowing my brain had gone for a walk down He's Hot Lane, was still talking. "She's so smart. Too smart for her own good, I think. She knows exactly how to manipulate me into getting treats. I'd show you a picture but . . ."

"But your portable telegraph machine doesn't take very good photos?" I guessed.

Ignoring my slam on his outdated technology he asked, "What about you? Do you have pets?"

"I travel a lot for work, so it hasn't really been practical. I have thought I'd like to get a cat. They seem more independent than dogs."

"And more rewarding, in my experience."

"What do you mean?"

He finished off the last of his drink before he answered. "There's something triumphant about a little sociopath deigning to cuddle with you. It's like winning a prize. Dogs love everybody. Too easy—"

"That's not true," I interrupted. "My mom's three rescue dogs hate me. She got them because I won't give her grandchildren. She treats them like they're her babies. They've gone on more vacations than I did growing up and I'm pretty sure they have nicer bedrooms and better food." Realizing that I might be revealing a bit too much about my issues with my mom, I shook my head. "But enough about that. I'm more of a cat person, too."

It seemed like I was talking a lot. Was I talking a lot?

"I feel like I should grab a notebook so that I could make a list of all the things it turns out we have in common."

"A list?" I echoed, my heart racing.

"I like making lists. It gives me the illusion of being in control."

That was seriously the sexiest thing a man had ever said to me. I could only sit there with my mouth hanging open.

He briefly brushed his fingers against the side of my hair. "My guess is you're that way, too. Everything about you seems a tad controlled. Even your hair."

Without thinking, I reached up to touch the same spot on the side of my head that he had. This wasn't about control, was it? It was about convenience. It took far less time to twist my hair and put it up than it would to leave it down and have to curl or straighten it.

And I liked being in control. Who didn't? "I can be flexible. Totally flexible. Just as long as everything is going exactly the way I want it to."

At that he laughed and the sound of it made me feel like my veins were full of fizzy champagne bubbles. "What's not going your way now?"

"So many things. The bride's mother is a total—" I caught myself and continued, "Has a strong affinity for liquor, and her ex-husband and his inappropriately aged fiancée make her nuts and in the past they've gotten into public fights and as Sadie's maid of honor it is my job to make sure that there's no *Real Housewives* moments."

"Nothing's happened like that."

"Yet. Because I'm keeping an eye on things. I really want this to go well for Sadie." And it wasn't just because I was hoping she'd refer other people to me, but because I genuinely liked her as a person and wanted her to have the wedding of her dreams.

Yep, I was definitely talking a lot and had almost said things I shouldn't have. It was like sitting close to him was just destroying all of my defenses.

He shifted slightly, somehow getting closer so that our knees pressed together. This caused a trembling sensation that started at my knee and climbed up into my stomach. I didn't move away, and neither did he.

He said, "You could get on a plane tomorrow, and everybody at the wedding could start throwing punches and hitting each other in the face with folded chairs and Sadie and Dan would still be blissfully happy."

"They really do love each other," I agreed. "But I heard you weren't much of a fan in the beginning."

"I was a little worried that . . ."

"What?" I asked innocently when his voice trailed off.

"That maybe she wasn't with him for the right reasons. But I was wrong. And I say when I'm wrong."

I appreciated that, too. I'd dated more than one man who, if they'd been under the penalty of death, still wouldn't have admitted that they somehow might have possibly been wrong at some point in time. "Me too. You can add that to your list."

His expression turned serious. "Rachel, listen, there's something I want to—"

Sadie and Dan had approached us. "We should do cake!" she exclaimed.

I was torn—I wanted to hear what Camden had been about to say, but I also really, really, really loved cake.

Dan brought it over and put it onto the table in front of me. It had white frosting with red icing roses—my favorite. It said *Happy Birthday, Rachel* in red writing. Dan grabbed birthday candles from his front pocket and started just putting the whole lot of them on top of the cake. There were so many I felt a bit insulted.

Especially when Camden added, "And exactly how old are you again?"

I was about to object to the whole blowing-out-the-candle thing. I hadn't done that in years. I almost never celebrated my real birthday if I could help it. It usually made me stressed.

But I saw how excited Sadie was and I didn't have it in me to resist.

Krista joined the rest of the wedding party. Mary-Ellen was laughing and hanging all over Vance and I tried to ignore the sense of relief that I felt.

Our waitress came in and offered to grab us another round of drinks and everyone said yes.

Once she left, Dan lit the candles and they all started singing "Happy Birthday" to me. Camden's voice was rich and surprisingly on key, and I found myself focusing on that sound and keeping my gaze pointed at the candles.

Probably because part of me felt like a fraud. I spent so much time lying to people, but I was starting to really hate it this time. And I was pretty sure that was mostly due to Camden.

I didn't want to lie to him, but I had to.

When they finished singing Sadie told me, "Make a wish!"

I wish things were different and that Camden would really like me and that I could be honest with him.

I blew out the candles in one shot and everyone cheered. I decided to shove those guilty feelings out of my mind and do my best to be present and enjoy myself.

Krista grabbed her gift. "Open mine first!"

It still seemed a little silly to be getting presents for this non-event, but I was surprised at how relaxed I currently felt. It probably helped that this wasn't my actual birthday. There was no pressure on me, no phone call from my mother to remind me that with every year that passed my eggs were edging ever closer to their Best if Used By date. There was no feeling like I hadn't met all the goals I'd set for myself that year. It probably helped that I didn't know half the people in this room. Being surrounded by mostly strangers made this strangely freeing.

I tore open the wrapping paper and saw that Krista had bought me a nice set of highlighters that would be perfect for my organizer. "Thank you," I told her. "This was really thoughtful. I will definitely get a lot of use out of these!"

She grinned back at me, pleased with my reaction.

"Us next!" Sadie said, handing me a small gift bag. There was a ton of red tissue paper on top and I found a small black box at the bottom. If I didn't know any better, I would have guessed that it was jewelry.

When I opened the box I let out a small gasp. There were a set of beautiful pale-pink pearl earrings. "This is too much," I protested.

Sadie waved off my protest. "You can't come to Hawaii and leave without pearls. We insist."

"They're so beautiful," I said. "Thank you so much." I'd had many brides give me gifts, but nothing like this.

"My turn," Camden said, reaching for the last present on the table. It was oddly wrapped, and he placed it in my lap.

"This isn't a flip phone, right? Because I don't need to chat with Ulysses S. Grant."

That made him laugh. "I'm not telling you what it is. You're going to have to open it up and see."

CHAPTER NINE

There was an outer layer of wrapping paper and inside were two items wrapped in tissue. I opened one and saw that it was a ceramic, four-inch-long potato.

"What?" I asked.

"Open the other one."

When I unwound the second item, it turned out to be a ceramic tomato, about the same size as the potato.

It took me a second to understand what he had done, and then it hit me like a tsunami. If I'd been standing, I might have fallen over.

Oh . . . how did he . . . I couldn't finish my thoughts, let alone say actual out-loud words.

Somewhere off to my right Krista said in a delighted tone, "Aww. So sweet!"

"They're salt and pepper shakers," he said and I could feel tears forming at the edges of my eyes.

"But why a potato and tomato?" Sadie asked.

Krista piped up with, "It's something Rachel says," at the same moment Camden said, "It's an inside joke."

An inside joke. We had an inside joke.

Something happened inside me. A break or a tear, where there had once been a firm commitment to a path I'd chosen for myself and my employees. Light was shining through, filling me up. It suddenly seemed stupid that I was staying away from Camden when he so obviously got me.

His present made me feel seen, and it had been a very long time since a man had done that.

"Do you like them?" he asked.

Like them? There weren't words strong enough to express how very much I adored his gift. It was so thoughtful and just . . . amazing. "I thought the no-interrogation thing was my present."

He nodded, looking very pleased with himself. "I figured this was better."

"How did you even get it?"

"Dan and I went out for a bike ride this afternoon and we stopped at this store that only sells salt and pepper shakers. It was easy enough to find a tomato set and a potato set. I bought both and mixed them up. Which means I have the only other potato/tomato set of salt and pepper shakers in the world."

"It's perfect. Absolutely perfect," I told him. "I kind of want to name my firstborn child Potato Tomato, now."

"I think we just got upstaged by produce," Dan told Sadie, who nodded and gave me a knowing smile.

There was a part of me that didn't ever want me to be happy. Maybe it was the same bit that sounded like my mother, always reminding me of all the ways I'd fallen short. Whenever things seemed good, there was always a way to mess up my potential happiness.

"Why did you do this?" I asked him.

"What? The present?"

"Yes." I needed to understand. Would Camden really take things this far? Was he so dedicated to unmasking me that he was willing to completely mess with my head and my heart?

Because he had definitely affected me. I wanted to show him what this meant to me, how my heart had been touched. And there was only one way I could think of to properly convey what I was feeling.

To kiss him.

Which could not happen.

He shrugged. "Like I said, I thought you'd like it."

But there was more to it than that. Even if he wanted to make it sound like it had been no big deal, it had been the biggest of deals ever.

I wondered if he had his own internal Mom Voice that was holding him back from saying more.

Sadie handed me a plastic knife. "You have to make the first cut of the cake," she told me. I was having a hard time holding my hand steady, keeping my breathing even. I didn't know what to do with everything—how sweet Camden was being, how I was reacting to him even though I shouldn't.

After I made the cut I handed the knife back to Dan and let him do the rest. He started cutting up the cake, handing me one of the corner pieces. That was always the best because it had the most frosting.

I took a bite and sighed. I licked some of the icing off my lips and turned my head just in time to see Camden's gaze focused on my mouth, his eyes dark and intense.

Gulping against the fiery lump in my throat, I again wished that we were alone.

I'd finished off my piece of cake before Dan had passed one out to everybody else. Well, everyone except Mary-Ellen, who said she didn't put empty calories into her body.

Since it was my faux birthday, I decided not to remind her about the champagne.

I heard Mary-Ellen say to Vance, "I don't understand that salt and pepper thing. The only good present she got was the earrings."

She was so wrong. All of my presents were incredible. This might very well be the best pretend birthday I'd ever had.

Carol returned with more drinks for everyone, and I grabbed at my daiquiri. I was feeling a tad overheated with Camden's general sexiness and needed something to help me cool down.

He smoldered at me again and I realized the drink wasn't improving my situation.

"What happened to your cake?" Camden asked me, and although he'd received his piece right after me, he'd had only like, two tiny bites of it. "Do you want more?"

I considered what I should say. Should I lie? What was worse—telling him that I hadn't liked the cake and didn't want more or admitting that I had already hoovered up my entire piece?

"Um, I already ate it because it was really delicious," I told him. I couldn't slander cake's good name.

"I can see that," he said, reaching over to clean a piece of rogue frosting from my lips. I caught my breath when he touched me, but then he lifted his thumb to his own mouth to lick the icing off and molten lava started pumping through my veins and I seriously almost passed out.

"Did you want more?" he asked and I had to clamp my teeth together so that I wouldn't call out, *Oh, yes, please, I definitely want more!*

Only it wouldn't have been about the cake. "I do. I would like to have like, three more pieces of it but I'm afraid you'll judge me."

He looked perplexed. "Why do you think I'd judge you? I like seeing a woman enjoy herself."

Okay, that was it. I was done. Somebody needed to stamp the word *finished* on my forehead and just put me to bed before I got any more bad ideas than the ones I was currently entertaining and spontaneously combusted. I felt dangerously close to that actually happening.

Camden got me another piece of cake while I drank more of my drink. Still not cooling me off. What did a girl have to do around here to not be in a state of constant heat?

"Get me one with the red rose on it. Those are my favorite. Both the frosting and real-life kind."

"You got it," he said and handed me a piece that had one and a half roses on it. I liked a man who listened.

I took my first bite and tasted something plasticky in my mouth, but I ignored it. "Ew."

"What?" Camden asked.

"There was a piece of melted wax on my cake but I don't even care. This tastes so good."

That made him laugh, especially since I kept eating without slowing down. He cut me two more pieces and I dug into those, too. I hadn't remembered to eat dinner. Cake counted, right? It had nutritional value. Eggs, milk, butter. Oh! And vanilla extract! Was vanilla extract healthy? I couldn't remember.

Krista spoke up. "So Rick knows about this place that does night-time paddle boarding. Apparently the bottom of the board lights up and attracts all these cute little fish. I thought it would be fun for all of us to head over and try it out."

"We're so in!" Mary-Ellen said, linking her arm through Vance's.

"Us too," Sadie said.

Dan gave her side-eye and said, "Do you not remember my issues with the ocean?"

"I promise that no fish will touch you," she said. "Come on, it'll be fun."

He didn't even put up a fight. "Okay, but if I fall in and some underwater creature brushes against my skin, I will remember this. And remind you about it every day for the rest of our lives."

"Deal." She kissed him.

"Do you want to go?" Camden sounded hopeful and I couldn't figure out why. My brain was getting fuzzier. I should probably slow down on the baked goods.

Did I want to go? Not really. I'd spent most of the night wanting to be alone with Camden, to see what would happen. It was like all of my issues and inhibitions had just flown away and I could think about only one thing.

His lips on mine.

And if we were alone . . .

Some part of my mind squeaked in protest that it was a bad idea, but for the life of me I couldn't remember why it was wrong for us to kiss. If everyone else went away maybe I could figure all this out.

"My stomach actually hurts a bit," I told him. "I'm not feeling too well. I think I'd like to sit here for a couple of minutes."

"It's probably because you ate four pieces of cake," he said with a wink.

"Such a shame!" Mary-Ellen called out loudly. "But we should get going!" She tugged on Vance's arm, pulling him from the room.

Both Krista and Sadie looked concerned, and I knew they were about to offer to stay with me. Which would wreck all of my very-well-thought-out and carefully laid plans.

"I'll make sure she gets back to the hotel okay," Camden offered.

"Why, Camden, that's a fabulous idea," Sadie said, pushing on Dan's shoulders, trying to get him to move. "We'll see you later."

"You're such a gentleman," Krista told Camden with a tiny smile, as if she were in on my game plan.

"I don't understand what's happening," Dan said and Sadie hushed him, promising to explain it later and it was like they couldn't leave fast enough.

Which suited me just fine.

"Can I tell you a secret?" I asked Camden. Now it was my turn to move closer to him, to get right next to his warmth and yummy scent.

"You can tell me anything you want."

There was something pointed to his words, as if he were expecting me to come clean about my supposed James Bond impersonation.

"I feel fine," I told him. "I mean, I feel a little light-headed but that's probably from all the sugar I just ate and drank. I just wanted to be alone with you."

"Really?" He sounded shocked.

"Yes. Why is that so hard to believe?"

"Probably because you've blown me off every single time I've flirted with you."

Silly man. "Only on the outside. On the inside, I wanted to say yes."

At that he paused, looking me over carefully. "You seem a little drunk."

Hmm. I had been remarkably truthy this evening. But I thought I'd know if I were drunk. However, there was the fact that I couldn't seem to shut up. "I am being talkative."

"I noticed. I just thought my natural charm had finally started to work on you."

"Yeah, I bet you did."

He smiled. "What do you mean by that?"

"Oh, you know exactly what I mean. You're just sitting here with your charm hanging out all over the place like women are supposed to be able to resist it. It seems very unsportsmanlike to me."

Although I'd basically just told him he was irresistible, he frowned. "Let's go get a car to take us back to the hotel."

"Oh, let's go paddle boarding!" It suddenly sounded really fun.

"Maybe you shouldn't be out in open water right now." He stood up, indicating that it was time to go.

Party pooper. I tried to stand up, too, but it was like balance and my body had parted ways. Camden grabbed me and I didn't even get a chance to enjoy the sensation because my head was really spinning.

"I might have misjudged that," I announced.

"You misjudged the floor?"

"In my defense, it was moving."

He tried to straighten me back up, but I liked being pressed against him. "Floors hold still," he told me.

"Not this one. It makes it hard to calculate where to step."

"Okay, you are definitely drunk." He sounded irritated, like I'd somehow wrecked all his spy-hunting plans.

"I don't know how. All I had were my smoothies." I tried to think of how this might have happened, but it was hard to focus on anything but him. Then I gasped loudly. "Do you think Sadie spiked the cake?"

He shook his head. "I don't get it. Even if there was alcohol in your drinks, you only had like, three daiquiris and enough cake to feed a kindergarten class. You should be fine."

"I haven't mentioned that I'm a total lightweight? Like, just looking at a bottle of wine is enough to get me buzzed."

Carol came in to check on us and Camden waved her over. "My friend's daiquiris—she ordered them without rum."

At that Carol's eyes went wide. "I am so sorry, I didn't hear her say that. Our club is known for our overproof rum in our famous daiquiris, and I thought that's what she was ordering."

"What's overproof?" I tried to whisper to Camden, only it was loud enough that they both turned to look at me.

"It means it has twice the amount of alcohol as regular rum," he said, still annoyed. "You didn't taste the liquor?"

"I think they use fresh strawberries here or something. That was all I could taste." Plus, I'd totally been distracted by him the entire evening. That didn't seem like something I should be blamed for. "I'm not drunk, though. I'm just buzzed and full of pizzazz! But don't try to text that to anyone because otherwise we'll be here all night."

Carol apologized again, asking what she could do to help and Camden asked if she could grab a taxi and some bottled water for us.

Camden leaned me against a wall, and it felt good against my face. He took out his wallet and I turned slightly to see him leaving like three hundred dollars as a tip. It was more impressive given that we hadn't had to pay for anything tonight. Carol returned with the water bottles and he put them into his pockets.

He came back over to me, put my arm around his neck, and supported my waist with his free arm.

"I like men who leave big tips. It says a lot about your character. Your mom must have raised you right."

"I don't have a mom. Come on."

Didn't have a mom? Everyone had a mom. If he wanted one, he could have mine.

But before I could ask him to explain, he was moving us forward and I had to focus on putting one foot in front of the other. The floor seemed to be moving, shimmering in front of me so that it was always a surprise when my foot made contact. I couldn't look up at the walls because they were definitely spinning.

"Okay," I told him. "If I injure myself at some point, please tell the EMTs that I'm O positive."

"Does that happen a lot when you're drunk?"

"I'm not drunk," I insisted.

"I can see that." It sounded like he was agreeing with me, but it was obvious that he wasn't.

I kept knocking into him, my hip slamming into the water he was still carrying. After the third time it happened I asked, "Is that a bottle of water in your pocket or are you just happy to see me?" He looked like he wanted to laugh.

I stumbled hard and he had to hold up my weight so that I wouldn't fall.

"You know what," I said. "I think I am drunk."

"You don't say," he responded in that teasing tone of his and I was glad he was more like himself again.

"Why were you mad earlier?"

"At the events we've gone to so far, I noticed that you didn't drink. At the brunch you even spit out your mimosa."

"You saw that?" Wow. He really had been trying to catch me from day one. "It's probably that control thing. Getting drunk makes me feel out of control and I don't like it. I mean, it's fine now. But normally it upsets me."

"I'm guessing it won't be fine tomorrow and you will be mad," he said. "We're almost there."

"Does that mean you don't like getting drunk, either?"

"Nope. I don't like having misunderstandings with the floor."

Ha. That wasn't why. He didn't want to be out of control, either. I knew the real reason even if he didn't want to say it.

A taxi was waiting for us, and the driver did not seem happy when he saw me. Which I thought was kind of rude. Camden had to promise to pay extra if I got sick, but I wasn't that drunk. It seemed like overkill.

As the taxi drove away from the club, I studied Camden's profile. He looked like he needed a haircut—the way his hair curled just behind his ear was really cute. I reached up to touch it, and he flinched like I'd hit him with an ax.

"What's wrong?" I asked.

"You're not really yourself right now and should probably just get to bed."

"I can't help myself. Do you know that you smell really good? I think it's because you smell clean, like soap. As if you shower routinely. Like, that's how low the bar is for women. That a man having good hygiene is what does it for us."

He smiled again, but shook his head. "You might want to stop before you say something you regret."

I probably should have listened to him.

CHAPTER TEN

Because the next thing out of my mouth was, "I'm just telling you the truth. Why would I regret that? Isn't it a good thing to tell the truth?"

"It is." He seemed surprised by what I'd said. "I think we should all tell the truth."

"Right." I nodded, encouraged. "Like how you said you almost ruined your whole life because of a lie. That's bad. What happened?"

"Do you think you'll remember any of this tomorrow?" he asked, and I didn't know if he wanted reassurance that he could speak to me without fear of me recalling it or if he wanted to make sure that I would.

"Possibly. Guess we'll just have to wait and see."

"When I was twenty years old, I was training for the Olympics, like I mentioned. I had a coach who had been involved in a scandal a few years before and was in danger of being banned from the sport. He put all his hopes on me. We trained and trained, more than what was even necessary. At a half marathon, I twisted my knee and we went to a doctor. The doctor advised that I stop running for at least six months to allow my knee to heal, but the Boston Marathon was only a month away. And that's a qualifier for long-distance runners for the US team." He let out a big sigh. "My coach lied to me. Told me it was fine and that I'd get better if I just kept running and pushing myself. It made everything worse and I permanently injured my knee and ended my running career. If he'd just told me the truth, let me decide what I wanted to do . . ." His voice trailed off. "He took that choice from me and ruined my prospects. I don't like being lied to."

"That sucks. I'm sorry." That was a little hard to hear, being a big massive lying liar myself who lied to everyone all the time about everything in my fake life. How sincere could my apology be when I was currently lying to him? To be fair to me, I wasn't going to wreck his life or anything, but dang, Camden was going to hate me when he found out.

Whether it was to distract him or me, I wasn't sure, but I went for one of my patented changes of the subject. "In addition to smelling good, I think you should know that, objectively, you are hot."

That made him raise both eyebrows in amusement. "Am I?"

"Mm-hmm. Krista said that if she had to repopulate the planet, she'd choose you to do it. That's like, a really big compliment to your genes."

"Does that mean you think I'm hot?" He could have asked the question seductively, but instead it was very matter of fact. It was like he'd decided I was off limits and more like his buddy than a potential love interest and I was finding it all highly aggravating.

"You know you're good-looking." As if that were somehow in question.

"Seriously, you are going to be furious with me tomorrow. Maybe you should drink some water and then we can play the quiet game." He handed me the water bottle and while I knew it was in my best interests to drink it, I didn't feel like it.

Nor did I want to play a game where I had to stay quiet. I had so many things to say to him. "You win the quiet game! You know, I think my inhibitions are very lowered."

"I know. And you're not really a lowering-my-inhibitions-is-a-good-thing kind of girl."

"I can have fun," I insisted.

"That wasn't what I meant. I have fun with you already. I just know how I'd feel if I were in your shoes saying things that maybe I didn't want to actually admit out loud."

"Everything I'm saying I want to say." That was right, wasn't it? "Do you know what the problem is with me? It's a riddle. I'll give you a hint. It starts with a *D* and ends with *aiquiri*."

"Despite how intricate and complicated your riddle is, I think I solved it. Would you please drink water?"

"Okay, fine," I said, dragging out the vowels in my words, like an ornery teenager. "But only because you asked so nicely."

He reached over to open the bottle for me, which was considerate because I wasn't sure I could have managed it. My coordination seemed to be a tad bit . . . off. I had thought I wasn't thirsty, but as soon as the water touched my lips, it was like I couldn't get enough. I drank half the bottle in one go.

We pulled up to the hotel and Camden paid the driver and said, "Stay put. I'll come help you." He got out, then shut his door. I saw him jogging around to my side and I let out a noise of disgust.

I didn't need his help. I was a grown woman more than capable of getting out of a taxi all by myself. I opened the handle and swung open the door. I went to climb out of the cab and I sprawled forward, falling down on my hands and knees. My purse went flying, emptying its contents on the ground.

Camden was right next to me, helping me back to my feet. "I thought I told you to wait."

"I was managing fine."

"Yes, I noticed while you were getting O positive all over the pavement," he said, leading me over to a bench near the hotel's entrance. "Please sit here for a second."

Since my head was still spinning, I sat. He went over to my purse and started gathering things up. I said a quick prayer of gratitude that I did not have any feminine products in my bag. I had the sneaking suspicion that I might not have been able to look him in the eye again if I had a mental image of him picking up my tampons.

"That thing in your hand is called a phone," I told him when he got my cell phone and put it back in my purse. "You might not recognize it since it's from this century."

He ignored my jibe and grabbed my presents. I hoped my salt and pepper shakers were okay. They were still wrapped in tissue paper, so I figured they had probably survived.

"I think your mints spilled everywhere," he said. "Wait, these aren't mints. What is this?"

"That's my happy box," I told him as he started gathering little rolled-up pieces of paper. He unrolled one and I didn't even object.

"'Nice job.'" He opened another. "'Great work.' 'You should be proud of yourself.'" He looked up at me. "I don't get it."

Camden put the pieces of paper back into the mint box I kept them in and brought the box and my purse back to me.

"My mom is very demanding," I told him as I returned the box to my bag. "I know she loves me, but I'm an only child. A child my parents never thought they would have. So it's like they have all their hopes pinned on me."

"The grandkids thing?"

"That's part of it, but I've always felt like I had to be the best. The smartest. The most successful. And sometimes my mom is critical. I know she's trying to help me, but it can be overwhelming and I can get mired in self-doubt. So when someone leaves me a nice note—a teacher, a friend, a client—I tear it off and keep it in my box. They're reminders that somebody appreciated me and thought I was doing a good job. That I don't always fall short."

He seemed to be considering my words, and I saw a flash of sadness on his face. "That's pretty deep for someone who's had enough rum to make Captain Jack Sparrow woozy."

"You're right." The night was far too beautiful and warm to be wasting my time talking about things that depressed me. "I'm going to go for a walk on the beach. Do you want to come?"

"We should go inside and clean your hands."

I looked at my palms. "It's fine. It's not bad." I flicked a tiny black pebble away. "It doesn't even hurt." My head seemed a little clearer, so I stood up and only wobbled a little.

"I don't think that's a good idea," he said.

Shaking my head, I told him, "I wasn't asking for your permission."

He stood up, too. "I'll come with you."

Secretly, I was thrilled. This was exactly what I'd hoped he'd do. But I didn't want him to think that I was trying to manipulate him. Even if I was. "You don't have to."

He ran his fingers through his hair in a very attractive way. Some part of my brain registered that the gesture and the loud sigh that accompanied it were probably due to frustration.

"Why are you sighing?" I asked.

"Because I'm having visions of you getting dragged out to sea and then Sadie blaming me for losing her best friend to the watery deep. So obviously I have to accompany you." His tone was light, but I could tell that something else was bothering him.

I guessed he would tell me when he wanted to.

"This way!" I said, walking across the grass to where it met the white sand. My heels immediately sank and I was having problems navigating the beach.

Camden came up behind me. "Why did you stop?"

I flailed my hands around, ending up pointing at my shoes. "I can't walk with these things on and I'm pretty sure that if I try to take them off I'm going to end up with a head injury."

"Sand's pretty soft. I think you'll be okay," he teased, but then he knelt down next to my feet.

His fingers made contact with the bare skin of my right ankle as he undid the strap and then carefully slid my shoe off, holding me in place with his warm, strong hand. I put my palms on his shoulders, just to keep myself steady. Not so much because of the shoe coming off, but because of the waves of sensation that traveled from my foot up my leg and settled deep and low in my gut.

I tried for humor. "Why are you keeping a ham under your shirt where your shoulder's supposed to go?"

He either didn't get it or didn't think I was funny. The second one felt like the most realistic reason, and he was probably right to ignore me. I'd also said it in an attempt to deflect the feeling of his skin on mine, and it wasn't working. Like, I was headed into eyes-rolling-into-the-back-of-my-head-from-pleasure territory.

Camden took off the shoe on my left foot in the same way, intensifying all the feelings, and I kind of wanted to tackle him into the sand and have my way with him.

But then a part of my brain that wasn't drunk from rum and/or high off his touch recognized that he wasn't into it. He didn't brush his fingers against my skin like he could have, or linger a moment too long holding me in place, or run his hand along the back of my knee, or a million other things to show his interest that I would have eagerly welcomed.

No, instead he was all business and respectful.

"Here." He handed me my shoes and took off his own loafers so that we could walk along the shore together.

It was like something from a postcard; a full moon hung above us, reflected on the water. A cool breeze chased away the heat and humidity left over from the day, and a salty smell surrounded us. The sparkling sand felt warm and soft under my toes. The palm trees that marked the line between the beach and the hotel's grass made a soft hushing sound as we walked by.

Beautiful.

"Tell me something about you I don't know," I told him.

He shuffled his feet for a second and I realized that he was trying to match my gait, slowing down his longer stride to stay with me. He stayed silent for a moment and I thought he might not answer. But then he said, "I don't just work at a tech company. I'm the CEO. Dan and I started it together in college and it's about to revolutionize the entire world."

It took me a second to realize that he was watching me closely, waiting to see what I would think. Maybe waiting for a specific reaction? I made a buzzer sound, like on a game show. "Thank you for playing, we have some nice parting gifts for you." At his raised eyebrows I added, "I already knew that about you. You were supposed to tell me something I didn't know."

"Sadie told you?"

"Well, I am her maid of honor," I reminded him.

"Yeah, and this whole wedding is just a big distraction from next week, when the company goes . . ." He let his voice trail off and I found it more than a tad enjoyable that I wasn't the only one who wanted to say things I shouldn't.

I decided to mess with him. "When the company goes public?"

"How do you know that?"

"Didn't we just establish that I'm Sadie's maid of honor? My guess is Dan told her and then she told me."

He looked upset. "Did you tell anyone?"

"Obviously I have all the local New York news stations on standby, waiting to get more information from me." Camden came to a complete stop. I reached back to tug on his arm, to get him to keep walking. "It's a joke. No, I didn't tell anyone, Mr. Paranoid."

"If this leaks out beforehand . . . there's so many things that could make this all go sideways."

"I'd never do anything that would hurt Sadie," I told him, and that was true. I'd also have a harder time than I would have yesterday doing something that would hurt him, but as I began to sober up I realized that some things were better left unsaid. "I don't know why you think bad things about me, but I'm actually trustworthy. I won't tell anyone." Other than Krista, but that shouldn't count. She was under the same banner of secrecy.

"I believe you," he said, and I wondered if it was real. Or if he was trying to placate me and win my trust. Even wasted, that suspicious part of me wasn't willing to just enjoy the moment. I had to question everything.

Including why he hadn't done exactly what I'd asked. "By the way, you still haven't told me something I don't know about you."

"A secret?" he asked. "I bet you have a lot of secrets."

As someone who made a living at turning around conversations so that I wouldn't be caught out, I was impressed by how quickly he shifted things back to me.

"A lady should, don't you think? How else are we supposed to maintain an air of mystery?"

He gave me a rueful smile and we kept walking in silence. The beach on this side of the hotel wasn't very long; it came to an abrupt stop at a large rock outcropping. We would have had to climb up to keep walking along the sand and I was obviously in no condition to do that.

"We should head back," he said and I was disappointed. Maybe he hadn't told me something I didn't know already, but I liked talking to him and I really liked that he had at least shared something with me. It wasn't exactly personal, just his real job, but it was something.

It made me feel like I should return the favor. "Do you want to know a secret about me?"

CHAPTER ELEVEN

He nodded, ready for me to share my deepest, darkest secret with him. "I do. Tell me."

Was he a little too eager? "It's not my birthday."

His mouth turned down. "That's not really a secret. Sadie's not a great liar."

"You knew? Why didn't you say anything?"

"What would I have said? It's not like I could have demanded proof. You would have shut me down with that enigmatic way of yours, where you answer but don't answer and you leave me feeling confused and like I'm not really sure what happened."

"You say that like it's a bad thing," I told him. It just meant I was very good at my job.

"Actually, I kind of like it. I never know what you're going to say and I look forward to finding out. I like how you try to subtly redirect me. It makes me feel like I'm playing a really great game of chess. Watch out."

We were heading back toward the grass and there was a large, pointy rock in our path. We could have easily gone around it, but Camden stepped over. Then he reached for my hand to help me across and I put my hand in his. The sensation of his hand engulfing mine, helping me to jump over, sent seismic waves through me and then . . .

He didn't let go. He kept holding my hand even when the path didn't have any more obstacles. I liked how this felt—secure, safe, like I was being looked after.

So many relationships I'd had were on one speed when it came to the physical—super fast. I liked that he was just holding my hand. With no expectation of anything else. I almost felt like a kid in high school again.

Although, to be fair, this might have been just to make sure that I didn't fall over and injure myself.

His voice interrupted my thoughts. "Tell me something you're proud of."

At the moment? That I hadn't tried to make out with his face even once. "In college my alcohol tolerance used to be quite a bit higher and it took me a lot longer to get drunk than it does now. Is that what you mean?" I asked with a grin, and was rewarded with a matching smile.

"Not quite."

"Okay. Um, I started my own business."

"As an event coordinator?"

"Yes." It wasn't a lie; it was something I had to protect. But I really was pleased with what I'd done over the last few years. "I have fifteen employees and all of them are women in need of a fresh start."

"Like former stay-at-home moms?"

I wondered how much I should tell him. Then I remembered his Olympics story and thought I could share this with him. "No. Like women who were hurt by their supposed loved ones. Or who were victimized at their jobs." My voice caught on that one, and I wondered if he noticed. "Or who can't get jobs because of some past mistake. They're my second family and I'll do anything to protect them."

"I understand that. It's how I feel about Dan and his family, and our employees. We've been working on building this up since our junior year in college and some of those guys have been with us from the beginning. Everybody had to sacrifice a lot. We do profit sharing so when this company goes public, we're all going to be well taken care of. I'm making sure that that happens."

"I suppose those are some more things we have in common. Starting our own companies, doing profit sharing, being loyal and willing to do anything to take care of the people that are important to us." Anything. Even keep away from him. After tonight we would need to go back to being just friends.

"Guess I better break out that notebook," he said with a radiant smile that tested my resolve.

We walked into the hotel, through the lobby in our bare feet, over to the elevators. When one arrived, we stepped inside and Camden pressed the button for our floor. The silence was comfortable and I found myself wanting to lean against him, to rest my head on his shoulder. If I only had tonight, then maybe I should make the most of it.

The elevator stopped on our floor and we walked to our rooms, still holding hands. We stopped in front of my door and I almost giggled. And whether that was from nervous anticipation or something else, I wasn't sure.

I wondered if he was going to tell me he had a nice time and he'd call me. Like, as if we'd been on an actual date. Something inside me was telling me that feeling that way was still a bad idea, but in that moment I didn't care.

He dropped my hand and I flexed, keenly feeling the loss of his touch. I glanced at his lips. I'd been wanting to kiss him for several hours. I rationalized that it was fine since I'd given myself a cutoff time—pretty soon this Cinderella night would be over and we'd turn back into pumpkins.

My heart began to hammer hard in my chest, like it was saying *bad idea, bad idea, bad idea* over and over again, but I ignored it, instead focusing on the swooping feeling in my stomach that made me giddy and excited.

I took a step toward him.

And he took a step back.

He cleared his throat. "So, I guess I'll see you tomorrow at whatever big, secret thing Sadie and Dan have planned," he said awkwardly. There was a distance in his words and I wasn't sure what had changed. He sounded dismissive. As if we hadn't been having a really nice time together.

As if I hadn't been about to make a move on him.

That sensation in my stomach turned sour, sinking down to my feet. I'd already made enough of a fool of myself tonight. There was no reason to prolong the experience. I dug through my purse looking for my keycard. I thought he'd do the same, get out his card, go into his room, and leave me alone with my uncomfortable embarrassment.

Instead he just kept standing there like he wanted to say or do something, but I wasn't interested in whatever that was.

I got more and more frantic, not able to find where my keycard had gone. I let out a sound that was a cross between a sob and desperation.

He reached out and circled his fingers around my wrist. "Wait a second. What's wrong?"

What was wrong? Seriously? We'd just had a magical, if slightly drunken, night together, where I'd had the best birthday ever and I wanted to kiss him and he'd looked like he'd been disgusted at the thought.

I wanted to shake off his hand but found I didn't have the strength to do it, even though I felt like an idiot for all the warm fluttery feelings that I'd been having for him. That had probably been due to the alcohol and not his supposed interest in me. Because he definitely wasn't into me. He couldn't have made that any clearer.

"You can tell me," he said. "Whatever it is."

That irritated me. Why was he acting like we were friends? He wanted something from me and even now, when I was humiliated, he was still trying to get it. Wanting me to open up and tell him what he had been waiting so patiently to hear.

Instead I thought I'd tell him something that would definitely make him run away. "My mother wants you to give her grandchildren."

He looked completely confused. "Like, buy them?"

"No. Remember when I took that picture of you and denied it? My mom asked me to do it and then decided you were handsome and smart and we should make babies together."

If that didn't send him running straight for those beautiful green Hawaiian mountains, I didn't know what would.

But instead of being freaked out, he seemed *amused*. "You talked about me to your mom?"

He was so missing the point. "No, not in the way you're thinking. I mean, yes, I did talk to her about you, but no, not like that. She asked if there were any good-looking, eligible men at the wedding—"

"And, of course, you immediately thought of me."

I wanted to stamp my foot at him. I settled on pulling my wrist out of his grasp. "You were the only man I'd spoken to besides Dan, and he's the groom, so don't flatter yourself."

"It's far too late for that. You already did. And so did your mom by insisting you pick me to father your offspring." He leaned against the wall with his arms folded. I briefly wondered how much time I'd get if I brained him with one of my shoes. So arrogant.

"I mean, if I'm going to be your baby daddy I should probably know your middle name first. But we can talk about all of that when you're more sober."

This was not a joke. "I'm plenty sober."

"Agree to disagree. It sounds like your mom's the interfering type, huh?"

Camden didn't deserve an explanation, but I just couldn't contain myself when somebody else recognized my mother's insanity. "You can actually hear the whir of her helicopter blades as she hovers over me."

He shrugged. "I don't think that would be so bad."

"You're probably the only man on earth who thinks that. Trust me, it's no day at the beach." Which made me think of our romantic moonlit walk that hadn't actually been romantic—the "romantic" part had only been a figment of my alcohol-addled brain—and I wanted to escape. I went back to my keycard search, and it was like it didn't want me to find it. As if it were hiding. My fingers brushed against it and I let out a sigh of relief. I inserted it into the lock and when the light turned green, I turned the handle and pushed open the door.

I stood in my doorway, facing him, ready to make a mighty speech. About how I didn't even need him. And I didn't like him. That despite my ovaries throwing a party every time I saw him, I did not want him to be the father of my hypothetical children.

My stomach roiled and lurched suddenly, and it was as if a bunch of warning lights went off inside me, all at once—*eject! Eject!* Like I was a pilot whose plane had just been shot down. One second I was a bit dizzy but relatively fine and angry, and in the next I was going to do a real-life reenactment of that scene from *The Exorcist*. I made a choking noise, put my hand over my mouth, and ran for the bathroom.

"Rachel? Are you okay?"

I threw open the door and knelt down in front of the toilet. I had just gotten the toilet seat up when everything that had once been inside my body started to come out of my face.

Camden turned on the light, and that made everything worse. "What can I do?" he asked, hovering behind me.

"Go away," I told him. What did he think he was going to do? My hair was already up and I didn't need a spectator.

He closed the door behind him and once I heard it catch, I continued to empty out my internal organs. I had one of those marathon vomiting sessions, where you kept throwing up even though you had nothing left inside you. It was like my stomach was a clown car.

When my gut stopped clenching, my throat loosened, and that nauseous feeling passed, I flushed the toilet. I brushed away the tears from my eyes, grabbed some toilet paper to wipe off my mouth, and threw it into the bowl. I closed the lid and rested my head against it, the porcelain cool and refreshing.

I knew I should get up, but I felt too weak to move.

There was a knock at the door, causing me to lift my head. He'd stayed? After I'd told him to leave? He'd just been standing there, listening to me retch over and over again?

"Are you done?" he asked.

When I didn't answer, he opened the door and I saw a look of relief. I could feel that my face was all flushed but I didn't know if that was from the straining I'd done while puking or the utter mortification I was currently feeling.

I must have looked like such a mess. I knew I had sounded awful.

Well, if I'd harbored any secret hopes that we might start to like each other, I'd just flushed all of those down this toilet.

"Didn't I tell you to go away?" I asked.

"I did go away."

"No, you're still here."

"I went away from the bathroom. Technically I did what you asked," he said. "But I thought you might need me."

"For what?"

Camden finally looked unsure of himself, a state of being he probably didn't experience very often. "I could, I don't know, help you get into bed."

"I don't need your help for that. I'm fine. I can . . ." I tried to stand up and it didn't work because my legs gave out.

He rushed forward to catch me before I hit the ground. He hefted me up, very carefully cradling me against his chest as he carried me back into the bedroom. It was so nice. I never would have told him that, but I loved being curled up against him, relying on his strength to help me because I currently had none of my own.

It was like that same feeling I'd had when he'd held my hand—that reassurance that I was safe and everything would be fine.

He'd already pulled down the covers and laid me against the cool sheets, which felt amazing. He gently put the blankets around me once I'd settled in and then he walked out of the room.

My hazy brain thought maybe he'd finally left, but he came back into the bedroom a second later carrying a large glass of water and some aspirin. He put them on the nightstand next to me.

"You're really dehydrated, so drink when you can," he instructed me.

I nodded to show him I'd heard.

"One more thing," he said, running back to the bathroom. He returned with a hand towel that he folded up. He placed it against my forehead and I realized that he'd run it under cool water and it felt amazing.

"Thank you," I croaked, suddenly realizing just how sore my throat felt.

"She thanks me!" he said with a smile. "I didn't know such a thing was possible."

I knew he was teasing, but I was in no mood for it. "I'm a polite person."

He said something that sounded suspiciously like, "To everyone else," but I chose to ignore it. I was the debilitated one here. I'd probably just wrecked this hotel's plumbing with what had poured out of me. The least he could do was not give me a hard time.

"I'm such a hypocrite," I mumbled, trying to find a comfortable position.

"What do you mean?"

"I have to keep Sadie's mom from being fall-down drunk and here I am. Fall-down drunk."

"It's not the same," he reassured me. "You didn't even know you were having alcohol."

"It's the same end result."

"No, it's not. Nobody's upset by what happened tonight. You didn't ruin anything."

Hadn't I? I'd had this good, reasonable, and logical game plan where Camden Lewis was concerned. I was going to be professional and courteous and do my job and not worry about him. I most definitely was not going to flirt with him.

It kind of felt like I'd ruined everything.

"So . . . ," he said, "I guess I'll see you tomorrow at that party Dan and Sadie are throwing."

"I can't believe they won't tell us what it is," I grumbled, pulling the covers up to my ears. I didn't care for surprises. "They owe us."

"Definitely. I mean, you just threw up half a cake in an attempt to make them happy."

I smiled slightly underneath my covers. "I guess it wasn't all bad. Frosting tastes the same coming up as it does going down."

"I did not need to know that," he said, sounding grossed out. "I'm taking that as my cue to exit."

"Wait." I pulled the blanket higher so that it covered my eyes. "Would you mind staying until I fall asleep?"

I couldn't have explained what made me ask, but I meant it. It wasn't like I could blame the rum this time—I had definitely purged all of it, along with most of my internal organs. This was just me. I did want him to stay. I craved that feeling he gave me, the one that I was looked after and things would be fine, to stay until I was asleep.

There was a long pause and I almost risked looking at him but was too chicken.

Finally he said, "Sure."

I let out a long breath as he turned out the lights. I heard him settle into the armchair that was situated by the foot of my bed.

"Good night, Rachel."

"Good night, Camden."

I closed my eyes and let out a deep breath, comforted by him being close by. Just one thing left to say before I lost my courage.

"Camden?"

"Yeah?"

"My middle name is Marie."

CHAPTER TWELVE

I woke up the next morning with a pounding headache and a fuzzy tongue. It was like something had crawled in my mouth and died. I let out a groan before pushing the covers off my face. I turned to my side and grabbed the aspirin and water and swallowed both.

In that moment, all of last night came rushing back to me.

Camden.

I looked at the armchair, but he was gone. The only sign I had that he'd even been here was the water and medicine. It was almost like I'd imagined the entire interaction. There was a hazy filter over my memories of last night.

Until there wasn't.

I sat up in bed and gritted my teeth at the jolt of pain that shot through my head. I thought of all the things I'd told Camden, how he'd seen me deposit daiquiris and cake into my toilet. I mentally scrolled through my memories, trying to see if I'd told him too much.

I'd for sure told him that he smelled good and was hot, and I'd attempted to kiss him. All totally humiliating, but I let out a sigh of relief when I realized that I hadn't told him the truth about my relationship with Sadie. So I'd shamed myself in such a way that I never wanted to see him again, but at least I hadn't broken the NDA.

It was like I'd become this totally different version of myself. A flirtier, freer, ready-to-spill-her-guts (both metaphorically and literally) kind of woman. I hadn't recognized myself.

What was I going to say when I saw Camden again? Because despite me wanting to hide in this hotel room for the next three days, that wouldn't be possible.

My phone rang and I had to get up, letting out another moan. My skull felt like it was trying to push my brain out the top of my head. I had dropped my purse on my way to the bathroom and I found it in the small hallway. I reached inside and grabbed my phone.

A New York number I didn't recognize was calling me.

My heart started thudding in time to my headache. It had to be Camden. Because outside of my parents, my employees, and my clients, nobody else had this number. I had created a contact for every number that had ever called me.

I didn't answer. I brought my phone back to bed and plugged it into the charger since it was nearly dead.

It stopped ringing and I felt oddly disappointed. I wondered if he'd call back.

Ugh. I had to get a grip on myself. This couldn't happen. I wouldn't let it. There was too much at stake here. I had people to protect. I did not need to dial the number to see if it was actually him.

When I looked at my missed calls, I saw that the same number had called two other times this morning and I'd managed to sleep through both of them.

Which wasn't surprising. I could sleep through just about anything. When everyone else complained about not being able to sleep with all the noise in New York, I honestly had no idea what they were talking about. Which also had its disadvantages. There could be a four-alarm fire in my apartment building and I wouldn't know.

Just like how I had no idea what time Camden had left. What had possessed me to ask him to stay? How had I let everything get so upside down?

I glanced at the time on my phone and realized it was almost noon. I had slept for so long. It was unlike me. I wondered what else I had missed.

As I scrolled through my notifications I saw that one of the missed calls was from Desiree, my employee working for the New Jersey bridezilla. I called her back and quickly determined that things were spiraling out of control there and she wanted to know if I could come to the wedding. They weren't sure they could manage.

The only way I could swing that would be to get on a red-eye directly after Sadie and Dan's wedding reception. Once the newlyweds had left for the evening, I'd ask Mandy to help Brandy get back to her room and my responsibilities would be over.

I got on the phone with the airline and had them change around the flights for me and Krista to the new day and time and to have my flight take me directly to Newark instead of JFK.

I texted Krista to let her know about the changes and she sent me back a thumbs-up. It surprised me a bit that she didn't ask me about last night, and that she didn't volunteer any information about her own activities. To gush if she'd had a good time or to complain if she hadn't.

It was very unlike her.

My phone rang again.

"I love the smell of wedding emergencies in the morning," I muttered.

Only this time, it was my mother. I wondered if she could hear me rolling my eyes over the line. "Hi, Mom."

"Hi, sweetie. Where are you?"

What kind of question was that? "In my room."

"With Camden?"

Matricide was still illegal, right? She was making my headache a thousand times worse. "No, Mother. Sheesh."

"Why not?"

It was actually a shock that I wasn't more messed up. "Nobody is making you any grandchildren right now."

She let out a dramatic sound and then said, "That's a shame."

I wondered what it was like to have a normal mother. "Mom, I need to get going. I've got a lot to do today."

"Okay. Do you want to say hi to your brothers?"

"Mom, they're not my—"

The next thing I heard was her three dogs barking at me angrily, still disliking me even thousands of miles away.

I'd never understood why she pushed the dog thing so hard. We lived across the country from each other. It was okay if her dogs weren't fans of mine. Teddy, Toby, and Tommy were free to be at war with me.

They were her "triplets" because she'd adopted them all on the same day (all different breeds) and she'd given them human names in what I could only guess was some kind of message of her expectations for me. I didn't have a degree in psychology or anything, but my mother was going to be what doctors commonly described as "deeply disappointed."

Nor did I understand her infatuation with Camden. I'd gone on real dates with actual men and she'd never been like this. Maybe she was getting desperate and was ready to foist me off on any guy who so much as spoke to me.

At this point I wouldn't have been surprised if she'd started offering them a dowry or something.

She got back on the phone once the barking had turned into a dull roar. "They love you so much!"

I had a scar on my left ankle from where Tommy had sunk his teeth into me and still mourned my favorite pair of high heels after Toby had defecated in them and I'd been forced to throw them away, but sure, the dogs loved me.

Before I could respond she asked, "Are you going to be spending some quality time with Camden today?"

"Mom, why would I—"

I didn't have long to wonder what she was up to, as she finally saw fit to enlighten me. "I had the loveliest conversation with him a few hours ago."

"What?" I mean, I recognized all of the words she had just used, but the order she'd used them in made no sense. How would she have talked to Camden?

"I forgot about the time difference because usually you're two hours ahead of me instead of two hours behind me and I called you and it was probably like four in the morning and you didn't answer your phone. I had the front desk connect me and there was this sleepy handsome man answering, telling me that you weren't feeling well and he'd have me call you later. I can't believe you finally listened to me and took my advice. It's better than Christmas!"

What was it about this man that made every woman who met him want to set him up with me?

"It's not what you think." Did one tell their mother that they were really drunk and were sleeping it off and that they had asked the man who had been nice and helpful to stay because one didn't want to be alone?

There was no way to describe this to her that wouldn't send her down the wrong path. No matter what I said or did, or how innocent I tried to make it seem, she would pole vault over me to get to the wrong conclusion.

"You don't want to know what I think!" she said, with that annoyingly chipper singsong tone of hers.

No, I most definitely did not. "Okay, I really do have to go. Love to Dad. Talk to you later."

I half expected her to call right back in an attempt to pump me for more information, but she didn't.

I had just finished using the bathroom when I heard my hotel phone ring. Was my mother trying to circumvent me from checking to see who was calling?

Or maybe she'd done it in hopes that Camden would answer again? "Hello?"

"Rachel? This is Troy. There is a wedding emergency and I need you down in my room right away."

"Is it Brandy?" I asked, the first place my mind went after I heard the word emergency. "Sadie? Is she okay?"

"Just get down here immediately." He told me his room number and then hung up. Troy was the kind of wedding planner who always prepped for emergencies. What could be so bad that he'd need me right away? I threw on some comfortable clothes, quickly brushed my hair, and twisted it into place. Troy had sounded like it was urgent, but I had to stop and clean my teeth. I half expected to see green fuzz growing on them, given how they felt and smelled.

I hurried toward the elevator and ran over a million worst-case scenarios in my head as I waited. It finally arrived and took me straight to Troy's floor. I sprinted to his room, banging on the door.

When he opened it he announced, "Finally!" and let me inside.

"What is it? What's wrong?"

"Lei," Troy announced. "We need lei for tonight and the florist made them in the wrong color. They have to be white. I told them white plumerias, but somebody messed up and they said they didn't have time to do new ones. I told them that was fine, I could do them by myself. But I need your help."

So, not technically by himself, then. "I thought you were only supposed to give them out as a welcome."

"There are several people arriving today for the party, and I don't want to overlook the new guests," he said.

His room was full of buckets of white flowers and he'd used his desk to set up a bunch of strings and a few long metal needles. He was kidding, wasn't he?

"Are you serious?" I asked.

"I never joke about weddings," he told me. "I'll show you how to make one. It's easy."

Troy and I had never worked together before. He'd heard about me from another wedding planner and, based on that recommendation, given my name to Sadie when she'd told him she needed a special type of bridesmaid at her wedding.

It was one of the things I focused on in growing my business—building reciprocal relationships with wedding vendors who would recommend me to their clients.

Which meant that I couldn't tell Troy no, even if his request was ridiculous. So I paid attention as he showed me the proper length for the string, how I should double it up and knot it at one end, hooking the free end to this foot-long steel needle. He pushed the needle through the bottom of the flowers.

"And you just keep doing that until the lei is full."

I looked around the room. "We have to make all of these?"

"Not *we*. My assistants and I are needed downstairs. But don't worry. I've called for reinforcements. If you haven't had lunch yet, please get room service. It's on me. I've left you my cell phone on the notepad there. Call if you need anything. See you soon!"

My stomach gurgled at the offer. It was past lunchtime, but I wasn't the least bit hungry. I still felt queasy and unsettled.

Then he left me alone. I sat down at the desk and sighed. I'd strung many a garland and arranged more than my fair share of floral centerpieces. A lei couldn't be that much different. It seemed relatively straightforward—just time consuming.

I'd finished three lei, pleased with how they'd turned out, when there was a knock at the door. Finally, Krista had arrived. I wondered if Mary-Ellen was going to show up, too.

Throwing open the door I said, "It's about time—" but immediately stopped when I saw who was standing there.

Camden.

CHAPTER THIRTEEN

He smiled at me like everything was just fine and normal and he hadn't woken up in my room at four in the morning, then announced, "I'm here about getting some lei."

"You are such a child," I told him. "And it's making lei, not getting . . . you know what? Never mind. I don't need any help." I still had several hours before the surprise event started.

I turned around and let the door start to swing shut on its own, but Camden followed me inside. "It looks like you need help."

Despite what I'd said, he wasn't wrong. "Fine. I'll show you how to make it." We didn't have to talk or anything. I put the desk between us as I gave him the exact same instructions Troy had given me. I didn't make eye contact with Camden, focusing on my task.

Fingering a flower on one of the completed lei he said, "You do good work."

He was not going to butter me up with compliments.

And I felt my resolve harden when he asked, "Should I write that down on a piece of paper so you can put it in your box?"

While I knew he was trying to be cute or whatever, his comment stung. It reminded me how much I'd shared with him last night. How I'd told him things I had never told another person.

Nobody else knew about my happy box.

"You can sit over there," I told him.

A strange expression crossed his face, but he took his needle and string and did what I said. I sat down at the desk, focusing on my task and doing my best to ignore him completely.

For a moment I considered texting Krista and having her join us. The only reason I hadn't so far was because when Troy said he had called for reinforcements, I'd assumed he meant the other bridesmaids. I never imagined that he would have contacted Camden.

And if I got in touch with Krista now? Once I told her what was going on she'd rush down here with a big bag of popcorn just to have the chance to enjoy watching my embarrassment. Then she'd probably say some inappropriate things.

Because this room was already chock-full of Grade-A one hundred percent awkwardness, and the longer our silence went on, the worse it got.

I was almost grateful when he finally spoke. "Are we just going to pretend like last night didn't happen?"

Feeling less grateful. "Can we? Because that would be great."

"It's kind of hard to forget you guzzling drinks like you were an eighteenth-century soldier about to have your leg amputated."

"That wasn't—" I saw that he was teasing me.

"How are you feeling today?"

"Sick," I responded.

"My guess is that comes from the duty-free pop-up you were running in your stomach."

"Ha ha," I told him although if I were being fair, it was a little bit funny.

"Did you need some aspirin? Or maybe a sledgehammer?" he offered.

He was relentless in trying to make me laugh, wasn't he? Like he knew humor would be his way in. "No, I took the aspirin that . . ."

That he'd left for me, but I didn't finish my sentence. I still didn't want to talk about what had gone on last night. I asked him, "Are you always this loud?"

"I'm not loud. You're just suffering from the aftereffects of rum flu."

I focused on the lei I was making. He knew how cute he was, and I was not about to be sucked into it.

Was. Not.

Then he said, "I'm aware that you're trying to change the subject."

"I prefer to think of it as gently steering our conversation in a different direction on purpose."

"You're not the only one who can do that. So, you didn't answer when I called you this morning," he commented, correctly guessing that I wouldn't be able to resist his bait.

"That's because unlike you, I have caller ID." I wanted to ask him how he got my number but knew that there were a handful of women who were supposed to care about me that would have happily handed it to him.

"Well, fortunately I'm not snobby like you, and when a phone rings, I answer. If I didn't, I wouldn't have had the chance to chat with Lindsey."

"Do not call my mom that."

"Her name?"

"Yes, her name. Like you guys are friends or something." As if I hadn't already had an earful from her this morning.

"What are you talking about? We are friends now. We're going to get lunch the next time she comes to visit you."

"You're not funny," I told him.

"Objectively, I believe that I am."

Did he not get how mortifying this whole situation was? Me not being myself last night, him having a chat with my overzealous mother, not being able to explain any of it to him. This whole thing was like a talk of shame.

To pile on, Camden offered, "Your face is all red."

Should I thank him for pointing out the obvious? As if I wasn't aware that my face was currently on fire from embarrassment?

Why could I not be around this man and just behave normally?

Because you like him.

I told Mom Voice to shut up and mind her own business. I'd heard quite enough from her today.

"We should focus," I told him. "A lot of people are paying a lot of money for all of this to go perfectly."

"Yeah," he said with a short laugh. "Including Dan."

So much for focusing. "What do you mean?"

"Can I tell you a secret?"

His words slammed into my chest, and I felt them twisting and turning inside me. They were the words I'd said to him. My secret had been harmless, but that desire had been there. To tell Camden about myself, to be seen by him.

He probably hadn't meant anything by it, and I knew I shouldn't overreact. "If this is something dumb like how much you can bench-press, I'm not going to be responsible for my actions."

"It's nothing like that. I probably shouldn't say anything, but not all of the sponsors are fully . . . sponsoring this event."

"I'm not following."

He put down the lei he was working on. "Some of them were only willing to offer a percentage off rather than the entire cost, and Dan stepped in and covered the rest."

"Sadie doesn't know that," I said, feeling a bit alarmed.

Camden nodded. "I know she doesn't know."

"But you told me." Was he not worried about me running off to tell her? I was supposed to be her best friend, after all. Should I tell her? This seemed like one of those things I might need to keep to myself. She might be devastated. Or she might be fine with it. I didn't know her well enough to accurately predict her reaction.

Maybe she'd see it as romantic, because I was sure that's how Dan meant it. She'd taken on those sponsorships to prove that she wasn't after his money, and he had secretly covered the missing portion because he loved her. He wanted her to have her cake and eat it, too.

Regardless of what was going on, this wasn't my secret to tell. Even if Sadie found out and got upset, I couldn't imagine them staying angry at each other for very long.

Camden spoke, interrupting my internal debate. "You're right. I did tell you."

There was something more to his tone, but I was apparently too hungover to appreciate subtle nuance. "Why would you do that?"

"Do you really have to ask?"

Why did he think he was being obvious when he was being the very opposite? He was making my headache worse. I didn't know what to say, so I said nothing.

When I didn't respond, he just shook his head. I got the feeling I had disappointed him. He started working on his lei again. The lei that he was wrecking.

"That's not how it goes," I said.

"It's fine. It doesn't have to be perfect, Madam Lei Tyrant."

I got up from behind the desk and walked over to him. "Despite your obvious insinuation, I'm not some kind of craft control freak. And you're doing it wrong."

"You're really proving that whole not-a-control-freak thing," he said as I reached for the lei.

He looked up at me and my heart started doing cartwheels. I'd been so busy avoiding making eye contact with him that I'd forgotten how beautiful his eyes were.

My breath caught and I forced it out of my chest. I wasn't going to pass out just because he was looking at me. "The, uh, flowers all have to be facing in the same direction."

"They are."

"No, you turned this one the wrong way."

He looked to where I was pointing and asked, "How did you see that all the way across the room?"

Because I'm becoming obsessed with you and everything you're doing and thinking and I was just waiting for an excuse so that I could come over and be close to you?

Obviously, I didn't say that.

I tried to take a step back, not willing to be sucked in by his sexy gaze. He reached for my hand and stood up, so close to me. So very close. A pang of crackling tension raced along my nerves, making it difficult to breathe.

I stared at his neck, thinking that would somehow make my pulse stop throbbing, but it didn't work. All I could think of was what it would be like to press a kiss against his throat.

What kind of sound he might make if I did.

Why did I want something so badly that I knew I couldn't have? It was like that time I tried to give up sugar and every bakery I passed gave me the shakes and I'd had to resist the impulse to press my face against the glass.

That probably wasn't a very apt comparison, considering that the sugar fast had lasted only three days. I could make it three more days again, right?

Only the desire in his eyes made me think I wasn't going to last three more seconds.

"Why are you afraid of this?" he asked.

What *this*? The fake *this* where he was trying to make me reveal that I was a spy? There was no *this*. "I don't know what you're talking about."

My stomach hollowed out when he somehow managed to get even closer to me without touching. I gulped hard, willing myself to resist.

"You know. This sexual tension."

I tried to remind myself about how he'd blown me off last night, hoping that would make it easier to keep my raging hormones in check.

But he stood in front of me all hot and lickable and what was I supposed to do? It was like a switch had been flipped inside me and there was no way to turn it back off.

No matter how much I denied it, I was so attracted to him. And even if things had been different for him before, unless he was the world's best actor, he was attracted to me, too.

But none of that mattered. It couldn't happen. "I think maybe you're unclear about the meaning of *sexual tension*."

He ghosted his lips over mine, and I felt it in my knees. He wasn't even touching me but my lips still burned and tingled as if he had. "Oh, I'm very clear about what it means," he murmured just above my mouth, making me blaze and shiver at the same time. "And it's been happening between us from day one."

"That's . . ." I was having a really hard time forming words as I no longer had control over the air coming into or out of my body. I wanted to melt against him. His teasing was driving me wild. It had to be stopped. "Nothing is going to happen between us."

"*When* I kiss you," he said, his lips still impossibly close to mine, making it so that I nearly missed the way he'd put an emphasis on *when*, like it was a foregone conclusion that it would definitely happen, "it'll be because we both want it. Nobody will be impaired. You won't feel sick. And there won't be any more secrets."

That was the cold bucket of ice water I needed to reengage my brain. Camden and his secrets. He really was a good actor. This had all been a lie to get me to confess the "truth."

There was a knock at the door and I didn't even care who was on the other side. Because whoever they were, they had just saved me from doing something really, really stupid.

I stepped back, trying to regulate my breathing.

"We'll talk about this later," Camden said in a voice that sounded both sexy and demanding.

Oh no, we would not. I ran for the door, yanking it open. Irene was there, and I was confused. Surely Troy wouldn't have called Dan's mom to come help us, would he?

She glanced from me to Camden and asked, "Am I interrupting something?"

He said, "Yes," at the same time that I said, "Nothing at all."

It absolutely had been nothing. And it had to stay that way.

CHAPTER FOURTEEN

"Come on in!" I invited her, a bit too eagerly. A chaperone would definitely ensure that I remained on my best behavior.

If I couldn't keep my traitorous body under control, and my brain wasn't willing to be polite but distant with Camden, then the only thing left was to make sure that I wasn't ever alone with him.

Irene entered the room and I couldn't blame her apprehensive look. Despite what I'd told Camden, the sexual tension between us was so thick that even a machete couldn't have cut it. She seemed to be sensing it, but only said, "What can I do to help?"

"I didn't want you to come down here," he assured her. "I was letting you know where I was going to be for the next few hours in case you needed me."

Again I wondered why he treated Irene like she was his mom, too.

The one thing I did know was that she probably should be resting. "We're okay. We don't need any help." Why did I like using the word *we* when it came to me and Camden?

No time to examine that weirdness.

Irene sat down on the two-person sofa near the patio doors. "I want to. I haven't gotten to contribute much."

I exchanged a glance with Camden and while we were both worried about her health, neither one of us was willing to take this away from her.

So I walked her through how to make the lei, and I felt Camden's gaze on me. When I glanced over at him, there was an indescribable expression on his face. When he caught me looking, he shifted to a slight smile, giving me a nod. He liked what he was seeing. It made him happy.

Ignoring the way that his approval made my blood thicken in my veins, I focused on finishing up my explanation.

"Easy enough," Irene said. "I used to do cross-stitch before the cancer, but given the pain and exhaustion from treatment, I haven't been able to do it lately. Once I'm cancer-free I hope to take it up again."

I dragged a bucket of flowers closer for her, bringing over the string and a needle. I sat in the chair next to the sofa, wanting to be close by in case she needed anything.

Camden seemed to have the same thought as he sat in the chair across from me, directly in my line of vision.

"Rachel and I got a chance to chat at the bridal shower," Irene said to him. "Did you know that she grew up in California, just like you did?"

"California?" he repeated, his "what is your secret?" look back on his face. "But I thought you went to camp with Sadie in New York."

Did this man ever forget anything he heard? "I did. My maternal grandparents live in New York so I'd visit them for a week and then go to camp. My parents liked the idea of family being nearby and I liked the idea of traveling across the country." I actually had gone to camp in New York for the reasons I'd just listed. I tried to keep my backstory as close to my real life as possible. It made it much easier to keep track of everything when I pulled it from my actual life.

"Which do you prefer?" Irene asked. "The East or the West Coast?"

My mom was on the West Coast, and so that kind of ruled it out. "I think I prefer living in New York."

Camden interjected, "I don't know how much you can trust her opinion. She roots for an awful school."

Irene's face dropped. "Oh no, you're a Wolverine?"

"I tried telling her, but she didn't listen," Camden said with a wink that did unmentionable things to certain parts of my body.

"Sorry, I can't hear you over the sound of our decade-long winning streak," I said, and it made them both laugh.

"Rachel also started her own business," Irene added and I wondered what she was up to.

"I heard," he said and I tried not to let those words affect me, remembering feeling close to him and sharing parts of my life with him.

"And you're . . ." Irene tried to remember. "A wedding planner?"

"Event coordinator," I said.

"How did you get into that?" she asked.

"I was a bridesmaid for several of my friends that I'd grown up with and realized I was really good at helping to coordinate things. I'm organized and work well under pressure." Well, usually, when the pressure didn't involve a handsome man trying to put me under his spell.

"So you kind of fell into it?" she asked. "It's not what you went to college for?"

"No, I started out in finance." I realized a moment too late what I had done. From the way Camden's eyebrows lifted, it was obvious that I'd set off his internal spy alarms. He opened his mouth, ready to ask me about it.

Irene accidentally intervened. "Do you do a lot of weddings, then?"

"It's what my business focuses on."

"What's the worst thing that's happened at a wedding? Just so we can be prepared," she said with a little laugh, but there was something behind it. Something she was concerned about.

"I don't want to freak anyone out, but things always go wrong at weddings. Usually they're little things, like a bridesmaid's bouquet going missing or people flubbing their vows. But I think I've seen everything. From medical emergencies, to brides and grooms running away, to actual fires and floods. There was the one where the bride and her sister were both in love with the groom and the sister showed up drunk and the bride had her in a headlock and we had to pry them apart. Lots of drunk people messing things up. Animals who were part of the ceremony peeing and pooping in the aisle. Mothers of the groom wearing white to the wedding. We had a best man once who was so drunk and so sick that he passed gas during the ceremony and made one of the bridesmaids throw up. Oh! There was the wedding where the bride, who ran a pet shop, insisted on having bowls with fish on each table, and her mother wanted to put floating lit candles on the top."

Irene's eyes went wide. "No."

"Oh yes. All those poor fish died and one of the flower girls wouldn't stop screaming when she saw it and had to be taken out of the reception. It was pretty awful."

She reached over to rap on the wooden table next to her. "Knock on wood, none of that happens with this wedding."

"I'll make sure it doesn't," I told her.

"You're a very good friend," she responded.

Camden's phone rang and he pulled it out of his pocket to look at it. "Excuse me a second."

He went out into the hallway and I could hear his muffled voice just beyond the door.

"I told him he works too much," Irene said, putting another flower onto her lei. "He doesn't listen, though."

"Children are funny that way," I said. "Especially when they're adults." And could make their own life decisions and didn't need a mother telling them how to live. "I feel like parents forget that part."

"We don't forget. We're just, unfortunately, very human. We wish we could be perfect for you, but we've got our own strengths and shortcomings, just like anyone else. We make a lot of mistakes, even when we don't mean to. But Camden does need to slow down. He's been obsessed with his company going public."

I wondered if he would have shushed her if he were still in the room. But she kept going. "He's especially concerned about the money he's going to get."

That surprised me. When I'd talked to him earlier, he'd made it sound like he was more concerned with his employees than himself. I found this disappointing. "He wants to be rich, huh?"

"Oh no, I'm afraid it's on my account. I'm the only parent they have left. Dan's father suffered a heart attack a few years ago and now this." She waved up to the scarf on her head. "There's an experimental trial that's not covered by insurance and it costs hundreds of thousands of dollars and Camden says they're going to pay for it after the company goes public."

I immediately felt ashamed for having rushed to the wrong conclusion about him. It might have been due in part to rich men in my life doing their best to destroy me, and I could have used that disdain to keep Camden at arm's length. Instead he had to go and be all noble.

"I'm so sorry," I mumbled. About her husband dying, what she was going through, and the bad things I'd thought about Camden.

"They wanted to wait a few years until after their first CPU hit the market, but decided to speed things up and do it now. With Dan getting married, there's all of these huge life changes happening at once. All I have to do is get Camden settled and happy." She told me this information like a concerned parent, not as someone who was trying to make me into that person in Camden's life. It was rather refreshing.

But I was still a bit confused. "Why do you talk about him like you're his mom?" I asked. It was a relationship I still hadn't quite figured out.

"That's not my story to tell." She reached over to pat my hand.

I couldn't help myself, even though she'd just politely told me to back off. "Was he living with you when he hurt his knee?"

She blinked slowly. "He told you about training for the Olympics and his accident?"

I nodded.

"He doesn't share that story with anyone. I think only Dan and I know it. It says a lot about you that he told you."

I decided not to share that the reason he'd told me was because he assumed I'd be too drunk to remember.

Still, her words somehow managed to make me feel both giddy and stressed. To find out that I was in possession of information that had a high level of significance to Camden, and then to fret over what exactly that meant. Was it part of his ploy? Did he really just think I'd forget? Or did it mean something more?

Something I hadn't considered during all of this mess was just telling Camden the truth. Not about the maid-of-honor gig, but about the spy thing. The downside was that it might make him angry with Sadie and Dan for having let it slip, but if I told him I knew, that would bring a stop to everything, right? He'd stop trying to seduce me and I'd stop being seduced. Win-win.

There was a knock at the door. Camden wanting to be let back in. Although I didn't quite feel up to facing him again after the information Irene had shared with me, I got up and answered.

"How was your telegram to the past?" I asked, trying to lighten my own mood.

"Your mom says hi," he said with a smirk, coming into the room.

A frozen panic wrapped around my heart. Had he really talked to my mom? I followed him back to the sitting room and tried to calm my racing heart. My mother could so blow all of this for me. I'd emphasized many times that she couldn't say a word to anyone. I probably should have clarified that it also included men she was considering as possible fathers to her grandkids.

There were many things she could have told him. Not just about my job. She had a whole lifetime of embarrassing moments to choose from. Like the Padded Bra Fiasco or the Spray Tan Incident.

Maybe Camden had some of those, too. "So, what was Camden like growing up?" I asked Irene. Even if I didn't understand their entire situation, it was obvious that she considered him to be like another son.

He made a face, but she either didn't see it or didn't care. "He was pretty normal. He read comic books and played video games. He was also terrible with girls."

"Really?" I asked, delighted.

"Untrue," he retorted, and his denial made me giggle.

Irene smiled, as amused as I felt. "What was the name of that girl that you had the huge crush on? Lara Croft?"

"Lara Croft?" I repeated. "The video game character with the really big . . ." My eyes drifted to Irene and I shifted to, ". . . desire to raid tombs?"

"You know that game?" he asked.

"You weren't the only kid with a PlayStation."

Shaking his head at me, he turned back to Irene. "The girl you're thinking of was Laura Hoff. And she didn't give me the time of day."

"It sounds like she was exceptionally stupid." The words were out of my mouth before I could even consider whether it was wise to speak.

"Why would you say that?" he asked.

Um, because she wasn't smart enough to date you? I kept it to myself.

"I don't like to speak badly about other women, but she was not very bright," Irene agreed with me. At least someone else in the room got it. "He didn't figure out he preferred smart women until he got into college. Then after he graduated he got so busy . . ." She let her voice trail off with a sigh.

Camden pointed at Irene's lei. "She's got a flower backward. Why aren't you telling her she's doing it wrong?"

"Now who's changing the subject?" I asked him. "Irene can do whatever she wants and it is perfect."

"Yeah, you weren't saying that ten minutes ago," he grumbled and I wanted to laugh again.

"Tell me more," I invited her, and it was all I needed to get her talking. She didn't explain their situation any further, but told me stories about Camden and Dan growing up, like how they got caught stealing gum from a store when they were twelve and how Dan's father had marched them back to the store to apologize. He'd made them promise they'd never be dishonest again.

It made me more than a little uncomfortable.

We got around to Dan's wedding, and how happy she was. "I've been trying to get them both married off. One down, one to go. I need some grandchildren."

"You should meet my mom," I told her.

"I'm not old enough to get married," he said and I did not mock him, which I thought was very big of me considering that he thought it was hilarious when my mom was doing it to me.

"Twenty-seven is plenty old," Irene disagreed with him. "I was twenty when I got married and look how happy I was."

"Back in the olden days," was his reply.

Not able to resist piling on him, just a little, I said, "Were those the days you got your phone from?"

Irene's whole face lit up in agreement. "Isn't that little flip phone just awful? He never sends me pictures like Dan does. And he doesn't have the Tweeter or Instagram."

"You should definitely get an account on Tweeter," I told him with a wink of my own.

He chuckled and said, "You first."

The rest of the afternoon passed that way—the three of us laughing and talking. I didn't get any more details about Camden's life growing up, but I noticed that as the hours flew by, that fear I'd felt earlier had totally passed. I was feeling peaceful. Happy.

I finished up my last lei, and was grateful for the help. I never would have gotten them all done on time without them.

A knock on the door prevented me from saying as much. Camden answered it, and it was Dan.

"My mom said she was here?" he said, sounding confused. He walked into the room, spotted me, then simmered with obvious annoyance.

Was he mad that we'd put his mom to work? I wouldn't have blamed him if that was the case.

"What's going on?" he asked. Definitely irritated.

Camden crossed his arms. "Nothing that's any of your business."

Dan frowned at him and reached for his mom. "Come on. We need to do some photos with just the mothers."

I stood up. "Do you need my help?" Would Brandy need to be wrangled?

"Considering you're not my or Sadie's mom, no." Dan's reaction surprised me. He'd been nothing but nice to me so far.

I wondered if Sadie had told him the truth about our arrangement and it had made him mad. If he was angry that we were lying to everyone he loved.

Dan helped Irene up, putting her hand on the crook of his arm. I thanked her for her help and she waved to me over her shoulder.

"Any time, dear."

They left and I was alone with Camden.

"What was that about? With Dan?" I asked—and whether I was trying to distract Camden or myself, I wasn't sure.

"Dan told us last night he doesn't want any of his groomsmen trying to hook up with the bridesmaids."

Since that was my plan as well, I silently agreed with him. "Why did he decide that?" And what was Dan going to do about Mary-Ellen, who seemed totally dedicated to finding someone to have a fling with?

"I think he's trying to limit the drama."

I wished him all the luck in the world. "Then he should probably tell his bride to stop trying to set everyone up."

Camden nodded. "And he's mad at me because I won't do what he says."

His words sent my pulse into overdrive, my nerve endings flaring and sparking, like they were trying to signal to him. Telling him to come closer.

Camden seemed to receive my message as he walked over to where I was standing, invading my personal space. My heart pounded slowly and loudly. Could he hear it? "Sadie is trying to matchmake us, isn't she?"

The part of my brain that could still think realized that while she'd been whispering in my ear, encouraging me to date Camden, she hadn't been doing the same thing to him. Even though I'd assumed she was.

That fire was back in his eyes, his voice again low and growly sounding, making the still functioning part of my brain short-circuit. "Now what do you want to do?"

I didn't ask what he wanted to do. I had a pretty good idea.

The only problem was I kind of wanted it, too.

CHAPTER FIFTEEN

"Now we go back to our room," I said.

His eyebrows lifted with interest and I realized what I had done.

"Rooms." I emphasized the *S*. "Rooms. You go to your room and I go to my room and we get ready for whatever Sadie and Dan have planned for tonight."

Why had I said *room*, singular?

As if I'd asked the question out loud Camden offered, "Freudian slip. You know how when you really want something but you're telling yourself you don't, and then you still say it anyways?"

"That's not what's happening here." Time for me to go and get clear of all this mess.

I made sure my key was in my pocket and headed for the door, letting myself out into the hallway. I texted Troy, telling him the job was finished. When I reached the elevators, I realized that I hadn't quite thought out my great escape plan. Camden approached and stood behind me, nearly touching me.

"Excuse me," he breathed, his words hot against the back of my neck. It sent shivers of delight skating across my skin. Then he leaned forward, not quite touching me, but it was like I could feel every single cell of his strong frame surrounding me as he pushed the elevator button to go up.

He stayed put, somehow sucking up all of the oxygen surrounding us so that I couldn't quite catch my breath. I thought I felt his nose against my hair, like he was breathing me in, but I didn't know for sure. What I did know was that having him so close overwhelmed all of my senses, making them go haywire.

All I had to do was turn around. Just turn around and push up slightly and I'd be kissing him. It would be so easy.

I'd never wanted anything more in my entire life.

The bell sounded and the doors opened.

I let out a deep breath that I hadn't been aware I'd been holding. Sadie's stepdad and his fiancée were on the elevator, their arms crossed, her expression angry and his apologetic.

Camden sent me a "what's going on?" look and I shrugged as we stepped inside. He pushed the button for our floor. Even though their mad vibes were uncomfortable, I was glad they were here. I definitely should not be alone with Camden in this tiny space. I'd seen too many music videos and perfume commercials so that I had a pretty good idea of the kind of trouble we could get into in an elevator.

"If you just let me explain," Geoff said, and Maybelle immediately hushed him. I wanted to exchange another silent conversation with Camden about what was happening behind us, but figured it was better to keep my eyes trained straight ahead.

Geoff and Maybelle's floor came up first, and Maybelle pushed past us, without saying a word. I heard Geoff say, "Sweetheart, wait . . . ," and then the doors slid shut.

"What was that? Why do you think Maybelle was so angry?" Camden asked.

"Maybe he forgot to buy her the new Furby." At his confused face I said, "What? That's what I played with when I was a kid. I don't know what girls her age are into."

"Older men, apparently."

I would not be swayed by his wit and charm. I would not.

The elevator doors opened and we started for our rooms. *Rooms, plural,* I reminded myself. "Do you think if Maybelle gets really mad she's going to uninvite him to the prom?"

He laughed and then said, "I don't know if she'll go that far. Then she might have to give back her life-sized Barbie Dream Car."

"You joke, but I could see her driving a pink convertible. I mean, if she has her license."

We stopped in front of our rooms. Once again, his laughter, his jokes, had disarmed me and I'd forgotten myself. So much for my resolve to not ever be alone with him.

Although it wasn't actually my fault—we were both going to the exact same place at the exact same time.

It was kind of my fault, though, for standing out here in the hallway with him instead of heading into my room.

"Here we are again," he said.

"Yes," I agreed, wondering why I was still standing there. "Just like last night. Only this time I promise not to spew all over the place like Mount Vesuvius."

I thought that might make him laugh, ease the tension a little, but it wasn't working. He moved closer. "And last night, you wanted to kiss me."

His words slammed into my chest, interfering with my heart's ability to beat. His nearness, his clean scent, was scrambling my brain and making my gut all tingly. "Why . . . I didn't . . . that's not . . . what would make you think that?"

I could hear the smile in his voice when he said, "Another non-answer. For the record, I wanted to kiss you, too. But I was trying to be respectful, given your situation."

Why did my throat feel so thick? And why couldn't I catch my breath? "Why are you being like this?" I asked.

"Like what?" He sounded genuinely puzzled.

I gestured vaguely in his direction, not able to get my currently too-heavy limbs to respond correctly. "Like this. Nothing can happen between us."

"Dan is not the boss of me."

Was that what this was all about? Some kind of rebellion against his best friend? Camden would show Dan that he could do what he wanted? "It's not because of Dan."

"Then why?" he asked, reaching up to softly stroke my cheek, his fingers pleasantly burning my skin everywhere he touched. I meant to tell him to stop, but couldn't make sounds. "When two people have shared what we've shared, things usually go in this direction."

"What did we share? A lot of gratuitous vomit?"

"That wasn't what I meant." His voice was soft, longing, and all that resolve I'd built up crumbled underneath it.

I'd been trying to distract him, get him joking again, but he'd stayed serious. I closed my eyes slowly, swallowing hard. All the pulse points in my body were throbbing from his touch and a few more seconds of this and I was going to melt into a giant puddle in the middle of the hallway.

His chest was almost touching me and he had his mouth just above mine, frustrating me with tension but no pressure. Just like earlier in Troy's room. While I considered pressing forward and ending the suspense, there was some part of me that was thrilled at the deliciousness of it all. The anticipation, the wanting, dying to know what it would feel like when it finally happened.

As if his brain were operating on the same wavelength he whispered, "I've imagined kissing you at least a dozen times."

His words were like fiery barbs that pierced my armor and my resolve. "You have?" Did I always sound that breathy?

"Mm-hmm. Your lips look soft and warm."

"They are."

"I think maybe I should be the judge of that."

He was going to kiss me and I wanted it so fiercely that it physically hurt me to put a hand on his chest, intending to stop him. My fingers ignored me and instead pressed against him, enjoying the hardness of his chest against my hand. He felt so firm and strong and I wanted to make a thorough exploration. But I could not afford to get distracted by extraneous and tempting muscles, so I yanked my hand back and said, "Wait."

Camden pulled his head back, giving me another one of those puzzled looks. I couldn't blame him because I was basically putty in his hands. "I thought we were on the same page."

"We're not even in the same book," I told him. "This can't happen."

"You don't want me to kiss you?"

"I . . ." I couldn't force out the lie. Because I wanted him so badly that I was quickly losing my hold on my sanity and sense of responsibility.

So I said the thing that would make him go away and stop tempting me. "I know."

His eyes lit up with amusement. "You know that I want to kiss you? I wasn't being very subtle about it."

"I know . . . that you think I'm a corporate spy."

With that he gave me what I needed—he let go of me and took a step back. And even though it was what had to happen, I missed his touch.

His entire demeanor shifted. "Who told you? Sadie? Dan?" Without waiting for me to confirm who had told me, he correctly guessed, "Sadie. How long have you known?"

"Since the cocktail party."

He shook his head, thrusting his hands into his pockets. "So, you've what, been having a laugh at my expense this whole time?"

"Nobody is laughing at you and I'm not a spy. I'm not trying to ruin your company. I literally don't care about it at all. I don't even know what it's called."

He studied me, a colder look in his eyes than I was accustomed to seeing. It made my stomach twist.

"I'm just supposed to believe you because you say it's true? Isn't this what you would say if you were a spy? Deny everything?"

"You could just think about it logically. Sadie would know, wouldn't she? Which would mean she was in on it and willing to betray Dan. Do you really think that's possible?"

He gave a slight shrug. "No. Sadie would do anything for him, and the last thing she'd ever do is hurt him deliberately."

"Right," I said, relieved he seemed to be seeing reason. "So if that's true and I'm Sadie's friend, then . . ."

". . . then you're not a spy." He rubbed the back of his neck, still seeming agitated. "But I still feel like there's something you're not telling me."

That one hit me, like a massive spear catching me in the ribs and piercing me against a wall. "There are so many things I'm not telling you. We barely know each other."

"What if I want to know those things?"

"Why?"

He gave me a wolfish grin and said, "It probably has something to do with that whole wanting-to-kiss-you thing."

While that made me even meltier, the need for the ruse was gone. "You can drop the act. You don't have to pretend to be interested in me anymore. I'm not a spy. There's nothing you have to get out of me."

"That's not—" He stopped himself, shaking his head.

I crossed my arms, hugging my chest. "I mean, it was a good plan. Make me like you and then trick me into confessing. That alone should prove that I'm not a spy. If I had been, wouldn't I have been more responsive to your overtures?"

"You've been pretty responsive."

"I have not." He had no idea how much I'd been holding in. I was about ready to pass out from the sheer effort of it.

Camden made a face I didn't recognize. "You're saying there haven't been vibes between us?"

"There are no vibes here. This is a vibe-free zone." I was totally lying. And the look on his face let me know that he knew that I was making excuses.

"So"—his voice took on that low, soft tone that made me want to collapse—"if I touched you . . . if I ran my fingers down your arm, across your hand, you would feel . . ."

It was as if he were actually touching me, and I could feel the phantom pressure of what he was describing, which sent my pulse hammering and my skin practically vibrating in anticipation. "I would feel nothing." I had to choke out the words.

"The goose bumps on your arm say something different."

So in addition to having perfect recollection, the man also had eyes like a freaking hawk. Fantastic. "I'm just cold."

"We're in Hawaii."

I gulped. "Air-conditioning."

"You're pretty committed to this lie," he noticed.

"I don't do things half-heartedly."

"I know"—he nodded, that sexy smile of his making me forget my own name—"and I wouldn't mind finding out for myself how true that is."

If I were Catholic, I'd have to go to confession for the kind of thoughts I was having right now.

When I didn't say anything, he decided to make everything worse. "Do you know why I thought there were vibes? Or why I thought that I could guess what you're feeling?"

My stupid face was an open book? I shook my head.

"I imagine that your heart beats faster when you're close to me. That your mouth might go dry while you feel like your knees are going to give way. That you can't wait to see me again. I can guess how you're feeling because those same things happen to me."

My only saving grace was that he was saying these words from a few feet away. If he'd been saying them with our bodies close, pressed against each other, there was no way I could have resisted him.

A door slammed farther down the hall, and the sound of it broke whatever magic he was weaving between us.

His expression turned rueful. "I don't know what it says about me. That I'm so ready to believe what you're telling me and ignore all the warning signs. How your and Sadie's stories never quite match. Why you don't have any social media. The things you've said since you've been here."

My voice finally returned to me. "I knew you suspected me and I said some of those things just to freak you out." Because I was annoyed that he was only spending time with me in order to expose me. "You aren't going to be mad at Sadie, are you?"

Camden turned his gaze toward the floor. "I need to . . . process all this. I'll see you later." He got out his keycard and went into his room, leaving me alone in the hallway. I waited a few heartbeats—for what, I couldn't have said. For him to come back? To tell me he believed me and everything was fine?

I couldn't wait for him to cause the very drama Dan had been trying to avoid. I went into my room and saw a card on the floor. It was a handwritten note in calligraphy, inviting me to come to the west lawn at seven o'clock for a night of fun. I wondered if this was one of the things Troy'd had to go work on.

I took out my phone and texted Sadie immediately. I told her what had just happened with Camden and his spy theory (leaving out all the almost-kissing stuff). She seemed unperturbed and texted back, **Great!** with a thumbs-up emoji.

I was concerned—it was like I'd just dropped a possible dramatic nuke onto her big day but she seemed fine with it. I texted back, warning that he might be angry, and she just sent me back a grinning emoji.

Sitting down on my bed, I let out an enormous sigh. Look at what I was doing. Prioritizing what Camden wanted over what Sadie needed. I wasn't here for Camden. I was here for her.

I couldn't let him make me forget what I was supposed to be doing.

CHAPTER SIXTEEN

Not having any idea how to dress for tonight's activity, I threw on a sundress with pockets, along with a minimal amount of makeup, and put up my hair. I'd just slid on my sandals when there was a knock at my door.

I let Krista into my room, and she was wearing a casual dress, too. I'd asked her to join me because I didn't want to accidentally on purpose run into Camden. Pathetically enough, I knew that if I stood by my door, I'd be able to hear when he was headed out and I didn't think I'd be able to prevent myself from joining him.

This was better. I'd told him about not being a spy and had to hope one, that he'd believe me and two, that he wouldn't have some kind of meltdown that would make things hard on Dan and Sadie. I again resolved that Camden and I would be distant but polite acquaintances.

Plus, he had no reason to hang around me now. Telling the truth had hopefully eliminated that issue.

But knowing it with my brain and dealing with the sense of loss in my heart were two entirely different things. Because I knew I'd miss his attention. That I'd grown to enjoy him and his teasing and his touch.

"What happened last night?" Krista asked, instead of saying hello.

"Hi to you, too." I knew what she was asking, and given that my entire brain seemed fixated on Camden at the moment, I didn't need her making things worse.

"At least you seem like you're feeling better. I'm glad you're not still sick."

It felt like it had been days since she and I had last spoken. "I wasn't sick. I was drunk." I explained about the mix-up.

"Then Camden, in his full knight regalia, swooped in and got you back here safely."

"He did." I nodded warily, not sure where she was going with this. "And?"

"And nothing. I vomited, he got me a glass of water. End of story."

She pursed her lips and then narrowed her eyes at me. "You know that I know you well enough that I can tell when you're lying."

"I'm not lying! I'm just selectively sharing the parts of the story I want you to know."

"Ha!" She pointed at me, as if she'd caught me doing something. "I knew there was more."

I tried switching back into business mode. "We should get going. I gave you Mandy's number just in case, right? She volunteered to help out with Brandy if we get to that point. I'm hoping we won't, but it never hurts to be prepared."

"I've got her number. And I've got yours, too."

Deciding that it wasn't worth responding to, I held open my door and gestured for her to go ahead.

As we walked down the hallway she said, "You haven't asked me about Rick."

It took me a second to place his name. *Oh, Dan's cousin.* "Is there something to ask about?"

"I've been waiting for your lecture on how we're not supposed to date wedding guests."

That would kind of make me a hypocrite, wouldn't it? "I didn't realize you two had gone on a date." I hoped it hadn't become more than that. Especially with Dan's objections. While Dan wasn't my main concern, he was Sadie's. And to keep her happy, I'd have to make sure that he was happy, too.

We arrived at the elevators, and one of them opened as soon as we pushed the button. We stepped in and Krista said, "We did that group hang last night. Sadie kept trying to push us together, but that man just broke up with his longtime girlfriend and they're a hundred percent going to get back together. Rick talked about her the entire night. It actually got a little depressing."

Was this what had made Dan put his foot down about no fraternizing? "We can thank Sadie and her matchmaking."

Krista nodded. "You know how people are at weddings."

I did.

She continued, "But if she wants to set me up with someone, they should at least be available."

We arrived on the ground floor and headed into the lobby. "He should also not be one of the guests at the wedding," I reminded her.

She just gave me an enigmatic smile as we walked toward the west lawn. I knew what that meant. She was aware of the rule but if she found someone she liked, I could stuff it. We headed outside and came around a row of bushes and saw a sea of white camping tents covering the lawn.

"What's going on?" I asked. "Did Sadie invite a bunch of Boy Scouts?"

Troy and one of his assistants (Anton? Antoine? I couldn't remember) stopped in front of us. "We're glamping," Troy announced. Glamping? Wasn't that just camping's older sister who wore too much makeup? "Hand over your keycards."

"Is this some kind of swingers thing?" Krista asked with a teasing lilt in her voice. "Because Rachel is not going to be okay with that."

"Why do you need our keycards?" I asked.

I watched as Krista handed hers over. Troy said her name to his assistant, whom he definitely referred to as Anton, and Anton flipped through a giant album and placed Krista's key in a pocket next to her name.

No wonder I'd had to make lei. This level of conspiracy to keep me from getting a good night's sleep had to have taken hours.

Troy tapped his foot impatiently at me. "I need your keys because Sadie doesn't trust you guys and doesn't want you to go sneaking off back to your rooms. We're sleeping out here tonight."

"Gee, why would anyone do that?" I would much rather go back to my king-size bed than be stuck sleeping on the ground. I'd never understood the appeal of camping. Or glamping. Whatever this nonsense was.

"Key," Troy said, holding out his hand. I took in a deep breath. He could find me new clients. This was not a hill to die on. I dug through my purse and found my keycard, giving it to him.

"Thank you," he said, his tone clipped. I guessed I wasn't the first person to give him grief. "Your tents are over there. Go and get changed and then meet me and the rest of the wedding party by the campfire."

"Changed?" Krista asked me. "This involves an outfit switch?"

I had no idea and shrugged as she and I walked to the tents Troy had indicated. My and Sadie's names were written on a tag, hanging on the tent to the right. Krista's name was on the left. She opened the flap. "Mary-Ellen! Looks like we're camping buddies," she said, in a tone of fake enthusiasm that only I would recognize.

It would be nice to be alone with Sadie. To check in with her, see how she was holding up, what she needed from me. To make sure that me telling Camden about the spy thing wasn't going to be an issue. That she was happy with how her mother was behaving.

Two cots with white sheets and blankets were set up in the tent. Small collapsible canvas totes sat at the foot of the cots, and I assumed that was where we were supposed to store our things. The tent was tall enough to stand in, and there were white Christmas lights strung around the interior. Above the two cots hung mosquito netting. Which seemed odd, because I was usually a magnet for mosquitoes and hadn't gotten a single bite yet.

On each cot there was a pair of pajamas. Button-down tops with drawstring bottoms. They were pale pink and the wedding's hashtags were written on them—#DanAndSadie and #SadieMarriedLady. There were also a pair of slippers and a note from the different sponsors who had provided the tents, cots, and clothing. I claimed the cot on the left and changed quickly, stowing my dress, sandals, and purse in the tote.

It was then that I noticed something on our pillows. Chocolate chip cookies inside plastic baggies. My stomach grumbled appreciatively and I devoured both of the cookies in record time. So, so good. I should probably go find something else to eat that had actual nutritional value.

I stepped out of my tent and found Krista waiting for me in her pajamas. "I thought we could head over together." There was a strained quality to her voice and I could hear Mary-Ellen singing off-key in their shared tent. I did not envy my friend.

"Come on, Mary-Ellen, let's get a move on!" she called out. Krista linked her arm through mine and I asked if she'd eaten her cookies. "Obviously."

"Do you think they were made here at the hotel, and if so, do you think we could get more?" I asked as we walked up to the campfire. Not exactly healthy, but maybe I'd throw in an apple or something.

Mary-Ellen was right behind us as we approached the campfire and found Sadie, Dan, and all of his groomsmen. The men's pajamas were white and I couldn't figure out who had thought that was a good color for camping.

Camden gave me a playful smile when we approached.

Krista let out a low whistle. "Do you see how he's looking at you? That boy has impure thoughts about you."

I shouldn't want that to be true.

She nudged me with her arm. "Don't bother denying that you think about him, too. It's pretty obvious he's living rent-free in your head. Because he has squatter's rights at this point."

I opened my mouth, intending to refute her statement, but had to admit to myself that it was true. Camden took up far too much space in my poor mind.

He said something to Rick, patted him on the shoulder, and then started walking over to me.

"Oh, look," Krista said to Mary-Ellen. "Come over here and see this."

"What?" Mary-Ellen asked as she was being dragged away. "What am I supposed to be looking at?"

Super subtle.

Every step that he took toward me I felt in my chest, my heart beating hard in time to his footsteps.

"Do you know why we're camping?" I asked as he approached, willing myself to calm down.

"Dan loves it. Sadie apparently did it as a gift for him."

That was very sweet of her, but not so much fun for me. "Why would someone love camping?" I truly didn't get it.

"I don't know. Nature, trees, peeing outdoors, bears, something-something one with the universe. I never really got it, either." He put his hands in his pockets and stood close to me, our shoulders nearly touching as we both faced the campfire, which seemed more like a bonfire. "Although, to be fair, this is only sort of camping. Still it could be fun, right?"

"Which one is it? Fun or camping? It can't be both. I mean, my idea of camping is a motel room that faces some trees."

He chuckled slightly, but before he could respond an employee of the hotel came by, passing out the white lei.

"Be careful with those," Camden said. "They were handmade."

She appeared puzzled, probably because all the lei we'd had so far were handmade.

The employee wasn't the only one who felt confused. He was over here bantering with me like nothing had happened.

Which I should accept and be grateful for. Instead I asked, "Have you processed yet?"

He raised both of his eyebrows, as if surprised by my question. "I'm taking things under consideration."

"Meaning?"

"Meaning . . . there are things that I'm feeling and I'm not sure how to deal with them and what you've told me."

My breath caught at his words, wondering what exactly those feelings were. "But you still think I'm a spy?"

"I don't know what to think."

Why couldn't I let this go? Maybe it was because I actually was lying to him and in this one area, at least, I wanted him to know the truth. "Why does it matter so much?"

"Because if you were a spy, and you found out things about us, you could sabotage us going public. We would lose the confidence of our investors if anyone stole our secrets—they'd think that our security was lax and that we were an easy target. It would devalue us, making our stock price drop, and I won't let that happen."

"I'm not here to hurt you or anyone else," I told him. That at least was honest.

I could feel him studying me, as if he wasn't sure what to believe. "I think there's something there. Something you're keeping secret. I understand that your secrets are none of my business—"

"Kind of feels like you don't. And while I respect your bachelor's degree from I'm Entitled to Know Everything University, not everything is about you." I'd hoped that confessing would throw him off the scent, but he was like some determined bloodhound, knowing there was something else to uncover.

If I could just keep my distance, this would all be fine. If I could storm off and be (rightfully) angry with him for prying, things might possibly get better.

Then he messed it all up. "You're right. I'm sorry. Will you forgive me?"

I turned to look at him and his eyes were like liquid green fire, burning hotter and brighter than the campfire next to us.

Say no. Make that chasm grow. Stretch the divide between you. This is your chance, I tried telling myself.

There was no part of me that wanted to listen.

"Can I have everybody's attention?" Hank, the director for the film crews, called out. "We would like you guys to start off by having a pillow fight."

One of his assistants started passing out pillows. I held mine by the edge. "Are you serious? We're not twelve."

Normally I wouldn't be so snappish, but I was currently wrestling internally with myself and neither side of me was pleased at being interrupted. There was what I had to do and what I wanted to do.

None of those included having a pillow fight.

"The viewers will love it," Hank said. "We'll edit it so that it looks really fun." He directed us to get into a circle. We all stood there, loosely holding our pillows. I could feel my dignity draining from my body.

"We got this," Camden said as he moved to my left. "We're going to win."

Hank yelled out, "Go!"

"I don't think it's a competition." But my words were swallowed up by Dan swinging his pillow at Camden's head, hard.

He ducked and the pillow glanced off my shoulder.

Camden turned toward me, looking utterly delighted. "You've got my back?"

Nodding, I said, "I do."

I should have blown him off and moved closer to the other bridesmaids. But it was like I couldn't stay away from him.

CHAPTER SEVENTEEN

One of Hank's assistants was throwing feathers at us as everyone started swinging their pillows in earnest. The men seemed much more into it, but the women quickly caught up. Camden stayed in position near my elbow, fending off potential attacks.

Despite me feeling stupid initially, and the blizzard of white feathers blinding us, I found myself squealing and laughing with everyone else. The men were enthusiastically raining blows down on each other, until Camden's phone rang.

He gave me that "sorry" expression of his and abandoned the battle, heading off into the night to take his call.

It surprised me that he left. He seemed to be having a good time.

Not to mention—selfishly—that it was not good for me that he'd taken off. Without him there as my wingman, I was getting pummeled by the other members of the bridal party. Mary-Ellen in particular seemed to take a huge amount of delight in whacking me.

Hank yelled, "Cut!" and Mary-Ellen got in one last lick before she set her pillow off to the side. "Bring in the chairs, and let's get the s'mores going."

Finally. Something I'd be good at.

The assistants brought in a bunch of white Adirondack chairs, seating them around the fire. Somehow I got downwind of the fire and it kept blowing smoke at me. I tried to scoot my chair over, but was blocked by the empty one. I dragged the empty one farther toward where Dan and Sadie sat.

"Trying to move my chair away from you?" Camden asked when he returned.

"No, just trying to get clear of the smoke. I like having eyeballs, thanks."

He smiled and pulled my chair closer to his, out of the smoke. I wondered why they hadn't set up the chairs so we were all seated together, but it was like Camden and I were in our own tiny little bubble.

He took his phone out of his pocket and started responding to a text.

"Was it really that important?" I asked him, not able to keep my opinions to myself like I should have.

"What?"

"The phone call. I know you're busy and have a lot going on, but Dan's only getting married once. He's counting on you. You should be here for it."

Camden put his phone back. "I am here."

"No, *here*, here. Not on your phone every ten minutes. You're going to miss everything."

For a second I thought he might tell me it was none of my business, and truthfully it wasn't. I just didn't want him to look back on this and regret that he hadn't been more present for his best friend.

"Maybe you're right."

"Those are words I do not hear often enough."

One of Hank's assistants handed us all the things we'd need for s'mores—the giant marshmallows, Hershey chocolate bars, graham crackers, and long skewers.

I got to work, preparing the chocolate and the crackers. Then I got my marshmallow on the skewer and put it over the fire.

"How do you take yours?" Camden asked. "Golden brown or flaming black?"

"It's sugar. I will take it however it wants to present itself. Burnt or otherwise. Plus, when it is burned, it means it's really melty inside." Kind of like how I felt every time I was around him.

My marshmallow did indeed catch fire, and I blew it out. I pressed it into the other components and let out a moan after I took a bite. So yummy. The marshmallow was oozing out everywhere, and it was getting all over my fingers. I started licking them off.

I noticed Camden watching me with that hungry look in his eyes that turned my spine to Jell-O. "Do you want a s'more?" I asked.

"I think I prefer a s'less," he said, then waved his hands. "Sorry, bad joke. I don't like s'mores."

"Don't like . . ." My voice trailed off. Who could say no to all these amazing ingredients combined together into a melted deliciousness? It boggled the mind.

"But I do enjoy watching you eat them."

His words echoed inside my chest, making it hard to breathe. Desire flared up inside me, like the flame surrounding the logs in front of us. "Why are you flirting with me?"

"Maybe I just enjoy flirting with you?"

"But why?" The jig was up. He didn't need to keep doing this.

He leaned across his armchair, so that he was in my space. "I like how your cheeks flush, how you grab your lower lip with your teeth, the way that you pretend you don't like it, but I can see in your eyes that you do."

"That's . . ."—*entirely correct*—"entirely untrue. And back to my point earlier: if I was a corporate spy, I would have willingly fallen into your honey trap."

"Unless that was your plan all along. Act as if you didn't like me so that I'd be even more interested."

I shook my head at him. "That is one messed-up dynamic that human beings enjoy."

"Agreed."

I focused on my s'mores, making a few more. Okay, five more. Ignoring Camden's intense gaze and eating my dinner.

Or, more accurately, *trying* to ignore his gaze and how it made me want to throw this chocolate-and-marshmallow concoction to the ground and leap into his lap.

That's how much my body liked Camden. It was willing to forsake chocolate and gooey goodness.

"I'm going to get a bottle of water," he said. "Do you want one?"

"No thanks." I needed one, but I didn't want to feel any more indebted to him. He got up and I realized that my right shoulder was aching. I rolled it a few times and it made a crunching sound. I had probably tweaked it during the pillow fight.

"Is that bothering you?" Camden asked. I wondered where the water bottles were located; he hadn't even been gone for ten seconds.

"Just an old acrobatic injury," I told him. When his eyes widened, I laughed and added, "I'm kidding. It's just a little sore. I'm fine."

"Do you want me to massage it for you?"

No. What I meant to say was *no. No, thank you. No, your hands on me is a very bad idea and no, you can sit over there and just not touch me.*

What I actually said was, "Yes, please."

He stood behind me and I was already shaky with anticipation before his hands made contact with my shoulders. I let my eyes drift shut slowly as his strong fingers kneaded my muscles. My head lolled forward and I had to struggle to not slide off the chair completely. It felt so, so good.

"You carry a lot of tension in your shoulders," he commented.

"I promise you it's everywhere." I meant of the stress variety, but I had no idea how my statement came across because I was too busy wondering what else I could claim was sore. I wanted more of his touch.

As if he could read my mind, he put his palm against the left side of my face, leaning me into it. Then with his right hand he began rubbing my neck, his slightly calloused hands causing a flood of warmth across my oversensitized skin.

"How's that?" he asked, his voice totally normal, like he wasn't in the least bit affected.

Meanwhile, the ability to speak had left me entirely. The sound I made was along the lines of, *"Viningrah."*

"Better?"

I tried to nod, but nothing in my body was cooperating. I was a heady mess of want and need, rendered speechless and immobile by his touch.

He let me go and I slumped against the chair, my skin still tingling where he'd touched it. Like he'd marked me. It was a good thing my entire skeleton had collapsed or else I would have attacked him then and there. Forgotten about my job, about my rule, everything.

I was in so much trouble.

Hank had us singing campfire songs next, and it was all bad and not very musical, but at least it allowed me to focus on something else as I tried to regain control over my body, slow down my breathing, and generally attempt to calm down the wave of lust that threatened to drag me under.

Friends, I reminded myself. We could be friends or I could just stay away from him completely.

At the moment the second option was sounding like the best one. That way I could stop thinking about kissing him and keep all of my body parts to myself.

"We've got enough here," Hank announced. "We'd like some footage of you returning to your tents."

I briefly wondered why anyone would care about us going to bed for the night, but it wasn't my job to question any of this.

To my surprise I was able to stand up all on my own. And walk forward. It was a miracle.

Camden waved at me before he walked off with Dan. Sadie came over to hook her arm through mine. "This way, roomie!"

I followed her as she talked about the events so far, and how Hank had wanted to take everybody out on some old rowboats that he'd found. "But Dan shot that idea down right away."

"What is his deal with the ocean?" I asked, glad I could talk again.

"His parents took him on vacation one year and they went snorkeling. Apparently some massive fish, it was like four feet or something, pushed up against Dan. It freaked him out and he's never liked the ocean since then."

"But he crossed an ocean and is having his wedding next to it."

"Hawaii was always my dream," she said. "This is how much he loves me."

I'd seen dozens of in-love couples and I don't know what it was about her words, whether it was the tone or whatever spell Camden had put over me, but my heart twisted so painfully at her words.

I needed that for myself, what she and Dan had. I felt that wanting fervently, so strongly, that it surprised me. I let out a big breath. "He's a good guy."

"The absolute best," she agreed as she pushed aside the left tent flap. "So are his friends."

"Dan may disagree with you. He told his groomsmen that they aren't allowed to date bridesmaids." Maybe that would put an end to her matchmaking.

"That's just because he knows about our NDA and he doesn't want Camden to find out about our arrangement because Dan's concerned this might blow up in my face and affect my career. But he worries too much."

I didn't know quite how to respond to that. I actually liked having the non-disclosure agreements in place. I liked the professional boundaries they created, the way they protected everyone involved. I had once let those boundaries be lax, and they'd caused me an incredible amount of pain.

This way was definitely better.

A couple wearing the official glamping pajamas passed us, and I didn't recognize them. I remembered how Sadie had told me that people were still showing up and would be up through the wedding. They were carrying champagne flutes and I immediately thought of Sadie's mother. "Where's your mom tonight?"

"My aunt Mandy promised to keep an eye on her. They're sharing a tent."

I should have asked about Brandy sooner. I kicked myself for not paying closer attention.

We entered the tent and she let the flap drop. Then she stuck her head back out. "Did you get everything? Are we all done?" she asked.

Hank called back, "We got what we needed. Thanks!"

I went over to sit on my cot and eyed Sadie's cookies. I was torn between curling up and trying to go to sleep and asking if I could eat them. She stayed put, peering out between the two flaps.

"What are you doing?" I asked.

"Making sure the coast is clear." She turned back to grin at me. "I'm sneaking over to Dan's tent. It's going to be like a real sleepaway camp!"

She'd told me she'd never been to one growing up, so I could understand her excitement. "That's not like any camp I went to."

"Didn't you ever sneak out to meet up with guys?"

"No, I wasn't a hot blonde. I had braces and a face full of acne."

She just shook her head at me like I was adorable.

"Why are you waiting?" I asked her. This was her event. She could put on a crown and have an official parade over to Dan's tent if she wanted to.

"Troy is being very dramatic over everything. I think he took me a bit too seriously and if I'm not in my own tent, I'm pretty sure he's going to make a scene. He and his assistants are out there practically patrolling to make sure nobody tries to go back into the hotel."

"That's not really possible, considering they confiscated everyone's keycards."

"Like I said, he's taking this whole doing-what-I-said-I-wanted thing a bit too far."

"Well, that's what we're here for."

But she didn't seem to be listening to me. "Okay, I'm off. This is so exciting! I'll see you first thing tomorrow! Unless I get caught!"

With that, she was gone. And she'd left her cookies. I figured that made them fair game.

I grabbed them and lay down on my cot. They were every bit as delicious as I remembered. I looked up at my mosquito netting and wondered if it was necessary or just some kind of accessory.

There was some rustling by the door and I wondered if Troy had discovered Sadie. Or if he was doing some kind of bed check.

"Is it okay if I join you?"

Camden.

I sat straight up in bed, getting my face and hair tangled up in the mosquito netting.

"What are you doing here?" I felt stupid as soon as I asked it. If Sadie had abandoned me to be with her groom, they obviously wanted some privacy.

"Dan kicked me out and there's no other empty cot but this one. Can I crash here?"

CHAPTER EIGHTEEN

I tried saying no again. Ran it through my mind. *No, no, no, no.* And *no.*

Instead my mouth formed the word, "Sure."

"What happened to my cookies? Dan made me leave mine behind."

"I ate them and I don't even feel bad about it. You should know better than to leave me in a room with sweet confections." I focused on trying to get the netting away from my hair. It was catching on a couple of the bobby pins.

"Do you need help?"

"I've got it," I told him, hoping that was true. If it wasn't, I was going to have to sleep sitting up because there was no way I could let him put his fingers in my hair. "Why do we even have mosquito netting? There's no mosquitoes."

He went over to his cot and lay down, his feet hanging off the edge. "There are, but they're farther inland. This part of the island has fire ants, cockroaches, rats, sometimes scorpions. The worst, though, is the foot-long centipedes."

I finally got the last bit of netting free from my hair, but his words made my hands drop down to my sides. "You're making that up."

"I'm absolutely not. They have a nasty bite and they're not afraid of people."

My eyes went wide and I clamped my mouth shut. I pulled my legs in close and wrapped my arms around them. I started surveying the ground and the tent walls. The ceiling. Centipedes could climb upside down, couldn't they?

Camden turned his head toward me. "Wait, are you scared?"

"Yes, like any reasonable person would be. Insects should not be twelve inches long!"

"Is it wrong that I find this cute?"

What was wrong with him? "Yes, that is wrong. I'm freaking out. Why would you think that's cute?"

"Because you always seem so ready to take on the whole world. It's cute that there's something that scares you."

"So many things scare me! Clowns! Crocodiles! Zombies! And now foot-long centipedes with venomous bites!"

He turned on his side, propping his head upon his hand. "The hotels do a really good job when it comes to pest control. I don't think you have to worry." He paused a beat and then asked, "Why are you scared of zombies?"

"Because if they ever become real, people should have a healthy respect and fear of them."

"Logical. I like that about you, too."

I grabbed for the blanket and shook it out, making sure there were no bugs of death hiding inside it. When it seemed clear, I wrapped it around my shoulders. "Does anything scare you?"

He looked down, like he was considering something. "Dan's mom dying."

This. I'd been wondering about this very thing. I knew I had to tread carefully, but I couldn't keep my question to myself. "What about your own parents?"

"My mom left right after I was born. She decided she didn't want to be a mother and I've never spoken to her. She signed away her parental rights. I don't even know if she's still alive. My dad was in a bad car accident and died when I was thirteen and since I didn't have any other family, Dan's parents took me in. They weren't well off, but Dan and I never wanted for anything."

"Wow. I'm really sorry." I'd kind of suspected something along those lines. I was struck by the passion in his voice, and how he would share something so personal with me. He had no ulterior motive for telling me about his life—the charade was over. He just wanted me to know, to share a piece of himself. It made me feel more connected to him.

"I feel like I owe Dan and his family. The company going public is my chance to give them the world. To make sure Irene has the absolute best medical care."

Did he not understand that he was enough for them? "You know you don't owe them anything. It's so obvious that she loves you like a son and that Dan thinks of you as his brother. I'm sure that all they want is for you to be happy."

He rolled onto his back. "I'll be happy when I know they're taken care of."

"I admire that about you." It felt like all I did was give him a hard time, so when he did something heroic that got me all weak kneed, I should probably share. "How hard you work for other people."

"Aren't you the same way?"

"I try to be. I don't know if I always succeed." Like now, when I was letting my own personal desires get in the way of the job I was supposed to be doing.

Although, if I wanted to be technical about it, the night was officially over. We'd put on a show for Sadie's followers—sung songs, made s'mores, had a ridiculous pillow fight.

I was off the clock. The rest of the night belonged to me and I could spend it however I wanted.

And what I wanted was to be here, in this tent, with Camden. I was understanding that illicit feeling of excitement Sadie had expressed. I had a handsome man in my tent. If only the girls I'd gone to summer camp with could see me now.

I'd just have to do my best to ignore the possible crawly, invasive predators.

Camden let out a groan and got up, stripping the cot and throwing his bedding on the floor.

"What are you doing?"

"I can't spend the entire night with half my body hanging off the bed."

This also meant that he'd gone from being four feet away to right next to my cot. I lay down, turning on my side so that I could face him. "But you're going to sleep on the ground?"

He could hear the distaste in my voice. "Weren't you the one who grew up going camping?"

"I went to camp, not camping. Very different things. But that's also how I know how much I despise the entire thing. Years of experience. This is why people made civilization. So that we wouldn't have to sleep on the ground anymore."

He put his pillow under his head. "Think of it as an adventure."

"I think of it as a pain in my butt. Do you know what doesn't have mosquito netting?"

"Is it your bed in the hotel?"

"It is my bed in my hotel room," I confirmed.

"But you don't get to be close to nature in your hotel room."

That was the entire point. "Nature and I already have a good relationship, thanks. I stay indoors and nature keeps to itself. Something about this feels unsafe."

He grinned at me, looking like he was enjoying our conversation. I was having a fun time, too. "What's unsafe? Besides the bugs, which I don't think will be an issue?"

"Um, have you never seen a horror movie? We're all sitting ducks out here."

"You think a serial killer is going to tear through here and get us all?"

I nodded. "That's exactly what could happen. We get lulled into a false sense of security by chocolate chip cookies and then bam!"

"You ate my cookies."

"I guess that means you'll be ready if it does happen. Honestly, you should be thanking me for not letting you get sucked in by them."

"Rachel, you do know that there's an entire children's fairy tale about not eating sweets that don't belong to you?"

I wagged my finger at him. "The moral of that story is about not eating sweets you find in weird places. Like attached to a house. Plus, there aren't any witches here."

"Just deadly centipedes and serial killers," he said with a smile.

"Exactly."

I put my hand over the side of the cot because I wanted to be closer to him. I saw the way he studied my hand, as if he were considering reaching out to take it. I held my breath, mentally encouraging him to do it.

Instead he folded his hands over his chest, looking straight up at the ceiling. "Are you planning on doing the sunrise yoga?"

"The only thing I want to be doing at sunrise is sleeping," I told him. "I'm not really one for greeting the sun, either. Which you can tell from me being so pale."

"Are you anti-yoga, too?"

"If I'm going to pretend to work out, it's going to be actual exercise."

He laughed and then said, "Yoga can be pretty intense. Have you tried it?"

"I've had to bend over to pick up the TV remote after I dropped it, and based on that experience, I don't think yoga's for me."

He tilted his face back toward mine, and there was something in his eyes I didn't recognize, a feeling that eluded description. "Putting everything else aside, I want to say that I like being with you."

"I like being with you, too." It felt safe enough to say. But those things he wanted to put aside? They were too big for us to ignore indefinitely.

My phone buzzed, reminding me that there was a real world beyond this one. I sat up and scooted down the length of the cot until I reached the canvas tote that had my things in it. I rummaged around and discovered my extra room key, the one I always kept in my pocket. I grabbed it and then located my phone in my purse.

It was a text from Mandy asking me to meet her in the lobby immediately. "Uh-oh. I have to go."

"What's up?"

"I think something's going on with Sadie's mom." I put my keycard and my phone into the pocket of my pajamas.

"I'll come with you," he offered. I knew I should probably turn him down, but I rationalized my negative feelings away by considering that I might need his help. I had no idea what I was walking into. And Camden seemed reliable enough.

"Okay. But we can't let Troy catch us. He's out there patrolling the border like he's in the secret police and apparently forcing people to go back to their tents."

"We're on a secret spy mission, then."

"I'm not a spy!" I protested but he ignored me as he crawled over to the tent entrance. He stayed low, peering through the flaps.

"It looks safe to me, let's go."

Then he grabbed my hand and I didn't even have a chance to register the sensations flooding through me because we were running across the grass toward the hotel, both of us crouched over. I wasn't sure how that was supposed to help, and I couldn't help but giggle as we ran.

When we got through the lobby doors, I noticed the curious looks from the different staff members and guests as Camden held up both his arms and yelled, "Made it!"

I didn't get a chance to laugh because Mandy was waiting near the front desk, looking serious. I made my way over to her. "What's going on?"

"She's drunk. The concierge is helping me get her room key. I know I could go ask that wedding planner, but then Sadie would find out and I want her to have this one night where she doesn't have to worry."

"Where is Brandy?" I asked.

"In the hallway on the fourth floor. She raided a mini-bar restock trolley. I'm so sorry. I was watching her and then she said she wanted to go for a walk and I believed her and—"

I put my hands on Mandy's shoulders. "You didn't do anything wrong and this isn't your fault. Camden and I will go get her to her room while you grab the key. Meet us there."

She nodded, wiping away tears from her eyes. I wished there were a way to make Brandy see the damage she was doing to her family, how much her addiction hurt the people she claimed to love.

Camden had come up behind me and gave Mandy his room number and full name. "You tell the concierge to bill all of the expenses to me. I don't want Dan or Sadie to know about this."

That made my heart flutter in my chest. If I hadn't been attracted to him before . . . this would have pushed me over the edge. "We have to go to the fourth floor," I said, telling my surging hormones to behave.

I tried to fill him in on how bad things had been with Brandy during the events this week, and how I'd taken it as my personal responsibility to try to keep her sober for Sadie's sake.

"That's not your job," he told me as we walked out of the elevator.

Only, it was. And I wasn't doing so hot.

We came around the corner and found Brandy surrounded by mini-bottles of alcohol. I glanced at them. Rum, vodka, tequila, whiskey—it was like she was trying to host a United Nations summit in her stomach. At some point her liver was going to declare its independence and flee her body in order to save itself.

I berated myself for my mental unkindness, but gallows humor had often been my go-to when I felt this stressed and upset. I knew alcoholism was a disease and that I should be more patient with her. "Come on," I said to Camden, "We've got to get her up."

Camden reached down and hefted her up easily, getting her into a standing position. It was so nice having an extra set of hands to help me. Somebody else who was willing to shoulder the burden. I was really grateful for Mandy and her personal connection to the situation, but having Camden here to help was making a world of difference.

He put one of her arms around his shoulders and I got on her other side, doing the same thing. We supported her weight between us, with him bearing most of it.

"This is why I like hanging out with you, Rachel. Nothing but nonstop excitement."

I told him to hush as we walked back toward the elevators.

"Are you trying to tell me I don't look good on this white horse?"

"Yes, and all that humility is very becoming," I said. His words reminded me of Krista's comments earlier about him being a knight in shining armor and made me suspicious that she might be having conversations with him behind my back.

Brandy decided to join the conversation. "Hey! What's happening!" Her words were slurred, but it was easy enough to make them out.

"We're taking you back to your room," I told her. "You were passed out in a hallway."

"I'm not drunk!" she yelled. "Do you hear me? I'm not drunk!"

"Yep," Camden said. "We hear you loud and angry."

She seemed to realize who I was, because she shifted from anger to glee and said, "Hi there, alcohol warden! I broke out of jail!"

The elevator arrived and we maneuvered her into it. I let out a deep sigh instead of responding to her jab. This whole situation just sucked.

Brandy wiggled against us, trying to break free but lacking the strength. "I don't need your help."

I let out a yelp as she stepped down hard on my foot. "Ow! This must be what it feels like to be the mother of an ungrateful child."

Camden appeared concerned. "Are you okay?"

"Fine. But at this point I'm worried that a smaller Brandy is going to come out of her mouth and try to bite my head off."

He grinned. "I always appreciate a good sci-fi reference."

Mandy was waiting for us at the door. Her relief at seeing us was evident, and she quickly opened the door. "In here."

"Mandy! How ya doing?" Brandy asked as we helped her into the room.

"I can't believe you've been drinking," her sister snapped back.

"Only liquor, I promise." Then Brandy laughed hysterically as we helped her over to the bed. She slid out of our grasp, collapsing on top of the blanket.

"What now?" Camden whispered to me and I shrugged.

Mandy overheard us. "I need to go back to my tent and grab my thyroid medication. I'm planning on staying here tonight to keep an eye on her. I'll make sure she gets to the sunrise yoga thing tomorrow morning."

"I can help," I offered.

"It's okay. I've been dealing with this my entire life and she's my responsibility."

Brandy should be responsible for herself, but it wasn't my place to say anything.

Mandy continued, "If you guys can stay here a second, I'll be right back."

"Sure thing," Camden said.

The sound of the door slamming shut seemed to rouse Brandy. She started taking off her glamping pajamas, throwing them on the floor. Camden shielded his eyes, and fortunately she was wearing underwear.

Then she leaned over the bed and threw up directly on her pajamas, as if that had been her intent all along.

The smell was almost enough to make me puke, too.

This, unfortunately, happened to be one of my areas of expertise. Taking care of drunk people. I looked around and spotted an empty bag in the trash can. I pulled it out and then placed the pajamas inside, tying off the bag.

I placed the bag inside the bathroom and then washed my hands.

When I rejoined Camden I felt like I needed to apologize. "I'm sorry you had to deal with me last night when I was like this."

"You were nothing like this," he countered. "But if she's supposed to go to that yoga thing tomorrow, isn't Sadie going to wonder what happened to her pajamas?"

I hadn't even considered that. "I'll give her mine. They might be a little big on her, but it's better than nothing."

"And how are you going to explain your lack of pink jammies?"

"I'll tell her I got marshmallow and chocolate on them. Better for Sadie to think I was clumsy than that her mother got wasted. But I don't really want to walk around the hotel half-naked."

"Here. Wear this."

Then he took off his pajama shirt, handing it to me.

My jaw practically flew to the floor once I witnessed the glorious hotness on display in front of me.

CHAPTER NINETEEN

I knew I shouldn't stare, but it was like my eyes had a mind of their own. All I could do was drink him in. I'd sort of guessed at his physique based on how he looked in his clothes and how strong he appeared to be, but I just hadn't been adequately prepared.

It was like someone had lovingly and painstakingly carved him out of marble and all I wanted to do was touch him. There were muscles and abs and planes and edges everywhere. A candy house in the woods might not trick me, but I'd discovered that a gorgeous, shirtless man was enough to get me to forget about everything else.

"Rachel?"

I blinked several times, registering both that he'd called my name and sounded amused. He was holding out his top to me and I hastily grabbed it, taking care not to touch his hand.

My throat felt thick as I told him, "Turn around."

"Right. Sorry." He presented me with his back, and that was somehow worse. I watched the way his tendons and muscles flexed as he put his hands on his hips and all I wanted to do was go over and press kisses against every bit of his flesh.

I ached with need and had to turn around, too. It was the only way I could control myself. I took off my pajama top and bottoms, folding them and placing them on the dresser. I grabbed my keycard and my phone. I put on Camden's shirt and inhaled deeply. It smelled like him.

"Okay," I said and he turned back around and it was a bit like the sun coming out from behind a cloud. I'd thought I was prepared for it, but nope. Instead I was drooling over here like I'd never seen a shirtless, perfect specimen before.

It wasn't one-sided, either. I saw his half-lidded gaze as he looked at the hem of his shirt against my legs. Awareness hung heavy between us, making me force air in and out of my lungs while my heart did a dance number. I found myself starting to walk toward him.

Fortunately, Mandy let herself back into the room. She looked faintly alarmed, and I quickly explained the situation, including pointing out where I'd left my pajamas for Brandy to change into tomorrow.

"I wouldn't have even thought of that. You're right, Sadie definitely would have noticed. Thank you," she said.

"Of course. What else can we do?"

"Nothing. Go and enjoy your evening."

I nodded and the Abdominal Snowman and I left the two sisters alone.

"Back to the tent?" he asked. That seemed like a solid plan. We would go back and sleep and let this night just fade into morning. Then two more days until we'd never see each other again.

That thought made me impossibly sad, and so I made a stupid decision. "I know this may sound hard to believe, especially given what we just witnessed, but I am starving. I haven't eaten all day." Other than cookies and s'mores, but that hardly counted.

"Did you want to go down to the restaurant? Or the bar?"

Neither one of those options seemed safe. Troy might expand his search. Or someone might see us and turn us in. "I have a secret weapon." I held up my keycard. "Let's get room service."

"How did you manage that?" Camden asked as we went back to the elevators.

I tugged at the bottom of his shirt, noticing how his eyes tracked my movements. "I always get two keys and keep them in separate places because I tend to lose them and lock myself out. This time it works to our advantage."

It took me a second to realize that I was presuming a lot. He might not be up for hanging out with me. Even if he had said he liked being around me. "I mean, if you want."

"I want," he said, his voice giving me impossible-to-ignore shivers. "Somebody has to keep an eye on you in case you slip up and reveal your nefarious intentions."

Teasing or testing? It was hard to tell. We exited the elevator and began walking down our hallway. "My nefarious intentions to make sure the mother of the bride doesn't humiliate said bride? Yep, whole lot of scheming going on there."

We got to my room and I opened the door, letting us both in. I was glad that housekeeping had come and the room wasn't in total disarray like it had been earlier. I grabbed a stray bra and shoved it into the top drawer of the dresser. Other than that it was fine.

The door slammed shut behind Camden and we were alone. Half-dressed. In a hotel room. With a giant bed.

Why had I thought this was a good idea?

"Changed," I blurted out. "I need to get changed." And give him back his shirt so that I wouldn't start finding excuses to accidentally brush up against him. I grabbed a pair of yoga pants and a T-shirt from the dresser. I could have gone into the bathroom, but I would have had to squeeze past him and I did not trust myself to accidentally touch him at the moment.

"Okay."

"Okay. So . . . I'm going to get changed," I announced for a third time, holding my clothes in front of me, like they were a shield that would protect me. Why was I repeating myself?

He gave me one of those sexy smiles of his and said, "I have no objections."

"Turn around, please." I made a circling motion with my finger so that he'd show me his back. He gave me an "aw, do I have to?" expression but did as I requested.

I took off his shirt, placing it on the bed next to me. I paused for a moment to study the broad expanse of his shoulders and torso, thinking about walking over to him, pressing myself against his back, wrapping my arms around him. Would he be warm? Or had his skin cooled from being shirtless for so long? I imagined how he'd react, thinking he might stiffen up in surprise and then relax into my embrace.

How he'd turn around slowly and after looking deeply into my eyes, he'd lean down to kiss me, his fiery lips devouring mine, gathering me up against him and lowering me down onto the bed and . . .

"Rachel?"

My heart beat so hard I was sure he could hear it. "What?"

"Are you having trouble with the buttons?" He sounded far too hopeful.

I grabbed my shirt and yanked it down over my head and realized that my face was currently stuck in one of my sleeves. "I'm fine."

He turned his chin toward his shoulder, as if he were going to look at me, but he didn't. "Did you decide not to put clothes on? I could understand why you wouldn't want to get dressed. I am pretty irresistible."

Now I managed to get both of my legs into one of the pant legs and I was bouncing around trying to get unstuck. "And yet somehow I've managed to resist you."

Barely, but he didn't need to know that.

I finally sorted myself out enough to get my pants on correctly and twisted and turned until my head was through the appropriate hole in my shirt. I got my arms into the right spot and announced, "All done."

When he turned back around, I threw his pajama top in his general direction because I was unwilling to get too close. It was better to have a lot of space between us.

Especially given that we were standing here in this half-dressed state where I was having inappropriate fantasies when nothing could or should happen between us. It forced me to make a deal with myself. I was allowed to spend time with him as long as I kept things strictly platonic.

"Your shirt's on backward," he offered and I glanced down.

"Oh. Yeah. That's how I wanted it." There was no way I was going to try adjusting it again. I might wind up strangling myself or something.

Then Camden would have to do CPR on me and I'd pull him down into a real kiss and . . .

I shook my head hard. I had to stop this. "Are you going to put that on?" I figured it might help my current situation.

He hesitated for a moment, as if he knew exactly why I'd asked the question, and he was enjoying my discomfort. "Are you sure you want me to put it back on?"

"I . . . yes." I'd said yes, right?

"Okay." He shrugged with a playful smile. "Your loss."

I mean, he wasn't wrong. Then he put it on over his head, where he did not get stuck in his sleeve hole, and pulled it down slowly.

I held in my groan of disappointment. It was like standing in front of the most beautiful painting you'd ever seen and the artist covering it back up with a drop cloth. I wanted to yell out, "Boo!"

Camden grabbed the menu and sat on my bed, leaning against the headboard with his legs straight out in front of him. I considered sitting in the armchair near the patio door, but figured that might make me look like a coward. I settled on perching on the corner of the bed farthest from him.

"Come here." He patted the bed next to him and I hesitantly crawled closer. He waved the menu in front of him. "What do you want?"

Food, I told my raging hormones. *He's talking about food.*

He held out the menu so that I could see it, but sitting so near him and all of his yummy warmth was making it so that I couldn't focus on the words in front of me. "I'll have a cheeseburger and fries."

"Maybe I'll have some of yours."

"Uh, no. You better get your own stuff. I don't share food."

He raised one eyebrow at me. "You think you can eat all that?"

"Not only can I easily finish off a burger and fries, but I can have some ice cream on top of it." Ice cream was like shoes or handbags. You could never have too much of it.

"What kind?"

"Mint."

He made a face. "How is that even a flavor? It's basically toothpaste with chocolate chips."

I considered what he said. "Honestly, I might eat that, too."

He laughed and grabbed the phone, pressing the button for room service. He ordered his own burger and fries and ice cream for both of us (chocolate for him). I had a brief fantasy of dropping some of the melty ice cream on his shirt so that he'd have to take it off again, and then oops, the chocolate would spill onto his chest and being the good person I was I'd have to help clean it off by—

"Rachel?"

"What?" I asked, blinking quickly.

"I said it'll be here in twenty minutes."

I nodded, hoping that my face wasn't saying out loud what I'd been thinking. He put his hands behind his head, and it lifted up the edge of his shirt, giving me another tantalizing view of what was being unfairly hidden from my view.

Clearing my throat I said, "If you don't want to wait we could grab something from the mini-bar. Although that Wheat Thins bag has like six crackers in it and costs twelve dollars."

"I don't mind waiting. I'm pretty good at waiting for things I want." There was that edge to his voice, the one that told me he was talking about something else.

Someone else.

I pressed my hands into my lap, mostly to keep them from lunging for him. "I can't believe we're doing this."

"Doing what?"

His questioning tone was understandable. We weren't actually doing anything. Not anything that I'd like to be doing, anyway. "Skipping out on Sadie and Dan's camping party."

He studied me for a beat. "Do you always do what you're supposed to do?"

"Usually."

"You never just throw caution to the wind?"

There was a time when that might have been true, but life had taught me a hard lesson there. "I've tried, but then I just freak out and try to gather up all the pieces of caution before they blow away."

He sat forward, getting even closer to me. I breathed him in, letting the feel of his nearness wash over me. "We should have some antics."

"I don't antic," I told him.

"Do you shenanigan? Frolic? High jink?"

"Not so much lately." Wow, that was depressing. I'd told myself I was just really dedicated to my career and the women who worked for me, but it was more than that. I'd shut down the part of my life that remembered how to have fun. Krista was right. I did always work.

"I happen to be a master of antics, and the first thing about having a good time is that you have to let your hair down. Both figuratively and literally. May I?"

For a second I forgot to breathe and then I nodded, not sure I'd be able to get the words out. He scooted closer to me and raised his hands slowly, cautiously. My pulse thundered inside me, heating up my blood.

His fingers made contact with my hair and I bent my head slightly, giving him easier access.

It was as bad as I'd feared earlier. His fingers running along my scalp were sublime in a way that was impossible to describe. He very carefully plucked the bobby pins from my hair, letting them just fall to the bed. One by one, and with the removal of each one, somehow my heart managed to beat faster and faster until I thought it might explode.

Then he reached the comb I used and tugged it slightly to get it loose, and my hair tumbled down in one big swoop. My hair was the one part of me that I was vain about. It was long and thick and curled slightly at the ends. I usually wore it up, like a piece of armor. It was my protection from people viewing me as anything other than a serious professional. I didn't let anyone see this side of me.

Except right now, with Camden. I raised my gaze to look at him and didn't understand the expression in his eyes.

"Beautiful," he murmured, his fingers still running through the ends of my hair. His touch made me dizzy, light-headed. I'd never had a man smolder at me before, but it was absolutely happening now. I had to grip the blanket underneath my fingers in an attempt to ground myself and remember where I was.

His face moved toward mine, sending prickles of heat marching up and down my spine. "Rachel," he breathed.

He was going to kiss me.

CHAPTER TWENTY

He was most definitely going to kiss me, and I couldn't let him.

I fled. Scrambled down to the foot of the bed and jumped off. It was like I'd torn off a piece of myself, leaving it behind, where it stayed next to him, wanting everything he was offering. "Wait. Just . . . wait," I said. "We can't."

"Can't what?"

"Any of that." I gulped in a deep breath. Why did it feel like there was no oxygen in this room? "Dan and I have the same rule."

"You're not allowed to make out with bridesmaids, either?"

How could he be calm enough to make a joke? I felt like my heartbeat was never going to return to normal. "I don't date guys I meet at weddings. It's a rule I have."

He lay back, putting his hands behind his head, the picture of ease. "Rules are made to be broken."

"Or they're made to be kept." I needed to keep this one. Not just because I had to be an example to my employees, but because at the core of my relationship with Camden I was lying to him and I was always aware of this fact. It wasn't fair to him.

Because I knew, I just knew, that if we kissed we'd be crossing a line we couldn't uncross. I could only imagine his face when I told him the truth about my relationship with Sadie. That he'd repeatedly questioned me about my life and I'd lied to him about it again and again. How betrayed he'd feel.

But it would be different if there were no romantic feelings involved. He might be hurt, but it would be so much less.

At this moment, friendship was all I had to offer him. Because it had become ridiculously clear to me that I wasn't going to be able to stay away from him. "I can be friends. Nothing more."

He didn't seem all that perturbed by my announcement, which did bother me. Shouldn't he put up even a little bit of a fight? "You know we've already met each other's parents. We're like, at Step 12 in our relationship."

"We're not even at Step 1," I told him.

"I don't think you're right about that," he said, but then he didn't push the matter. "So if we met somewhere besides a wedding, you'd go out with me?"

I wanted to date him now, even though I knew how badly it would all end up. "It's not just wedding guests. I haven't really dated anyone in a while."

"Because of work?" He asked this like it was a totally reasonable explanation, and I supposed in a way it was. I could have agreed and kept that part of myself hidden.

But I wanted him to know. "No. My dating karma hasn't been great. I figure in a previous life I caused a lot of damage that I'm paying for now. Like I must have been like a CrossFit instructor or Mussolini or something."

"I think I've said this before, but I find that hard to believe."

Crossing my arms, I warded off the chill I was feeling. "So does my mother. But if I'm being really honest . . ." My heart warned me not to do it, thudding hard so that I'd stay silent. "I find it hard to trust men."

At that Camden sat up. He patted the bed next to him and I understood his invitation. It was drawing me closer, but letting me know that I had nothing to fear from him.

"Do you mind if I ask why?"

Debating within myself, I walked to the edge of the bed. I'd just decided to join him and try to explain when there was a knock at the door.

"Room service," Camden said, swinging his legs off the bed and padding over to the door. He wisely checked the peephole before letting the hotel staffer into our room. The scent of fried food hit me hard and my stomach grumbled. Camden took care of signing for the bill while I reached for my tray, lifting off the lid. I wasn't sure what to eat first, but the cheeseburger looked delicious so I chose that.

Camden handed over the little folder and the staffer wished us a good night and let himself out. Camden grabbed his tray and sat next to me on the bed.

He picked up one of his french fries. "The sweet smell of heart disease," he said, before popping it into his mouth.

"Don't tell me you like to eat healthy." At his expression I pressed on. "Are you the kind of guy who loves avocado toast?"

"What's wrong with avocado toast?"

I started laughing, not able to help myself.

He tried to frown at me, but it quickly turned into a smile. "Does that mean you don't eat healthy?"

"Well, there's this"—I gestured to the food next to me on the bed—"and the four chocolate chip cookies and six s'mores I ate before this, so feel free to draw your own conclusion."

He watched me attack my burger, while he absentmindedly ate a fry here and there. "You enjoy eating."

"Doesn't everyone?" It was one of the best things about being alive.

"I've dated more than my fair share of women who didn't. Who preferred to deny themselves."

"Not me." I mean, food, no, other stuff, yes. "What about you?"

"It's why I work out. So I can eat the occasional cheeseburger and fries when I feel like it."

"Yeah, someday my metabolism's going to give out and then . . . I don't know what's going to happen." I assumed it wouldn't be great. But I'd still be happy and eating what I wanted.

"I think it's sexy when a woman enjoys herself. So tell me, Rachel Vinson, what else would you like to enjoy tonight?"

His words turned my blood into liquid fire. I knew exactly what he was asking me, and I very much wanted to say it.

I didn't, though. "For now? The rest of this burger. And then the ice cream. I can't do anything else. I'm not in a place where I can date anyone."

"I don't remember asking for that."

Maybe not, but he was heavily implying it. "I can only be friends with you."

He seemed to be considering my offer as he tore open a packet of ketchup, adding it to his burger. "I could always use another friend. Can't you?"

I nodded. Someone to hang out with and talk to and not kiss no matter how much you wanted to? There was room in my life for that. Regardless of how torturous I found it.

Because the other options weren't acceptable. "Just so long as you understand that we're the kind of friends whose shirts don't accidentally slide off?"

He looked far too amused. "But what if my buttons just spontaneously come undone?"

"They won't," I instructed him in a determined voice. My heart couldn't take it. I would go up in flames. Ones that reached to the moon.

"Are you sure? Stranger things have happened." He took a bite of his burger and then swallowed it down. "And please know that if your shirt was to accidentally slide off, I don't have any objections to that."

Whew, I knew that he was teasing but that silky tone of his made my skin feel heated. "Thanks for the update."

"Any time. And don't worry. I promise to remember that we're only good buddies."

Even though it had been my decision, his words felt vaguely disappointing. There was a decent amount of space between us and I imagined climbing over our food and telling him I'd been wrong about that silly friend thing. I needed to change the subject. "So earlier today, what was with Irene being worried about stuff going wrong at weddings?"

I grabbed a bunch of fries, needing to sublimate this desire I felt for him with greasy, delicious food.

"Oh, easy," he said. "Dan used to date Satan and I think Irene's afraid she might try to wreck the wedding."

I stopped midchew. "What?"

"Her actual name is Lilith."

"Like . . . the woman from mythology who was the mother of demons?" When he nodded I asked, "Why do parents do stuff like that?"

He finished off the last of his burger in a single bite, and I found it impressive. "It was an old family name. Anyway, she made his life miserable. She was always accusing him of cheating on her and he had to constantly prove himself by buying her gifts he couldn't afford. He was deep in debt for a long time. She kept demanding more and more stuff and he couldn't see that she was using him until one day he finally woke up."

"What pushed him to end things with this delightful-sounding creature?"

"Dan wants kids, and she'd spent years telling him that she wanted a family, too. During a fight she finally admitted that she'd lied and never planned on having children and that was it."

"Obviously it's her choice whether or not she wants a family, but she definitely shouldn't have lied to him for years." She'd tricked him and led Dan on. I ate my last french fry and started eyeing Camden's. While I didn't share food, I wondered if my new friend was amenable. "Don't tell my mom, but I want to have kids, too. Like, six of them. My own little basketball team."

"Don't worry. I won't tell her."

It took me a second to register that he actually could snitch on me and it was another layer of weirdness added to everything else that was happening. "What about you?"

"I definitely picture myself being a dad. I've thought about how nice it would be to have people in my life who were related to me. I miss that."

His words made me ache for him, that he didn't have relatives. It must be so hard; I couldn't even imagine. Then that sympathy turned to an odd kind of joy, that he would want to have children. I had to remind myself that his words had no bearing on me or my future life.

Then, as if she somehow sensed that hypothetical grandchildren were being discussed, my mother called. I couldn't let her know what was happening.

"You have to be quiet," I told him, very stern in my warning. I shifted my tone as I picked up and said brightly, "Hi, Mom!"

His eyes got comically large and he mouthed, "It's your mom?" He held out his palms, moving his fingers back and forth like he wanted me to hand my phone to him. Fat chance.

"Hi, sweetheart! How are things going?"

I glanced over at Camden. My mother would have a coronary if she could see that he was here. "Good. I'm just getting ready for bed."

"I was calling to see if any progress had been made. How's Camden?"

His eyes lit up and he started to speak. I clamped my hand down over his mouth.

"Fine, I guess."

He mumbled something against my hand and I tried not to think about how soft and warm his lips were on my skin. I had to close my eyes against the sensation.

My mom was talking, but I wasn't registering anything that she was saying.

"Sounds great, Mom. I need to get going. I've got sunrise yoga and need to get to bed. I'll call you later!" I hung up the phone and waited a moment to see if she'd call back. When she didn't, I slowly moved my hand away from Camden.

"That wasn't funny," I told him.

"It was from my perspective," he said, still clearly enjoying himself. "Your mom likes me."

"That's not really saying much. My mom likes anyone who has the potential to impregnate me." These words were out of my mouth before I could wish them back inside my head, because it brought back that thick, weighted feeling. Where we were both feeling something, but I had to deny that it was happening.

"Why not tell her I was here?" he asked, and it was more than just simple curiosity. He was asking me something that I couldn't answer, because I had feelings about him that I wasn't ready to share, so I kept things light.

"Because she would have flown here to hog-tie you and force you to marry me."

"That doesn't sound so bad."

I knew he was kidding, and maybe it was because I was in this wedding environment, or just because of how attractive he was, but there was a superdumb part of me that wanted to believe such a thing was possible.

When I didn't argue with him, he added, "You totally lied to your mom."

I wished I could shrug it off, but he wasn't wrong. "It was necessary. Sometimes, in my life, I have to do that to protect people I care about."

It felt like a major confession, the closest I'd come to telling him the truth.

We finished up the rest of the food, and he did indeed allow me to have some of his fries. They were a little cold, but I didn't even care. Camden cleared the trays and plates from the bed and he lay down on his side, facing me. "Let's play a game," he said.

"What kind of game?" I asked. I lay down across from him.

"The kind where you tell me something."

"Like what?"

"Something about you that I don't know," he said, and then added, "I don't want to know about how much you can bench-press, either. Something real. Something you haven't told someone else. Maybe what you were going to tell me earlier before the food arrived."

"I can't even bench-press the bar, so there's nothing to tell you about that," I said, aiming for lightness when all I felt was a slight sense of dread. Would Camden think less of me if I told him why I didn't trust men?

"In our game we can trade truths," he said. "You tell me something, I'll tell you something."

Why? I wanted to ask him, but wasn't sure I was ready for the answer. Because deep down, I knew why. "How will we know if we're actually saying the truth?"

"We're going to have to trust each other."

It was a big ask, even if he didn't know that.

"Okay," I said. "I'll play."

CHAPTER TWENTY-ONE

I took in a centering breath, then spoke. "Right after I graduated from college, I was offered a job in one of the most prestigious brokerages in New York. There were ten of us hired at the same time, and I was the only woman. I loved everything about it. Including my thirty-five-year-old boss, who took a liking to me."

Grabbing one of the pillows from under my head, I moved it against my chest so that I could hold on to it. "I'd been so eager to please, wanting everyone's approval, because I was determined to succeed. To make my parents happy, I suppose. He took advantage of that. Lots of late nights and things that I now understand were entirely inappropriate and we had an affair. He preyed on my inexperience. It was such a cliché that it feels ridiculous that it happened to me."

It was the first time I'd ever seen Camden look truly angry. That it was on my behalf was a little thrilling. "Did he get fired?"

"No, I did. He was married, something I didn't know. And when evidence of our relationship came to light, he threw me under the bus. He'd been very careful the entire time. He told the firm that I was harassing him. When the partners reviewed the footage, it was me going into his office, sitting on the edge of his desk. They didn't know that he was the one who called me in. They didn't see our emails, which he got someone in IT to destroy. There were no texts or anything that I could use to prove my innocence. I looked like the aggressor, and they fired me."

Camden somehow managed to look even angrier, but he stayed quiet.

"It just about destroyed me. I had spent four years in college working toward this goal, getting internships every summer, and one man's lies made everything go away. There were a rough couple of months, but then I decided that I was never going to let someone else dictate my career. I wanted to go into business for myself. Some friends had asked me to do events for them and I realized that I had a talent for it. I had a high demand right from the beginning and was worried that I couldn't do it all alone. I had started doing volunteer work, because my mom was always saying that the best way to get over your problems is to help others, and that's where I met—" I had very nearly said Krista's name, which would have been so bad. He had no idea she worked for me. "My first employee. She had just gotten out of an abusive marriage and couldn't find work. I hired her and now, here I am."

"That must have been really hard, but good for you for finding a way forward," he said, and I appreciated that he hadn't jumped into my story with all the things I should have done differently, like my father had. I knew my dad had been trying to help me, but the situation couldn't be retroactively fixed.

"I also promised myself that I'd never date anyone from my workplace. It was such a stupid mistake and I wanted to make sure that I'd never make it again."

"And since you mostly work weddings, that's why you don't date wedding guests," he correctly surmised, even if my reasons why were a little bit different than what he imagined.

"Pretty much."

"I can see why you'd be afraid to trust men," he said. "I don't blame you."

That made tears well up in my eyes, and I wasn't sure why. Maybe because I felt understood?

"I know I should be past it. I have dated, but like you said, my trust was so thoroughly violated that I find it hard to give it again. But it's not the worst part. The worst is how hard it is to trust myself. When someone else makes you question everything—your judgment, your decisions, your intuition—that's hard to recover from. He undermined my belief in me."

At that Camden reached out his hand, resting it on top of mine. He squeezed gently. "I would like to be a man you could trust."

"I'd like that, too," I confessed.

"And if I were a different type of guy, I might ask you for this lowlife's name and address so that I could invite his face to meet my fist."

That made me smile. "And you're not that kind of man?"

"Not one that would go searching for him, but if we just happened to accidentally run across him someday by total chance and coincidence, yeah, I'd enjoy punching him."

"I think I'd enjoy that, too."

He took his hand away and I almost reached for it, wanting his warmth and support back.

The look in his eyes made me think he knew exactly what I was feeling. "You did trust me, you know. Last night. When you asked me to stay."

"I did. But that's because you're . . ." I trailed off, trying to think of the right word to explain why I'd done that.

"Amazing? Good-looking? The most intelligent and impressive man you've ever known? Hilariously funny?"

"You're different."

The teasing light died in his eyes. "Good or bad? Like, good in that I'm different from the other men you've known or bad as in you're so not interested that you felt like you didn't have to worry about me?"

"Just . . ." He was asking for too much. I couldn't give him what he wanted. "Different."

His phone rang and he didn't even take it out of his pocket, which surprised me.

"You're not going to get that?" I asked.

"Nope."

He wasn't even going to look at it? "What if it's important?"

"A very wise woman told me to be present in the moment, and there's nowhere I'd rather be than right here with you."

His words touched my heart, and as much as I tried to suppress the feeling, I couldn't let him in like this. "So basically we're giving each other the same advice."

"Sounds like." He shifted then, making the entire mattress dip, and I nearly rolled into him.

"Your turn," I said. "To give me a truth. Like why you're single."

"That's easy. Too busy. I mean, it's been a long time since I've been serious with someone. The last time was probably in college but it turned out that she was sleeping with my roommate whenever I traveled for meets. She blamed me for leaving her alone."

"That doesn't sound fun."

"It was a long time ago," he said, making a small shrug. "I haven't been avoiding relationships; I've just been focused on other things. It doesn't help when your best friend is marrying the woman of his dreams. Dan once told me that the night he met Sadie all he wanted to do was to keep talking to her for forever. It made me realize what I was missing out on. A woman I could stay up all night talking to."

Like you. He didn't say the words, but he didn't have to. I felt them. Again my heart lurched happily.

"My turn," I said, my throat feeling a little tight. "My truth is . . . I'm not a spy."

"Honestly, I don't think you're a spy, either."

"That's not really a truth. It's more of a 'you decided to stop being dumb and believe what was right in front of your face.'"

He seemed to take that as some kind of challenge and said, "Okay. Truth from me that I haven't told anyone else—earlier tonight when I was rubbing your shoulders? I had to stop and walk away because you leaned your head to one side and you exposed your neck and the only thing I wanted to do was press my mouth against your skin."

Warmth pooled in my gut; my breath stuttered in my lungs. "Just friends, remember?"

"That was a friend thing to say."

"Um, no."

"Being honest is friendly," he insisted.

Saying stuff that made me want to pounce on him was not friendly. This conversation needed to be stopped. I turned over to reach for the TV remote on the nightstand next to the bed. "Do you want to watch a movie?"

He seemed to be at ease and completely aware of the fireworks that were going off inside me. "Sure. What did you have in mind?"

What I had in mind and what was going to happen were two entirely different things. "Something with Noah Douglas or Chase Covington in it."

The hotel had the option to log in to my personal Netflix account. I made Camden cover his eyes while I entered the password and pulled up a romantic comedy I'd watched a dozen times already.

"I know it makes me sound old, but nine times out of ten I'd rather stay home and watch a movie than go out," I told him.

"That sounds like a perfect night to me."

That made me feel a bit giddy. With a smile plastered on my face, I started the movie. We were about a minute into it when he asked why the heroine was wearing so much makeup despite the fact that she'd just woken up and it set me off. "Right? Like there's not enough pressure on women to always look perfect, now we have to be models when we roll out of bed."

There was a look on his face, like he wanted to say something to me. Based on the way his gaze traveled from my head to my feet, I guessed it was going to be something nice about how I looked. I wanted to hear what he might have said, and it was my own fault for shutting all that down.

We kept up our commentary while we watched the movie, and it turned from being about what we were watching to us talking about our lives. I walked him through how I'd set up my business and the mistakes I'd made and things I wished I could do over, as well as the successes. At first I felt a little dumb, given that his company was operating at such a higher level than mine. He could have been a jerk about that, but he wasn't. He listened intently, commenting and praising me. It made me feel . . . significant. Like what I'd done mattered.

That led to him telling me why he hadn't applied for patents for Dan's central processing unit—his reasons lined up with what Sadie had told me a few days before. Which was why it had been so important to him to fend off any potential spies.

After we talked about the ins and outs of his plans, the conversation moved to us trading stories from high school and college, which led to us talking about bad dates we'd gone on (I was pretty sure I won that particular contest) and finding out how much we both liked to read. He told me how he would sit with Irene and read her favorite stories to her while she was having chemo and it made me like him even more.

Hours passed, and they felt like minutes. And with each shared laugh, every thing we discovered we had in common, we moved closer to one another. We both kept adjusting our positions so that we edged nearer, until we were almost touching.

But Camden didn't cross that line, and I didn't want him to.

Well, I did, but I had promises to keep.

Like the one my alarm reminded me of as it beeped. "It's time to grab Brandy and get back to pretending to camp," I told him.

Our faces were so close together that we were taking in each other's breaths.

"Can we stay here for one more minute?" he asked, and I nodded slowly. I didn't want to leave, either.

Even though I knew we had to, I loved being in this bubble with him. I didn't know how many minutes had actually passed as we lay there, looking into each other's eyes, but it was time to get back to reality.

"We should go," I whispered.

"Are you sure I can't kiss you?" he asked and his words turned my insides to hot liquid.

"Yes." I meant that as *yes, kiss me*, but I verbally fixed it to, "Yes, I'm sure we can't kiss."

It was better this way. Even if I couldn't tell him why.

He nodded and got up first, breaking the spell, and I was glad that he did. It made it easier for me to stand up and walk away from the bed where we'd spent the entire night getting to know each other.

Which had only made everything worse. Because I'd been interested in him before, definitely attracted to him, but now I really liked him. He was fun and funny and challenged me and . . . crap. My mom was going to be so disappointed when she found out that I was not going to fall in love with him.

Because that could never happen. I couldn't allow it.

We took the elevator up to Brandy's room in silence. We didn't need to talk. That connection was there, so strong that words weren't necessary.

Mandy opened the door for us and Brandy was sitting on her patio, drinking coffee.

"We're here to help get her back downstairs," I said.

"She's embarrassed over how she behaved last night," Mandy told me. "And I won't have any problem getting her to the yoga thing."

"Okay," I said. "But like always, give me a call if you need anything."

We left and Camden took me by the hand. "Friends hold hands," he told me.

I didn't protest, even though I hadn't held hands with one of my friends since I was five years old.

We got out to the west lawn, where people were starting to wake up and move around.

I was surprised at how beautiful the sunrise was—I didn't usually get up this early. Although, technically, I'd never actually gone to sleep.

Funny thing was I didn't even feel a little bit tired.

"Maybe greeting the sun's not so bad," I said.

I turned slightly to see Camden watching me and he said, "Yeah, I was thinking it's pretty great."

We walked over to the tent that we hadn't gotten the chance to share and gathered up our things from the tote bags.

There was a finality to it, and I realized that I wouldn't be seeing him again until the wedding. I probably wouldn't even get to talk to him until the reception.

Which was for the best. I knew that, but it was like I couldn't get that logical message to the rest of my body.

"What are your plans after this?" Camden asked, making small talk that felt a little awkward after everything we'd shared.

"We've got a spa day for the bridesmaids and the moms. You?"

"The boys and I were debating on whether we should go paintballing or play golf."

I gasped. "No paintball!"

"Why not?"

Why were men so dense? "All it takes is one of you idiots missing and smacking Dan in the face and leaving him with a giant bruise that will be in all of his wedding pictures forever."

"Nobody's going to—" He sounded indignant, but then switched to a more sheepish tone. "You're probably right. I'll make sure we play golf. Do you have any objections to that?"

"None other than it's a stupid sport. I don't get that game. It's just walking around in a huge yard and hitting tiny white balls while wearing dumb clothes."

"I don't know," he said, that teasing lilt back in his voice. "It kind of sounds like you get it."

That surprised me. I had a guy break up with me once because I'd dared to say that fantasy football was stupid. "You're not going to defend golf?"

"Any sport that's been around for five hundred years doesn't need me to defend it."

He probably had a point. "As my dad likes to say before he plays a game, make sure you bring an extra pair of pants in case you get a hole in one."

Camden grinned at my cheesy joke, but we were interrupted by movement just outside the tent. Anton, Troy's assistant, lifted the flap. "What are your names again?"

We gave them to him, and he opened that massive album, found our names, and returned our keycards to us. We thanked him and he left.

"Well," Camden said. "This is it. I'm going to go now."

"It's not an airport. You don't have to announce your departure."

He nodded and started to walk to the front of the tent and stopped short. "What are you doing tonight after the bachelorette party?"

"Sleeping would be my guess."

He reached into his jeans pocket and pulled out a quarter.

"You carry change?" I asked. "Why?"

"To pay for stuff," he said, like it had been a dumb question.

I just shook my head. "An outdated phone and you have cash? You're like a fugitive from the 1990s."

Ignoring my words he said, "Let's flip for it. Heads you hang out with me after the parties and tails I hang out with you."

"Ha ha. That's the same thing."

He winked at me. "I knew you were smart."

"Yeah, I heard you like smart women." I had to stop being flirtatious. Normally this was never an issue for me, but it was turning into a big one.

"Fine. Heads we hang out, tails we don't."

He flipped the coin in the air and I found myself silently praying for heads. Camden caught the coin and flipped it onto the back of his other hand.

But he didn't reveal it. Instead he said, "Tell me that you feel it, too. That something's changed."

"It can't." I felt silly saying it. Like a kid sticking their thumb into a dam, trying to hold back the oncoming flood.

"But it did."

I didn't disagree with his statement. I couldn't. It was true. But I just let his words hang there in the air, not responding.

With a rueful smile he headed out of the tent. Without telling me the outcome of his coin flip. I wanted to say *wait, come back*, that the suspense was going to kill me.

I sank down on my cot, realizing the enormity of my situation. It wasn't just the coin toss. Everything that man did and said was going to wreck me.

How was I going to make it through the next two days?

CHAPTER TWENTY-TWO

Krista found me sitting on my cot. "Was that Camden that I spied coming out of this very tent? Carrying his clothes?" She came to a stop in front of me. "Look at your hair! I'm so happy for you!"

Before she could get carried away I held up my hand. "Hold your horses, there. Nothing happened."

She pshawed me and said, "Your hair's down and your shirt's on backward? I call BS that nothing happened."

"I get how it looks, but we just talked the whole night."

"Is that what the kids are calling it these days? I bet he's a great talker." She waggled her eyebrows at me.

I groaned and collapsed back onto my cot. I was having enough problems dealing with this Camden stuff without Krista making it worse.

She sat on Camden's cot, waiting for me to say or do something, but I was feeling a little overwhelmed at the moment. So she said brightly, "I'm surprised you're up and ready for yoga. Given that it starts earlier than you're probably used to. It's this magical time of day we call morning."

"I didn't wake up. I never went to sleep."

"I bet you didn't," she said, and then immediately switched gears. "Sorry, I can't help it. I know I shouldn't give you a hard time, but it seems like you like him and that just makes me kind of giddy for you."

She wasn't wrong, no matter how much I tried to deny it. "It doesn't matter if I do."

"Of course it matters!" she protested.

"I don't believe in boyfriends and I have to stay true to my beliefs," I said. It was something I'd jokingly said to her before, but now it just felt weak and inadequate.

Because after last night . . . things couldn't be the same. Like he'd said, something had changed. That connection, the one that had been there since the beginning even though I'd denied it, felt so strong now. It was as if I'd known him and liked him for years. I didn't know how I was going to walk away from him once this was all over. Sadie and Dan were getting married tomorrow and I was catching a red-eye right after. That would be it.

She put her hands over her face before sliding them down slowly. "I blame your mother for this. Not every guy you meet has to become something more serious."

That was what she didn't understand. I wanted that something more with Camden and I couldn't figure out a way to make it happen without betraying his trust. "If I kiss him, then I've done something wrong."

"Why? You're not going to see him again."

"It's not a matter of seeing him again, it's a matter of integrity. I wouldn't want to get involved physically with someone that I was lying to. If I keep things platonic, then it doesn't matter."

She looked annoyed. "It matters if you missed out on something great."

"Great? He exercises, I don't. He likes being outside, you know I'm basically allergic to the sun. He eats avocado toast on purpose and I don't need to explain to you how I eat." Whether this was to convince her or me that there was no future here, I wasn't sure.

"From an outsider's perspective, who is getting information from all sides, I can see the things the two of you have in common, the shared interests, and how well you seem to get along. You and I have been doing this for a long time and I think you know as well as I do that what this all boils down to is do you like being together, do you want the same things, and are you interested in each other's lives?"

Everything about Camden fascinated me and last night I'd happily listened to his half-hour-long story about what training for the Olympics had been like, and could have listened to him for hours more. "Other than his loyalty to Ohio State, yes." To all of her questions.

She looked far too satisfied with herself. "I don't even have to ask if the physical connection is there, because anybody can see that."

True.

Krista continued, "I'm not sure what your whole denial thing is about, but you like him. What you choose to do with that information is up to you, but know that I'm here for you." She stood up. "Now, should we get out there and say good morning to the sun?"

I didn't have it in me to tell her that I'd already had that experience once this morning and nothing else could compare.

～

I made a quick appearance at the yoga session, explained my outfit change the way I'd said I would, and got back to my room. I set an alarm and then crashed hard, a dreamless sleep that was difficult to wake up from. I refused to let myself think about how Camden's half of the bed still smelled like him. If questioned, I never would have admitted that I slept on that side so that in a small way it was like he was still there with me.

Our spa day was pretty typical and something I'd experienced in many wedding parties. Sadie seemed happy and bright, which was my only goal. To make sure that expression stayed put.

I enjoyed my facial, my massage, and the pedicure that took off so much dead skin that I might have gone down an actual shoe size.

Afterward we were free to spend the day how we wanted, until the bachelorette party that evening. It should have been my job to plan it, but the hotel wanted her to have it at their bar and she had agreed.

The only instruction she'd given me was to keep away from anything that might seem tacky or low-class. She'd said to me, "I grew up poor, feeling like I was always being judged. I want this to be above reproach. I mean, trolls are always going to find fault, but my brand is aspirational. It should be more elegant and refined. No strippers, no anatomical cakes or balloons. Just us having a good time."

It was her day and anything she wanted was fine by me. I'd gotten in touch with the hotel before we'd even flown to Hawaii and they had assured me they were going to take care of everything, including the food. All we had to do was show up.

Showing up was definitely in my wheelhouse.

Sadie had apparently told Dan the same thing—she'd asked that he not let things get out of hand, because the camera crews would be there. He had told her not to worry because he didn't even want to have a bachelor party. He'd said, "Why would I want to celebrate my last day of being single? All I want is to be your husband and I can't wait for that to happen."

I may have sighed happily when she told me that. I'd heard that the men planned on having a nice steak dinner with cognac and playing some poker.

Most weddings I'd been involved with had a rehearsal dinner the night before, but Sadie told me she wasn't interested in her mom and stepdad having to sit at the same table for any length of time. At the reception they were going to be seated separately, something she could get away with there and wouldn't have been able to at a rehearsal dinner. It sounded like a good plan to me.

I also spent my day wishing that Camden would call me. Or stop by. I kept an ear out for his door, my gaze drifting repeatedly to our shared wall, but I never heard him return to get ready for the bachelor party.

Deciding this was beyond pathetic, I got ready myself, keeping the bathroom door shut and the fan on. For good measure I turned on some music on my phone just so that I wouldn't know if he was back.

I picked out my favorite red cocktail dress for the party and was in the midst of putting my hair up when I stopped, almost hearing Camden's voice telling me to have fun and not take myself so seriously. I could be professional and still have a good time. I wouldn't need my armor tonight, so I left my hair down.

And if I was going to admit it, I was hopeful that his quarter had landed on heads and that I'd see him after and he'd get to appreciate it.

I made my way down to the bar and saw one of the camera crews in a corner, talking among themselves. I found Krista sitting in a chair near the door, waiting for me.

She grinned when she saw me. "Your hair's down! It looks pretty. You did that for a boy."

Feeling embarrassed at being caught out, I said, "I did not. I'm not even seeing Cam—any boys tonight."

"You almost said his name!" she told me in a singsong voice. "Because you like him and yes, you did do your hair that way for him."

"What are you drinking?" I asked, wanting to change the subject.

"The bartender got out champagne." She held up her flute.

A waitress came over and asked me what I'd like, and I told her I was fine. I'd order something when the other girls appeared.

It took a few minutes, but Mary-Ellen and Sadie came down together, their arms linked. There were hugs and air kisses exchanged and the manager of the bar approached us, leading us to the private table they'd set up for us. It had a bunch of finger foods—things like kalua pork sliders, shoyu chicken kebabs, grilled pineapple.

It was delicious and I didn't even care that somebody was filming us eating. This food was worth it.

The waitress brought over a tray with more champagne flutes. To my surprise, Sadie took one. "It's a special occasion!" she declared. "Only don't let me get too far gone. My wedding is tomorrow."

"How do you define *too far*?" I asked. I was happy to be her babysitter tonight if that's what she needed.

"If I start dancing on tables, definitely cut me off," she said, reaching to clink her glass with Mary-Ellen's and Krista's.

Krista held up her glass for the toast and said, "May we have so much fun that we don't even notice how annoyed the other bar patrons are!"

I'd thought the bar would shut down for the evening, but it was still open to other guests. Given the looks I was seeing already, we probably were going to annoy our fair share of people.

"Can I get a soda? Something lemon-lime?" I asked the server and she promised to be right back with it. I figured it was better to order a drink that had no chance of being accidentally spiked.

"Do you know how bad those are for you?" Mary-Ellen asked. "Artificial sweeteners eat holes in your brain. It's basically death in a can."

The fact that she said this unironically while munching on buffalo wings and potato skins and drinking champagne as fast as they could bring it to her was not lost on me. The server returned with my soda and I carefully drank the entire thing in front of Mary-Ellen, just to spite her. It was a spite Sprite.

As we ate, at the director's urging, Sadie recounted how she'd met Dan in Rome. He'd been there for a tech conference and she was there to do a photo shoot and they met at a restaurant after she dropped her napkin and he returned it. They spent the rest of the night talking and walking the romantic, moonlit streets of Rome.

"I knew that night I was going to marry him," she told us and Mary-Ellen sighed so loudly and wistfully that I wondered if I should tell the bartender to slow down on serving her.

Sadie shared more stories about their courtship, how he'd proposed to her by flying her back to Italy and asking her to be his wife on the Spanish Steps, which was where they'd first kissed.

She had gone over this information when she hired me, but it had been matter-of-fact then. It was like I was seeing a different side of her—she was so unguarded and free, and obviously in love. Again I felt that pang, that sensation like I was missing out on something big.

After drinking a sixteen-ounce glass of soda as quickly as I had, I needed to use the restroom. I excused myself and stayed longer in the bathroom than was strictly necessary.

I glanced up at my reflection as I washed my hands, not able to come up with a reasonable explanation for my current feelings. I'd been to dozens of weddings and had seen so many people happily in love who promised to spend the rest of their lives together. I'd never felt like this before, like I'd lost a limb and wanted it back. How could I be missing something I'd never had?

And why did Camden's face keep popping into my head?

"You've got a job to do," I reminded myself, reaching for the paper towels. It was time to stop throwing my private pity party and get out there and support Sadie.

I walked back into the bar and smiled when I saw how much fun Sadie and the bridesmaids were having. They looked happy. My shoulder twinged slightly, probably from my purse pulling on it, and I switched the strap over to the other side. I rubbed my shoulder slightly, my mind drifting back to when Camden had massaged it, and the reason he'd told me that he'd had to stop.

"Do you need help with that?" Camden asked.

CHAPTER TWENTY-THREE

As if I'd conjured him up, Camden was standing behind me. I twirled around and saw the way his eyes darkened, how his chest went up and down a bit faster, like I was the one making him feel like there wasn't enough oxygen in the room.

"Wow," he said. "You are stunning."

I resisted the urge to preen a little, enjoying his appreciation more than I should have. It wasn't too long ago that I didn't want any men to look at me, but like I'd told him, he was different. "Thank you."

"Didn't anyone ever tell you not to wear a red dress to a bullfight?"

I laughed and asked, "What does that even mean?"

"We already established that you're a smart woman, Rachel."

Was I about to get run down by a randy bull? Maybe Camden would pick me up and throw me over his shoulder to have his way with me. I tried to tamp down the little thrills rising up inside me.

While I was busy trying to calm my rampaging heartbeat, he pointed at my shoulder. "Maybe I should finish what I started. It looks like I didn't do a good job of massaging your shoulder."

If he'd done it any better, I might have died. "It's fine, thanks." I noticed that he was carrying a bottle of water. "You're not drinking tonight?"

"Sadie asked me not to. I'm not the designated driver since we're not going anywhere, but I'm the designated nobody-gets-a-face-tattoo-or-a-black-eye guy. I've got to protect those pictures, right?" When I smiled at him, he asked, "What about you?"

"I'm drinking soda to spite Mary-Ellen."

He just nodded and I actually kind of loved the fact that he didn't even ask me why. Krista would have done the same thing because she knew me so well. It felt a little like he did, too.

"So," I said, "what are you guys doing here? I thought you had some big boys' night planned."

"We did. But Dan didn't want to be away from Sadie. She told him she was going to drink tonight and I suspect he was afraid things might get a tad out of control."

"He doesn't trust her?" I asked.

"Of course he does. He's just protective."

"Nothing says 'I trust you' like a combined bachelor and bachelorette party."

Camden shrugged and said, "I told him not to worry, but he didn't listen. I knew that you were here and that you'd have things in hand."

His words stung a little. Like I was some fuddy-duddy stick-in-the-mud. "Because I'm the boring one?"

"What? No. Because you're the loyal one who puts her friends above everything else."

Only I wasn't really friends with Sadie. I mean, I was, we liked each other, but it was a lie. Maybe I should have considered it more of a white lie. Like, "I really like your new haircut," or "We should definitely catch up soon," or all of Instagram.

Either Vance or Rick made a huge whooping sound and the entire table broke into laughter. They all definitely seemed to be feeling more than a little happy.

"We should get back over there to keep an eye on them," I said and Camden nodded. I hurried back, not wanting to linger too close so that my body didn't get any bright ideas.

I slid into the seat next to Krista and she said, "Ooh, the man you obsess over is here."

"I don't obsess," I corrected her, speaking softly so that we wouldn't be overheard. "I think about him the exact right amount." Which was all the time, so maybe she was right about the obsession thing.

"Well, know that I'm here as your best friend. How do we play this thing tonight? Am I going for polite but cool toward him? Or super friendly? Do I make myself scarce? Or are we going to end up in jail tonight? You know I'm down for anything."

This was why I loved her. "I'll be fine."

And I truly believed that right up until the moment Dan said, "We should do something fun. Play a drinking game."

Mary-Ellen pounded on the table with her open palm and said, "No! We should play something even better. Like Truth or Dare!"

I wanted to say that was not really a game for adults, but then she added, "I'll go first. Camden?" It was obvious what her dare was going to be, that she planned on manipulating this situation, and I couldn't stop the jealousy that swelled up inside me. "I dare you to ki—"

"Wait!" Sadie interjected, cutting her off. "I'm the bride. Shouldn't I get the first turn?" Her gaze turned toward me and I knew. I just knew. "Rachel! I dare you to kiss Camden!"

She was trying to protect her fiancé's best friend, in her own way. I could recognize that, even if all the blood had left my head and pooled at my feet. She was doing her best to head off Mary-Ellen. Sadie turned to me, apologetic and pleading and more than a little drunk.

"Aren't you supposed to give me a choice in the matter?" I asked, already knowing what was going to happen. "Don't I get to decide whether I'm telling a truth or doing a dare?"

Dan was mumbling something, looking annoyed, but Sadie ignored him. I couldn't look at Camden. I didn't want to see his reaction. My pulse was already throbbing so loudly in my ears that I couldn't think straight—if he had that smoldering "I want to kiss you" look in his eyes, there was no way I could resist him.

"Wait, I get to go first and do my dare," Mary-Ellen insisted, zeroing in on Camden and missing all of Sadie's very blatant cues.

"Did you not just hear me say that I'm the bride?" Sadie said, sounding both determined and apologetic. She was definitely trying to help keep Mary-Ellen far away from Camden, even if I didn't like the way she'd gone about it. "You have to do it!"

"Rachel's the shy type," Krista offered. "She'll need privacy."

I'd never been more grateful for her. I'd get away from prying eyes, rationally explain to Camden why this was a bad idea, and everyone would be none the wiser.

"How do we know they won't just lie about it?" Rick asked, obviously noting my slight sense of utter panic.

"Camden won't," Dan said.

"Rachel totally would," Sadie said, making my panic increase a hundredfold. Was she about to break the NDA herself and upend everything we'd been working toward? It would be better for me to just get this over with than to have a drunken Sadie try to explain herself and put my business in danger.

"There's a storage closet!" Mary-Ellen shrieked with excitement, seeming to forget that she had just wanted to be the one making out with him. "I saw it when the bartender was getting more champagne!"

At this point it seemed like everyone was a bit overexuberant and I was going to say as much, but Sadie had jumped up and grabbed both me and Camden by the wrists and was pulling us back toward the storage closet.

"Sadie, wait a second," I tried. This was truly the stupidest thing that had ever happened to me. I attempted to pull my wrist out of her grasp, but she was surprisingly strong.

Mary-Ellen raced ahead, opening the door for us, and Sadie pushed us inside, shutting us in. "Don't come back out until you've smooched!"

It was a very tiny closet and Camden was pressed against me. I tried to back up but hit shelves and heard the clanking of glass bottles.

"Careful," he said.

I felt something metallic brush against my face and realized it was a chain for the overhead light. I pulled on it and a very dim light bulb came to life.

"What is that?" I asked. "One watt?"

He didn't answer. I finally made eye contact with him and realized that the fading light made shadows over the planes of his face, hiding his eyes from me. This somehow made him more exciting and this moment both thrilling and nerve-racking.

"Is it happening?" I heard Mary-Ellen ask.

"I don't know!" was Sadie's reply. I leaned over and hit the door with my fist, their fading giggles letting me know that they were scurrying off.

"You didn't put up much resistance," I said to him.

He reached up to rest his hand on the shelf just above my head, effectively boxing me into place. "Why would I?"

His words burned inside me, melting away my rational thought.

"This is stupid," I protested, attempting to ignore the way my internal body temperature seemed to keep rising. "We're not thirteen."

"No, we're not," he agreed.

"We don't have to actually kiss. They wouldn't know."

"We would know. We wouldn't want to be dishonest." He had shifted closer to me and my heart throbbed so hard in my throat that I was afraid I wouldn't be able to speak.

I held on to the one argument I could think of. "What about Dan?"

Now he was nuzzling my hair on the side of my face and even though he technically wasn't touching my skin, it felt like he was. "I don't want to kiss Dan."

"No." I gulped. "I meant he doesn't want anything like this to happen."

"Then they shouldn't have put us in a tiny closet together."

It wasn't like we could hold them accountable. "They're all tipsy."

"That sounds like a them problem." He reached up to push my hair behind my ear, then ran his fingers down the side of my face.

Sighing with delight, I said, "They don't know what they're doing. We do."

"You're right. We do. We're adults. We can make our own decisions. Any decision we want."

Everything he was saying made such complete and total sense. Here I'd been so proud of myself for keeping my urges in check. I'd spent an entire night next to him and totally resisted his overwhelming magnetism. I'd counted that as some kind of win.

But there was about to be a total upset.

I could feel it. I knew he could, too.

This was what had changed between us.

He reached out with his left hand, resting it on my waist and pulling me closer to him. The shock of his body pressed fully against mine made my brain stop working.

"We should kiss," he murmured next to my mouth and I burned for him to press his lips against mine.

"We *should* kiss," I said, like he was using some kind of Jedi mind trick on me.

"It would be a good idea."

I nodded. He was totally right. "Yes, it would be a good idea."

"Onomatopoeia."

"What?"

"Sorry, I thought you were going to keep repeating everything I said."

"Maybe . . . ," I said, pushing forward, wrapping my arms around his neck. "Maybe this isn't a time to joke."

"I wish you were always this agreeable."

"No, you don't."

"You're right. I don't. I like you just the way you are," he said.

The anticipation was literally killing me. Even though a part of my brain was screaming that I was headed for a hormonal Chernobyl—that there would be a huge explosion and then a ton of fallout—I didn't care.

I knew I should care. Maybe it was because the time we had left together would be so short that I was rationalizing why this would be okay, despite what I'd said to Krista. Or because I'd wanted to kiss him for what felt like an actual eternity that doing so suddenly seemed reasonable. Logical, even.

His hands pressed into my back. "Do you feel sick?"

Other than taking a total leave of my senses? "Nope."

"Drunk?"

"Not even a little."

"Good." His lips made contact with my forehead, kissing me gently, almost like he couldn't resist doing so for one more second. I let out a soft noise, loving the way that felt.

He pulled back. "Rachel, do you want me to kiss you?"

I was so focused on the physical sensations he was creating that it took me a second to register what he was doing. He was making sure I wasn't impaired in any way and then giving me the option to say yes or no. He knew what he wanted and now he was telling me the rest was up to me.

There would be no backtracking on this, no "whoops, we made a mistake, I didn't mean to put my tongue in your mouth, I was just caught up" kind of situation. I was here, so was he, and we were both agreeing to this.

The words *just friends* kept repeating in my head, reminding me of the boundaries that I'd set for myself and what I should be doing. But I forgot about everything else. About Sadie and Dan with his rules, about the wedding, the NDA, my responsibilities—everything beyond that door ceased to exist for me.

There was only here and now with him.

Pressing my fingers against the back of his neck I whispered, "Camden, I want you to kiss me."

CHAPTER TWENTY-FOUR

I caught a glimpse of his wicked grin, as if he were imagining exactly what he was going to do next. My heart leaped in excitement at what his plans might be. His phone started ringing in his pocket, but he didn't seem to hear it.

"Your phone's ringing," I told him, disappointed that our moment was over before it had even begun.

He took it out of his pocket and threw it over his shoulder, where it landed with a thud on the ground.

I understood that gesture and had a burning need to know what he'd do next, now that he had his go-ahead.

Given what I already knew about him, would he tease me? Ghost his lips near mine without actually touching? Or would he brush his mouth gently against mine over and over again until he had me begging for more?

Would he softly explore my lips as we learned each other's rhythms and how we liked to be kissed?

Or did he expect me to make the first move?

Camden slipped his hand up to my neck, holding me in place. Out of utter frustration I was about to ask him about his intentions when he pressed his lips against mine, making a sound that was a mixture of relief, gratitude, and desire.

We were like two asteroids colliding into each other. Slamming with full force, debris flying everywhere, cores melding into one another. There was intense velocity and a shock wave as his mouth devoured mine, and I feared that in the aftermath there wouldn't be any part of me left. I'd just be tiny pieces of rubble all over the floor because his kiss was utterly destroying me.

Every move of his lips against mine set off a wave of pure starlight, filling me with a silvery, glowing warmth that made my whole body light up. Like I'd been living in darkness for my whole life and someone had just figured out how to flip the on switch.

That light quickly turned to a smoldering fire that made me feel raw with want and need, burning its way through me. I wondered if he was on fire, too.

His mouth was wild on mine, and he was making sounds in his throat that collapsed my spine, making it hard to stay upright. The explosion of nerve endings along the surface of my lips spiraled out, spreading that fire through every part of my body.

I marveled at how well we fit together, like a key fitting perfectly into a lock. Like we belonged together. Had been made for each other.

His kisses were so hard, so hungry, and full of a sureness that surprised me. No hesitation, no curiosity or wondering. Like he knew where we both belonged and it was here, with each other.

Krista had been right. There was no questioning the scorching chemistry between us.

I was desperate for him, and the way he shuddered against me made me think he felt exactly the same. I was a freaking saint for not kissing him before this. Somebody should have canonized me.

His mouth moved away, like my lips weren't enough to satiate him. He started pressing kisses along my jaw until he reached the spot where it met my neck and ran his lips along the edge. I didn't know it was possible to burn and shiver at the same time. My heart was beating so hard it was like it had turned my entire body into one giant drum.

I clung to his shoulders, loving the way he felt under my hands. There was so much strength there.

He kissed his way down my throat, his breath hot against my skin, and my eyeballs rolled so far back in my head I was afraid I might not ever be able to see again. He made the fire inside me so intense I could feel beads of sweat forming along my hairline, along my back. At this rate my legs were going to melt clean off my body.

"Do you know how long I've imagined this?" He asked the words against my skin and I couldn't respond. All I could do was hold to him tightly, like I was caught in a storm. Or a solar flare that was going to burst and consume me.

"You," he said, punctuating each word with a kiss, "are sexy and smart and amazing and I want to see you again."

"What?" My question came out breathy and confused since I wasn't sure what he meant.

"When we get back to New York."

There was no pretense on his part. He was being serious and honest with me. No more spy stuff, no more going along with what Sadie wanted. "This isn't part of the game," I told him, needing to know that he understood what he was offering.

"No, it's not." He stopped kissing me and I wanted to whimper in protest. He rested his forehead against mine. "This isn't about this game, or any other kind."

"Okay." Why was he talking when there were other far more interesting and amazing things we could be doing?

He started pressing kisses against my face, on the delicate skin of my eyelids, my temple, the bridge of my nose. "This is real. You and me. I want this. I want you."

I wanted him, too. But there were other things to consider. Things he didn't know.

Things I was having a hard time remembering at the moment, given how he was stroking my back.

I finally settled on, "I can't . . . I can't . . ." I couldn't promise him anything. Especially not when my brain was hyperventilating and reason was impossible. "Just kiss me."

"That I can do."

It was what I could offer—to be in this moment, here with him. His smoldering kiss engulfed me again, but the desperate ravishing of a few seconds ago was gone. Now he was gentle and sweet in a way that brought tears to my eyes.

He had feelings for me, and he was showing me. With his tenderness, his softness.

I was never going to forget this moment. The way his lips felt on mine, how every part of my body that he touched felt indelibly marked—as if I would have those marks forever.

"Rachel." He said my name reverently, almost like a prayer.

It felt like too much. I couldn't think of emotions right now. I pulled on the back of his head, deepening the kiss. He responded immediately and that hungry, intense kiss was back. The stubble of his chin rubbed against my face, sensitizing my skin, heightening every pass he made. I found myself reaching for the bottom button on his shirt, not caring where we were or what else happened. I had to touch him, to feel more of his heated skin on mine. Fire raced up and down my veins as he pushed me into the shelving unit behind us.

And I knew that fire could consume. It could ravage and devastate. I remembered that all of this would be destroyed when he found out the truth.

That cold reality—along with the sound of a bottle crashing to the floor—was what brought me back to myself. The shattering glass broke us away from one another. He stepped back and it was like someone had wrenched me away from him, and I hated the distance between us.

We were both panting, and the sound of his harsh breathing was doing funny things to my stomach. The only thing I wanted in that moment was to throw myself back into his embrace. I felt so stupid that I'd missed out on the opportunity to be doing this the entire time.

I had to clear my throat so that I could speak. "We should go. We did what they wanted."

"We did what we wanted," he corrected me. "What I want to keep doing."

A wave of guilt and regret enveloped me. He was going to be furious with me. There was a reason I was holding back from him. Maybe if he'd just said this was a hookup it might have been okay. But with him saying he wanted things to continue? There was no future here.

Now I had tears in my eyes for an entirely different reason. My chest hurt. I wanted so badly to just tell him the truth. I couldn't. I reached for the door handle, pushing it open.

No matter what I told myself earlier, I'd wanted this. The door wasn't locked, nobody was standing guard outside it. I could have left at any time. I'd willfully gone into this situation knowing what the end result would be.

I walked back to where the group was sitting and felt Camden on my heels. I had no explanation to offer him about why I couldn't let things continue.

The bridal party let out a loud cheer when they saw us.

"Was it everything you ever dreamed?" Krista asked as Sadie ran over to hug me.

"Are you so in love?" the now slightly drunk bride asked me. "You're going to invite me to the wedding, right?"

Hank was packing up the camera equipment. "You guys should probably call it a night. It's after midnight and you don't want everybody sick tomorrow at the ceremony." Given how the level of inebriation had increased among several people at the party, it seemed like that was a good recommendation.

"I'll help get Sadie back to her villa," I said, but Dan stopped me. "She's my almost wife. I think I can handle this."

I felt bad—I hadn't been trying to imply that he couldn't. I was just looking for an easy excuse to leave and focus on something that wasn't Camden and his magic lips.

"I love you so much," Sadie cooed at him. "You're my hero."

They left together and I said to no one in particular, "But it's bad luck."

Camden was still standing right behind me. "What is?"

"Technically it's their wedding day. They're not supposed to see each other." Camden wasn't doing anything in particular, but standing this close to him made me feel awkward and stupid.

"I guess if Dan keeps his eyes closed, it'll be okay."

I didn't have a response to his joke so I just announced, "I'm headed to bed. Good night, everyone."

That was meant to be a hint to Krista, one that she either didn't get or was ignoring. "See you tomorrow morning!" she called back.

"Okay, then." So much for that plan.

"It's getting late for me, too. I'll walk with you," Camden said and there wasn't a way for me to decline since we were going to the exact same place.

We spent the whole time in total silence, not touching. I could feel his confusion, and I didn't blame him. I was definitely giving off some very mixed signals.

When we reached our rooms he asked, "Is everything okay? Did I scare you off down there?"

This was a switch. Usually I was the one panicking about saying or doing too much and freaking out my date. "No. It's just . . . I don't see a way for things to continue."

Was that vague but final enough?

"Tonight or ever?"

"Both?" I asked it like a question, clearly indicating how conflicted I felt. Because when I looked at his lips all I wanted was to have them pressed against me. I wasn't picky where.

"Are you sure about that?"

"No," I confessed. "Everything is so confusing. I'm not sure what to think."

He took me by the hand, and my nerve endings were very happy at this development and tingled in response. He tugged at me, wanting to pull me closer but letting me make the call.

I walked into his embrace and I could feel how happy my actions made him.

"So let's not think," he said and then his mouth was on mine. Desire roared to life inside me, twisting low and hard in my gut. How was he so good at this? How did it take him just fractions of a second to render me totally senseless? Make me go fluid and pliant against him, desperate for more?

He had me floating dizzily in a world of heat and darkness, where nothing but the next wave of pleasure or sensation mattered when he stopped the kiss.

"Rachel, it's late. We've got an early morning."

"But . . ." I reached out for a reason for him to stay put. "The coin flip. Aren't we supposed to spend time together after the party?"

He grinned and said, "It landed on tails. Which is why I'm off to bed."

"You are?" Did I sound as pathetic as I felt?

"Yep. Do you want to join me?"

His words plunged me into a want so thick and desperate that my whole body was shaking with the need to say yes.

There was no way. "I can't."

I'd expected him to show the same sort of disappointment I was feeling, but he seemed perfectly fine. Almost as if he'd expected my answer. "Then I'll see you tomorrow."

I felt compelled to explain. "I have to draw this line in the sand." I might not have been able to tell him why, but it had to be done. I'd already drawn a line before, saying I wouldn't kiss him, and now I'd done that a whole bunch.

But this line . . . this one had to stay firm. I couldn't be with him like that when I was lying to him. Not to mention that it was way too soon, even if my body heartily disagreed with me.

Camden took a step back, his hand still around my wrist. "Do you know what happens whenever I draw a line in the sand? The tide always washes it away."

Then I'd have to make that line in concrete. Or steel. In whatever substance Captain America's shield was made out of.

He lifted my arm and pressed his lips to the inside of my wrist and my knees buckled underneath me.

"I may have mentioned this before," he said, "but in case I didn't, I'm a very patient man. And I'm very good at waiting. I'm happy to wait for as long as you need me to."

Then he pressed one soft, perfect kiss against my lips. "Good night, Rachel. And if you change your mind, you know where to find me." He disappeared into his room.

I stood in the hallway for a moment, trying to collect myself enough so that I could find my keycard and let myself into my own room. I will admit that I considered knocking on Camden's door more than once and it was only through sheer force of will that I didn't.

Grabbing my keycard, I let myself into my room and slumped against the wall, going down until I sat on the floor.

Obviously, I was willing to ignore my own rule about not dating anyone from a wedding. I'd moved past that line a long time ago, even if I'd kept denying it. And even though I usually felt like men were untrustworthy, that wasn't at all true when it came to Camden. I knew I could trust him.

But it wasn't just about trust. It was about me literally not being able to tell him the entire truth. I racked my brain, trying to remember the details of Sadie's non-disclosure agreement. If it hadn't been so early in New York, I would have called my attorney.

Camden said he was willing to wait. Would he wait ten years? Because that might be how long the NDA was going to last.

It was so frustrating because this was entirely my fault. I had insisted on those non-disclosure agreements for so long, wanting to keep things totally aboveboard and professional, and now it had come back to bite me in the butt. Maybe if I could have been more relaxed, more open, I wouldn't be in this situation now.

I was leaving in twenty-four hours. Maybe I should be focusing on that instead of trying to come up with a way to have everything I wanted without breaking anybody's rules—either mine or the legal system's.

There had to be something. A way around this.

All I had to do was come up with it.

CHAPTER TWENTY-FIVE

Apparently my subconscious mind took my challenge seriously, because when I woke up the next morning, the answer was clear.

I couldn't break the NDA, but what if Sadie could? I sent a text to our lawyer, asking for the specific language. I used the bathroom and came back out to find a response from Gerald—a quick runover told him that while I couldn't disclose, there wasn't any kind of similar language for Sadie. She was free to tell whomever she wanted.

At the combined bachelor/bachelorette party last night I'd been so worried about Sadie accidentally exposing the truth and it sounded like I should have encouraged her. Then I could have cleared the air with Camden, explained everything to him, and things would all be okay.

That might have been overly optimistic, but it was the one hope I had right now. Because the alternative, that I'd have to cut him completely from my life when we got back to New York, was too overwhelming for me to think about. I didn't want that.

But could I even ask that of her? I hoped that she'd be amenable to it, but I would still feel like a very selfish person for asking. It was her wedding day and everything should be about her and her happiness.

Maybe once she was home from her honeymoon I could check in with her and see if she was open to it. Despite how hard she was trying to push me and Camden together, I had to admit to myself that there was the very real possibility she might not want this information to ever get out. She was so protective of her online image and I knew this might hurt her.

One thing at a time. I put on the outfit Sadie had selected for us—blue T-shirts with the word *bridesmaid* on them. She would be wearing one that said *Mrs.* We were all going to wear the same black yoga pants so that we'd look oh so cute in her videos and pictures.

I made my way down to Sadie's villa. Both she and Dan had been given villas on the beach, with their own private pools. The nice thing about it was that she had several rooms, which helped with the absolute zoo that was happening when I got there.

There were several hairstylists and makeup artists, a camera crew, Stefan and his dress team, one of Troy's assistants, Irene, Mandy and Brandy, and then me and the two other bridesmaids. The crowd surprised me because I was twenty minutes early.

Somehow Sadie sat in the midst of the chaos, looking serene and happy. I opened my bag, putting some of the contents on the table. "Okay, I've got acetaminophen and Visine if you need it."

"Grab something to eat first," she said. "I'm feeling great. You don't have to worry about me."

"That's my job."

She took my hand, squeezing it. "You've done amazing so far. I'm so grateful for you. Now, go eat!"

I checked to see what Brandy was up to, and she was chatting with her sister. She appeared to be sober and so I turned my attention to the massive brunch spread. No alcohol, which was wise. But a ton of everything else. Pancakes, eggs, bacon and sausage, muffins, doughnuts, fruit, slices of bread, deli meats, and several different kinds of salads. Knowing that I had a long day ahead of me, I piled my plate high.

Krista was sitting by herself, checking her phone, and I sat down next to her. "Carb-loading, I see," she commented. "Same."

She knew as well as I did how exhausting everything was about to be. Despite the frenzied excitement currently taking place, this really was the calm before the storm.

"Are we laying odds on what goes wrong first?" Krista asked and I shushed her.

"No. Sadie's going to have a perfect day and we're not going to jinx it."

"I think you just did by saying that. Everything's gone too smoothly so far. You know as well as I do what that usually means."

Shaking my head, I dived into my blueberry muffin. It was almost as big as my whole hand, and so delicious. When I got a mouthful down I said, "Things are going to be just fine."

It was then that I glanced up and saw Mary-Ellen's face. Her eyelids and her mouth were swollen. It looked like she'd just gone three rounds with the heavyweight champion of the world.

"Mary-Ellen?" I asked, trying not to sound as alarmed as I felt. "Are you feeling okay?"

"My mouth's a little itchy, but other than that I'm fine. Why?"

I reached into my bridesmaid bag and pulled out a compact, passing it to her. When she saw her reflection, she shrieked. Everybody stopped what they were doing to look at her.

Mandy came over and asked, "Did you eat any almonds?"

"Of course not, Mother!" Mary-Ellen shot back, putting her hand up to her swollen mouth. "I'm not stupid."

One of the servers at the brunch said, "The pancakes are cinnamon and almond flour."

"Is this an anaphylactic situation?" I asked. I knew I should have brought an EpiPen with me, but Krista had talked me out of it, telling me my Mary Poppins bag was fine as it was.

220

"No, she just needs some antihistamines," her mom said. I had some in my bag and I dug them out, but Mandy shook her head and named a specific brand that Mary-Ellen responded to.

"I'll get them," I volunteered. "I'll go over to the gift shop right now and see if they have them." Otherwise I'd have to use a grocery delivery app.

"The pictures are going to be ruined!" Mary-Ellen said with a whine.

Not if I had anything to do with it. I ran out of the villa, headed toward the lobby. My phone rang and I answered without looking, thinking that they might need me to grab something else. "Hello?"

"Rachel?"

It was Camden. I came to a complete stop at the sound of his voice. "What's wrong?"

"It's Dan. He's missing."

I felt my stomach bottom out. No way. There was no way that Dan had taken off. Even if he had, he would have told his best friend / brother. "Okay. Come down to the lobby and I'll help you look for him. I just have to take care of one thing."

I hung up my phone and ran for the gift shop. Fortunately, they had the brand Mary-Ellen needed. I sprinted back to Sadie's villa and made my way inside, handing off the meds to Mandy.

With everyone watching us, I realized I couldn't just go back out without explaining. "I forgot something in my room. I'll be right back."

Krista gave me some serious side-eye, which was warranted. I didn't forget things when it came to weddings. But there was no way I was letting Sadie know that her groom was missing.

Camden was waiting for me in the lobby and without thinking, I rushed up and hugged him tightly. I could see how worried he was. "It will be okay," I told him. "We'll find him. When did you see him last?"

"At the bachelor party thing last night. When we left."

I had to force back the memories of what had happened outside our rooms after we'd left—something much bigger was happening here.

"You haven't heard from him since? He didn't text or call this morning?"

"No, but that's not unusual. Dan is bad about charging his phone." Camden ran a hand through his hair out of frustration. "He's not in his villa. I knocked on the door for fifteen minutes and called his room. No answer."

"Did you check in with the groomsmen?"

s"Vance says that something happened with Rick last night and that he said he was going over to Dan's villa to talk. Apparently Rick was pretty drunk and mad that Dan hadn't chosen him to be the best man."

"Maybe if they're not at the villa, they're someplace nearby? The beach?" I said. I still refused to believe that there was any possibility that Dan had taken off.

"Let's go check."

We got to the sliding doors before Camden stopped and put his hand on my shoulder. "Hey."

I turned, my expression questioning.

He put my face in his hands, looking at me with such incredible tenderness. Then he pressed his lips on mine, kissing me with so much passion that somebody behind us yelled, "Get a room!"

"Sorry," Camden said as he pulled back. "I just realized that I hadn't greeted you properly this morning."

"Uh-huh."

He started walking away but I just stood there for a second because I was pretty sure that kiss of his had disconnected my legs. I took a tentative step forward and was relieved when I didn't fall flat on my face.

"Come on," he said, reaching for my hand, holding on to me tight.

We made it down to the beach closest to the hotel and did find Dan and Rick. Who were on their hands and knees.

"That's not good," I said.

Camden didn't get it right away, and as we approached them I braced for the worst.

Dan glanced up at us as we approached and announced, "My idiot cousin lost Sadie's wedding ring."

Rick looked bleary-eyed and sheepish.

This was why people shouldn't get drunk right before a wedding: they so often did stupid things. Like lose the bride's freaking wedding ring.

"Aren't you supposed to have the ring?" I whispered to Camden.

"Dan was going to give it to me this morning."

"We've been out here for hours," Rick complained. "We're never going to find it."

"Keep looking," Dan said. "People who lose expensive rings don't get to complain when they have to search for it."

Much as I didn't want to admit it, Rick was kind of right. "I know what to do." Dan probably wasn't in the mood to hear it, so I turned to Camden. "Believe it or not, this is not the first time this has happened to me. Get a real phone that has an actual data plan and look up the Ring Finders and give them a call. Tell them it's an emergency, and I bet they'll get someone out here right away to help. Finding lost rings is what they do. But don't text them on your phone, because you want them to respond this century."

"I can do that," he promised.

"Great. I'll check in with the front desk and see if a ring's been turned in. I'll also ask the concierge to keep an eye out for it."

Camden nodded and I glanced at Dan. His face was pointed down, so I kissed Camden quickly. His face lit up with delight at my small gesture. At me making the first move. I told him, "I have to go. I'll see you later. Let me know how things turn out. We'll figure something out if it doesn't turn up."

I had to hurry. I had to stop in the lobby and talk to the concierge and then get back to have my hair and makeup done. If I didn't get back soon my absence was going to be noticed. I said a small prayer that they'd find the ring and hoped that this was the worst thing that would happen today.

If I'd only known.

CHAPTER TWENTY-SIX

I sneaked into Sadie's villa and was glad to see that Mary-Ellen's face had continued to improve. Krista was getting her hair done and patted the seat next to her so that I could wait my turn. Sadie was with the makeup artist and everybody seemed calm, which was what I was going for.

Getting ready for a wedding was a bit like what I imagined a theater actor went through—putting on costumes, getting their hair and makeup done, going out to a beautiful set/backdrop, standing up in front of an audience to put on a show that was going to make them laugh and cry and cheer.

"You have Camden face," Krista told me.

"What?" My thoughts had been in such a different place that I wasn't even sure what she meant.

"There's this expression you get when you've just seen Camden."

"That's not true," I disagreed.

"It is. And you did see him." When I didn't argue back she grinned, sitting up straighter in her chair. "What's going on? I want all the details."

I was supposed to be her boss. Setting the example. Not breaking the rules. I didn't have many rules for my employees, but this was one of the big ones. It made me feel like such a hypocrite that I not only had fallen for a wedding guest but also was now actively looking for a way that we could be together.

But I thought it would be so nice to talk to someone who had all the information and who would have my best interests at heart. I glanced up at her hairstylist, but she had earbuds in, so I figured it was safe to talk.

"Okay, there is something I want to tell you."

"This isn't going to involve the location of a body, is it? Camden's still alive somewhere out there, right?"

"It's not like that. I like him."

I expected some kind of reaction from her, but her expression didn't change. "Oh. Sorry. Imagine that this is me making a performative gasp."

"What?"

"It means I'm not surprised."

Oh yeah? I could fix that. "I made out with him. Multiple times."

Now she looked utterly delighted. "Seriously? I wish I was drinking something so that I could do the spit take this moment so obviously deserves. Oh, I am one hundred percent behind this. I'm going to be so supportive of you two that I'll be like your own personal Spanx."

"I can't let anything happen. He doesn't know about . . ." I let my voice trail off as I looked around the room, making sure that nobody was paying any attention to us. "He doesn't know about what we do."

"So?"

"He has this thing about lying. A big lie wrecked his knee and his Olympic future. His dad had qualified for the Olympics when he was younger and Camden wanted to honor him by—" Realizing that I was about to go on and on, I stopped myself. "He's going to feel betrayed."

"Shouldn't you let him decide how he's going to feel? You don't get to preemptively decide how people will react before you even give them the chance."

I shook my head. I had done that before in my life—given people the benefit of the doubt, and it had screwed up everything. I hadn't done that in years. I predicted how people around me were going to behave and then acted accordingly. I saved myself a lot of heartache that way.

Before I could argue my viewpoint with her, she added, "You always want to control everything, including relationships. That's not how this stuff works."

"This isn't a control issue. And maybe it's not just about him," I admitted. "Maybe I don't want to see the look in his eyes when he finds out. I was going to ask Sadie if she could tell him. According to Gerald, there's nothing in the contract that prevents her from telling the truth."

Krista gasped and reached for both of my hands. "That is so great! That's the answer to everything! Sadie can tell him and then you won't see the disappointment and he'll get over it and declare his undying love for you and you guys will live happily ever after!"

"Isn't that kind of the cowardly thing to do? Letting Sadie take the brunt of it?"

"The cowardly thing is to walk away from the first guy you've had feelings for since I've known you."

It was scary to take a chance again. Part of me didn't want to. It would be easier to just go back to my quiet, ordered life.

I pictured Camden's face and realized that giving up like that would also be much sadder. I resolved to talk to Sadie when she was alone. Which, given the way so many people were fussing over her, might not be for a while.

The stylist finished with Krista and gestured for me to take her spot. As she started brushing through my hair, I heard Stefan bellowing behind me.

"Where is the bride's other shoe?" He put out his hand. "Somebody better put it in my hand right now or heads are going to roll."

I got up out of my chair and Krista came to my side, ready to offer me silent support as we figured out a way to calm this situation down. Sadie didn't need the stress. "What's happened?" I asked him.

"Sadie's left shoe is missing." He enunciated each word carefully.

"Did you—" I was about to ask him if he'd looked for it but figured that might cost me a limb.

"It's not here," he retorted. "Somebody took it."

"Why would someone take just one of Sadie's shoes?" Krista asked me under her breath. "Like there's a Shoe Fairy who takes your heels and instead of a quarter leaves behind drama?"

Valuing my life, I knew better than to laugh. I put a hand over my mouth in order to hide my smile. When I knew I had my face under control I asked him, "Didn't you bring multiple sets of shoes?"

"Yes." He rolled his eyes so hard I half expected them to detach and flop onto the floor. "But I chose this pair because they match her dress."

"The dress that goes all the way to the floor? Where no one's going to see her feet?" This didn't qualify as a tragedy. They could use a different pair of shoes. "You could put her in hiking boots and nobody would know."

Stefan looked like I'd just announced that I wanted to murder his entire family. In an imperious tone he announced, "It's fine. I will figure it out. I don't need your help."

Okay then. He'd kind of just made it everyone's problem by freaking out, but whatever.

"Rachel?" I turned to see Sadie waving me over from the doorway to her bedroom.

"What's up?" I asked her as I followed her into the room.

She closed the door and said, "I need to get changed into this robe before I get put into my wedding dress. Would you mind helping me get my shirt up over my head so that I don't screw up my hair? It has a wide neckline, so I think it'll be okay, I'm just scared of doing it alone."

"Anything you need," I said. Sadie went over to the closet to retrieve her robe. "And while I have you alone, I was wondering if I could ask you for a favor. I feel bad even asking. I don't want to take away from your day. It's so selfish."

"You haven't done a single selfish thing since I've met you," she said as she laid her robe on the bed. "What do you need?"

"I . . ." How would I even phrase this? "I think you were right about the Camden thing."

"How so?"

"I have feelings for him. I want to spend time with him. But I'm deceiving him. He thinks that you and I . . ."

". . . that we're best friends," she finished.

"Right. And I can't try to be in a relationship with someone I'd have to lie to. I would never, ever break our NDA, but my attorney tells me that you can."

"Rachel! I would love to do that! I will tell him first chance I get." Her eyes sparkled brightly, her smile lighting up the whole room. "The fact that you're falling for Camden and want to date him adds to my day. Just think—someday we might look back on my wedding photos and tell our kids this is how you two met."

"Well, let's not get ahead of ourselves. Stick your arms up."

She held her arms over her head and I lifted the shirt. I moved it carefully around her hair but gasped when I saw what the shirt had done to her skin.

"What?" she asked, sounding alarmed.

I yanked the shirt up over her hands. "Your skin . . . you're blue."

The shirt obviously hadn't been made of an expensive material and it had stained her armpits and the sides of her bra a faded indigo. She ran over to the mirror, holding up her arms. "This is not happening. It looks like I tried to smother a Smurf under my arms."

With her arms still held aloft she added, "I can't get in the shower. It will wreck my hair and makeup. But I can't get married with blue armpits."

"This is fine," I told her. "Let me grab Krista and we can clean this up." I hoped regular soap would be enough to get her clean. I lifted my own shirt to check out my skin, but there was no blue.

"I bought the shirts from different websites," she said.

That was good at least. We only had to worry about getting blue off her skin. Conscious of the camera crew still filming in the room just beyond us, I opened the bedroom door and called Krista's name calmly.

She came quickly and when she saw Sadie's armpits she gasped. I closed the door, hoping no one had heard her.

"I need your help washing this off," I said. Krista nodded and they both followed me into the bathroom. I got two washcloths wet with warm water and grabbed the bar of soap from the counter. I laid down a bath towel and had Sadie stand on it. I took her left side and Krista the right.

"You know, when they said you needed something blue for your wedding, I don't think this is what they had in mind," Krista said.

It made Sadie laugh. And laugh. She laughed until she almost started crying. When she was able to catch her breath she said, "I'm sorry. When I thought about what things could go wrong today, blue armpits did not make that list."

"It's coming right off," I told her. "Everything will be fine. We just have to make sure we get all of it or else Stefan is going to have a full-blown cardiac event."

Within a few minutes it was like the blue had never been there. The bra was toast, but fortunately it wasn't the one she'd planned on wearing with her wedding dress.

"See?" I said to her reflection. "Gone. Are you feeling okay?"

"I am," she said. "This was just a silly bump on my road to getting married."

Sadie had no idea that another one of those bumps was her groom's cousin losing her wedding ring. Now was definitely not the time to mention it. "What else can we do?"

"Nothing. You already saved me from having the most humiliating wedding photos ever. I'll get changed and meet you guys in the other room."

I nodded and left with Krista, shutting the door behind us. The camera operator closest to us spun his camera in our direction and I fought the urge to put up a hand in front of my face. I reminded myself that this was all being broadcast live and now was not the time to be camera-shy. I smiled instead, hoping he'd lose interest in us.

Mary-Ellen was almost completely back to normal, and I was glad for that. The problem was she had started whining when her face was swollen and apparently hadn't stopped. At the moment she was loudly talking to her mom and her aunt. "Sadie has everything. Now she gets a rich, handsome husband, too. When is it going to be my turn?"

Before Mandy could reply, Brandy said, "I don't know why everyone's making such a fuss. Most marriages end in divorce. What is the point?"

This was just lovely. I walked over and said, "The point is this is your daughter's wedding day and we're all here"—I focused in on Mary-Ellen—"to celebrate with her and make sure she has the best day ever."

That seemed to shut them down, at least temporarily. I didn't need Sadie to see this later. It would crush her.

I went back to getting my hair finished while Krista sat with the makeup artist. Things generally seemed to calm down and Sadie rejoined us in her satiny white robe. The photographer was taking pictures of the wedding gown on a special hanger and having Sadie stand close to it, looking up at it, looking away from it, everything.

The stylist had just put on the last touches when I got a phone call from a New York number I didn't recognize. I answered tentatively. "Hello?"

"Is this Rachel?"

"Yes."

"This is Anton. We're having a slight problem with someone not being on the list." I heard a woman's voice, loudly demanding to be let in. There was a light lunch taking place just before the wedding for the guests to enjoy. The hotel had provided extra security for today. Now that Sadie was streaming live, she had some, shall we say, overexuberant fans who might show up, given that they had her exact location. Everybody wanted to be cautious.

"What's the name?" I could check with Sadie to see if somebody had been inadvertently left off.

"She says it's Lilith."

That name sounded vaguely familiar, but I couldn't place it. "Let me call you back."

"Was that Camden?" Krista asked me and the mention of his name made me put two and evil ex-girlfriend together.

Oh no.

"I'll be right back. Hold down the fort for me."

At this rate I was never going to be able to finish getting ready for this wedding. I texted Anton back and told him to keep her there, that I was on my way to help.

I wanted to text Camden but couldn't because his phone might eat my texts, for all I knew. I wondered if he used a horse and buggy instead of a car, too. So I called him and he answered immediately. "Hey, you. There's good news. That ring finder lived nearby and with her metal detector found the ring in under five minutes."

Okay, that was great news, but something bad was happening. "Lilith is here. She's trying to crash the wedding."

His voice went totally serious. "Where?"

"At the luncheon. Can you meet me there?" I told myself that I didn't know what she looked like and if she wasn't still throwing a fit when I got there, I'd never be able to identify her and tell security to keep her far away from the wedding. I totally dismissed the fact that I'd just told Anton to hang around. Much as I wanted to rationalize it to myself, I just wanted Camden to be with me.

"On my way," he promised and hung up.

I'd been the one telling everyone that things always went wrong at weddings. Just usually not this often or this big. I wondered which plague of Egypt was next. Locusts? The ocean turning to blood? Frogs?

One problem at a time, I told myself. I had this.

And I had Camden as my backup.

CHAPTER TWENTY-SEVEN

I arrived outside the luncheon and saw Anton, but no woman making a scene. I was about to approach him when I felt a pair of strong arms go around my waist. Camden pulled my back against his front, resting his mouth against the crook of my neck.

"Do you know that I haven't been able to think about anything else besides you today? I was out there digging through sand and spent my time imagining being with you. Talking to you. Hearing about your day. Touching you, holding you, kissing you. I don't remember ever feeling this way before."

His words made me catch my breath. My heart flittered with excitement and happiness, but guilt swirled in my gut, too. There were secrets we had to share first and, more importantly, wedding crashers we had to stop. "Which one is Lilith?"

If he was put off by me not responding to his words, he didn't show it. He quickly kissed my neck, released me, and scanned the area. "Over there. Talking on her phone. Speak of the devil, and she appears."

"Do you think she's calling Dan?" I asked as we walked in her direction. I took out my phone, texting Samuel, the concierge, and asking him to meet us with some security.

"He blocked her a long time ago, so I doubt it."

Lilith was a tiny woman, and I had honestly expected her to look like Sadie, but she was dark-haired and dark-eyed and sporting a serious scowl. She hung up her phone when she saw us approaching.

"Camden! Are you surprised to see me?" There was so much venom in her supposedly nice words that if he wasn't feeling surprise, I certainly was.

"I didn't say *Bloody Mary* three times, so yes."

She narrowed her eyes at him. "I want to speak to Dan and I'm not leaving until the two of us talk."

"That's not going to happen," I said and she transferred her reptilian stare to me.

"And who is this? Your flavor of the month?"

I knew her words were designed to hurt and intimidate, and I had to admit that it worked. Because I was immediately wondering how many women Camden had dated. He said he never got serious. The sweet stuff he'd just said to me—was that the kind of thing he said to everyone he went out with?

"I'm the maid of honor," I said, determined not to let her get under my skin. "And you're not welcome here."

"Sadie's friend," she muttered, and then immediately dismissed me, turning her whole body toward Camden. "Go get Dan."

It was a good thing that everybody had been concerned with Sadie's overexuberant fans trying to sneak into her wedding and that there was security in place, because only Irene had correctly anticipated that Lilith might try to do something like this.

"No," Camden replied. "You need to leave."

Lilith crossed her arms. "Things have changed and Dan needs to know that. I do want to have a family with him. Once he finds out, he's going to dump that . . . thirsty, ridiculous excuse for a woman and come running back to me."

I was about to protest on Sadie's behalf, but Camden was too busy laughing. "Do you really think that? He's in love with Sadie. He's totally devoted to her."

This was not what she wanted to hear. "He'll leave her when he finds out I'm pregnant." She put her hands against her stomach.

A jittery surge of adrenaline slammed into me and I actually panicked. Pregnant? Sadie was going to die.

Thankfully, Camden was there to save the day. "Dan hasn't seen you in two years. So unless you're a whale or an elephant, there's no way you're pregnant with his baby."

Now that my fear was subsiding, it was easy to see that this had been her final card to play, her last-ditch attempt at forcing an audience with Dan. I was so glad that Camden was there with me.

"You don't know what you're talking about," she hissed. "I'm not leaving. I'm a guest at this hotel and I have every right to be here. Dan and I are meant to be."

"The only thing you and Dan are meant to be is over," Camden retorted.

The concierge finally arrived, and he'd brought one of the security guards. "Is there a problem here?"

I pointed over at Lilith. "This is the groom's ex-girlfriend and she's trying to crash the wedding. We'd like her to leave."

"You can't make me," she insisted. "I'm a guest."

I turned to Samuel. "Your hotel is depending on positive publicity from this event. I think the last thing you want is some rogue guest ruining the festivities."

He nodded. "You're right." He turned to Lilith and addressed her. "Kai here will escort you back to your room while you pack up your belongings. We will help you find another hotel to stay at."

Lilith crossed her arms again, making it clear the security guard was probably going to have to pick her up to get her to move. "I don't think so."

"Given that she's trespassing, you could call the proper authorities," I offered.

That seemed to sink in and she glared at me. "Fine." She spat out the word. "But you can't hide him from me for forever."

I didn't need to hide Dan for forever. Just for the next few hours. Then Lilith would be free to try casting a spell or sacrificing a goat or whatever it was that she did for fun.

She gave us one final glare and marched away with Kai following close behind. I let out a sigh of relief and thanked Samuel for his assistance.

I hugged Camden. "I'm so glad you were here. I mean, I would have handled it on my own, but having you here with me made it so much easier."

"You can do anything," he agreed. "But dealing with Lilith happens to be one of my specialties. We'll have to keep an eye out for her. I'm still surprised she showed up."

"Irene won't be. But we won't tell anyone until after everything's over, right?"

"Definitely. Nobody needs to know yet."

Much as I enjoyed having him hold me, we had a wedding to get to. "We need to go finish getting ready."

He kissed the tip of my nose. "Yep. Time to go get our best friends married to each other."

That caused a twinge in my gut, and I tried to brush it off. Sadie was going to tell him and then we'd deal with it from there. "So we should go."

Problem was, neither one of us was moving.

"I do have one wedding-related concern. If you could step with me into this hallway over here we could discuss it."

"Of course." I nodded, playing along.

We entered the empty hallway and he spun me so that he had me pinned up against the wall. "The problem is that I want to kiss the maid of honor and I'm going to have to keep my lips to myself for several hours."

"That is a serious problem," I agreed, reveling in the delicious tingles making their way through my body. "You should probably get your fill now."

"Not possible," he breathed before pressing his lips to mine. That fire he caused, the one that threatened to overwhelm me every time we touched, roared to life. He kissed me with hot, superlative strokes, and I loved the way he subtly responded to everything I did. Every time I met his feverish kiss, the way I ran my hands through his hair, pressed my body against his, he let out sounds that were an intoxicating and inexplicable mixture of frustration and satisfaction.

Was I ever going to get used to the way this felt? Like being engulfed in a waterfall of pleasure, not being able to breathe, but completely not caring?

He broke off the kiss and stepped back and I leaned against the wall, needing the support.

He took in a few deep, shaky breaths before he grinned and then had the audacity to say, "I hear you're always supposed to leave them wanting more."

Then he *left*.

I couldn't believe it.

Camden needed to stop messing with me. I wasn't strong enough to take it.

I arrived back at Sadie's villa to find total chaos. I located Krista and quickly filled her in on what had just happened. The wedding crasher, not the kiss. I had taken a picture of Lilith while she was throwing her fit and forwarded it to Krista so that she could be on the lookout, too.

She pulled up the photo on her phone. "I don't want to say this wedding might be cursed, but . . . know that I'm thinking it."

"Everything will be fine," I reiterated for both of us. Even though I was kind of starting to think the same thing. Relatively speaking, these had all been minor fires that had been quickly put out. Nothing we couldn't handle.

I just had to hope things stayed that way.

The makeup artist waved me down, insisting I sit in her chair. I looked around at the rest of the bridal party and the moms and realized I was the only one who wasn't made up yet.

My phone rang and I tried to brush off the pang of dread that lanced me at who it could possibly be. We'd had our drama for the day, things were going to be fine now. I saw that it was my mom calling me. I didn't know whether to be relieved or annoyed.

"Hi, Mom. I'm a little busy."

"Close your eyes," the makeup artist told me and I did as she asked.

"It's the wedding day, right?" my mother asked. "I want you to take some pictures of the bride and send them to me."

"Why?"

"So I can live vicariously and pretend like you're the one getting married."

It was too bad my eyes were closed because they could have used a good roll to the back of my head. "Mother, I'm not sending you a picture of Sadie. I have to go. Goodbye." That woman. It was a good thing I loved her.

"Okay, go ahead and open," the artist said and in the mirror I noticed Sadie standing near my shoulder.

"Was that your mom?" she asked.

"Yes. And she wants me to send a picture of you in your wedding gown so that she can pretend it's me."

Sadie looked sadly at our reflections. "At least your mom wants you to get married."

Oh crap. Had Brandy been making more rude remarks while I was gone? No, Krista would have put a stop to it. "Your mother wants you to get married, too."

"I don't think she does. And I'm not really sure why."

Ignoring the makeup artist's request that I close my lips, I turned toward Sadie. "Well, I want you to get married. And Dan *definitely* wants you to get married."

That made her laugh and it lightened my soul a little bit, too. I wished I could do more. I wished I could give her a different mom, one who would be happy and excited for her.

And as long as we were returning our mothers for new ones, maybe I could put in a request for a mom who wasn't obsessed with the state of my uterus.

"Thanks for being here," Sadie said. "I know this all started out a little . . . unusual, but I don't know how I would have done this without you."

Regardless of how it had all begun, the fees paid, the contracts signed, the lies we'd told, I was genuinely glad to be here with her, and felt lucky to have the chance to stand up with her when she married the love of her life. "Same," I told her.

She'd leaned over to hug me when there was a loud sound, like a cannon exploding. It made the villa shake.

"What the—" I said, standing up.

There was a flash of blinding light outside the windows.

Everyone in the room stopped what they were doing and collectively we held our breath.

The next sound was that of the constant, incessant drumming on the roof. The rain was pouring down, streaking the glass and making it impossible to see outside.

This was every wedding planner / bride's worst nightmare when it came to an outdoor wedding—unexpected rain.

"Oh no," Sadie said.

"We're on an island," I reminded her. "This happens, these little flash tropical storms. I'm sure it'll be gone in a minute or two. It will let up." I tried not to think about her flowers getting pelted by this heavy rain, or how it would make the sand wet, or the way it would drench the gauzy fabric being used on the chairs and the arch that they were planning on getting married under.

We waited. And waited.

The rain didn't stop.

CHAPTER TWENTY-EIGHT

Sadie went into her room and sat on the foot of her bed. I followed and plopped down next to her.

"Of course it's raining," she said, her voice catching, and I could see how she was struggling not to cry. "My shoe is gone, Mary-Ellen almost died, I looked like I was going to audition for the Blue Man Group, and now there's torrential rain."

Some irrational part of my brain wondered if Lilith had somehow caused this. Like she'd summoned the storm, or something. "I know it's probably hard to see right now, but according to legend, this is a good thing."

She gave me an incredulous look. "How in the world is this a good thing?"

"In lots of cultures rain is lucky on a wedding day. It symbolizes washing the slate clean and how strong your union will be. You've heard of the phrase 'tying the knot'? There's some debate over where it comes from, but one of them is from the Celtic tradition of handfasting. The husband and wife would literally have knots of cloth tied between their hands and if it rained . . . do you know how impossible it is to undo a soaking-wet knot? It means your marriage will be solid and no one can unravel it."

"It's not. And given all this experience and knowledge that I possess, I can tell you that I understand this is not what you were hoping for, but it's going to be okay. The only thing that matters today is that you and Dan get married. The rest of it is all fluff." Like cotton candy. That would melt in seconds in this weather.

I put an arm around her shoulders and squeezed and said, "Sometimes when everything gets messed up, all we can do is embrace the storm and ride it out. Rainbows come after the rain." I was wandering into cheesy platitudes, but I would have said anything if it would cheer her up.

She gave me a weak smile, and I hoped that meant it was working.

The main door of Sadie's villa slammed shut, and I heard Troy calling for Anton. "I'll be right back," I told her. I grabbed the box of tissues from her nightstand and handed them to her, just in case.

Troy was soaking wet and looked a little like a drowned cat. I almost asked him how things were going, but decided not to given his current expression. I tried for helpful instead. "Is there anything I can do? Do you have a backup plan?"

His glare was like two giant laser beams, set for destruction. "Obviously I planned for the completely unexpected rainstorm that didn't show up on any weather report."

I couldn't tell if he was being sarcastic. I hoped he was serious.

He put my fears to rest by adding, "There's already a large tent up on the west lawn, next to the ballroom so that the reception would have an indoor/outdoor feel. I'm going to move the ceremony there. I just need some time and manpower to set it up."

"Tell me what you want me to do." I'd happily get out there and set up chairs if that's what it took.

"Right now I need you to keep Sadie calm while I figure out what to do with a van full of peacocks."

For a second I thought I'd misheard. "A van full of peacocks? Why do you have a van full of peacocks?"

"For ambience, Rachel!" he yelled and I knew I shouldn't have asked. I got the kind of stress he was under.

Troy sighed and said, "I'm sorry. I don't mean to take this out on you. I just need to get Anton so we can come up with a new battle plan. Keep your phone within reach so that I can call you if I need to."

"I will absolutely do that."

He rushed off and I squared my shoulders back, ready to do what I did best. Keep the women in this villa calm. I didn't know how long it would take Troy to move everything over, but I'd have this bridal party ready when he was.

$\sim$

There were a couple of hiccups as we got ready for the ceremony—Mary-Ellen mistook spray deodorant for hair spray and there were little white flecks on her gray bridesmaid dress and Krista lost one of her pearl earrings—but in the grand scheme of things they were minor issues.

The wedding was delayed by only forty-five minutes. Troy's assistants had umbrellas for us, including a massive one to cover Sadie's dress, and we went to the spot he'd designated for us to wait in.

We stood there in anticipation as the music started and everyone followed Troy's detailed instructions. The flower girl and the ring bearer made it down the aisle without any issues. Mary-Ellen walked down the aisle with Vance, followed by Krista and Rick. Then it was my turn. Camden waited for me and put out his arm so that I could put my hand through it.

Troy was an absolute magician. Somehow he had managed to move everything over and nothing seemed like it was out of place or missing. Flowers decorated the archway that the officiator stood under, and there were pale-pink and white flowers attached to the chairs closest to the aisle. A white runner had been staked to the ground for us to walk down. The rain outside gave everything surrounding the tent a misty, hazy quality so that it all seemed even more romantic.

The overabundance of romance made it hard to calm down my overactive imagination as Camden and I walked down the aisle together. I wanted this fantasy. This belief that love could conquer everything and that there was a happy ending waiting for me.

We separated once we reached the front and then everyone stood when Sadie entered the tent. Despite everything she'd gone through that morning, she looked absolutely radiant. I glanced at Dan, and saw that he had gotten choked up, and was trying to fight off tears at seeing his luminous bride.

To my surprise, she walked down the aisle with her stepfather and mother, but then I saw the wisdom in her making certain that they were on opposite sides of her and not able to interact. It seemed as if someone had forgotten to measure the aisle properly as her dress was hitting every row of chairs as she walked. A couple of the floral decorations tumbled down, but it somehow made the whole thing even more endearing.

When she got to the front her parents kissed her cheeks before taking their seats, separated by the aisle, and she handed me her bouquet before she took both of Dan's hands.

"They're totally going to make it," Krista whispered to me, and I nodded. There was no doubt.

Now I was the one getting emotional as they said their vows to one another. Dan still seemed either nervous or overcome with emotion as he fumbled a couple of the words, like promising to love Sadie "in thickness and in health."

Krista leaned in to say, "We're witnesses. She never has to worry about gaining weight."

I almost giggled, and my gaze slid over to Camden. I found that he was watching me with a knowing smile. His eyes didn't dart away, like they would have if he'd been embarrassed that I'd caught him. It was more like he didn't care if I knew that he was watching me, admiring me.

He was so handsome and amazing and fun that it made my breath stutter as I marveled at the fact that he liked me.

I just had to wait for Sadie to talk to him to see how all of this was going to shake out. I hoped he would give me a chance when he found out the truth.

The officiator announced that they were husband and wife and all the guests broke into applause as Dan kissed Sadie sweetly.

They made their way back down the aisle, waving to everybody as they went. Camden was there to escort me and we followed them, my heart thrilled at the idea that another happy couple had gotten married. I really did love weddings and everything they represented.

Troy was waiting for us, shooing us off to go with the photographer and videographer to do photos. Someone had found a pair of rain boots for Sadie, and there were all kinds of adorable shots of her with them on and everyone holding their black umbrellas.

That shifted into the family photos and I kept an eye on Brandy and Maybelle, hoping that everybody had the good sense to behave. So far, so good.

After an hour or so the photos were finished, and I wondered if Sadie was disappointed. They'd put double that amount of time on the schedule to do pictures, but with the wedding being pushed back and the weather, I supposed we had to make do with what we had.

Troy directed all of us into the ballroom so that Sadie and Dan would be able to make their grand entrance as Mr. and Mrs. Zielinski.

The reception had been going for a little while. Sadie had specifically requested that the food be served buffet style because she didn't want there to be a time period where people were confined to their tables, thanks to her parents. I actually preferred being able to choose what I wanted to eat instead of being forced into something.

I started toward the food, but Camden stepped in front of me. "I seem to recall asking you to save a dance for me several nights ago."

Trying to be nonchalant, I shrugged one shoulder. "That rain check has expired."

He gestured toward the open ballroom doors. "It's raining, so I think it's still good."

"Well, you do make a compelling argument."

I let him lead me out to the dance floor, where there were only a few other couples dancing. The song came to an end and a slow one started up. Camden put his hands on my waist and I slipped my arms around his neck.

Initially there was a bit of distance between us, but he quickly took care of that.

"Have I told you how beautiful you look tonight?" His mouth was next to the top of my ear, and his warm breath sent shivers across my skin.

"You clean up pretty well, too," I said.

I closed my eyes and leaned my head against his shoulder. I loved being close to him like this. His arms tightened around me, as if he were feeling the same way and wanted to draw me in even more.

He brought back those tingles when he asked, "So . . . have you thought more about what I said? About seeing where things go when we get back to New York?"

"Have you talked to Sadie yet?"

"Sadie? Why would I talk to Sadie?"

I leaned back so that I could look in his eyes. "You have to talk to her first."

He seemed thoroughly confused, but that was all I could give him. I went back to resting my head on him, and he raised one hand up to the back of my head, as if he were cradling me, keeping me safe.

I reveled in every second of it.

"Do you have your speech prepared?" Camden asked.

"More or less." I could make a maid of honor speech in my sleep, given that I'd done it so many times. I had figured out a long time ago the formula to a good wedding speech: it would have something that made the crowd laugh, something that made them a little weepy, and something that would make them cheer for the happy couple.

"I've got mine in my pocket and I've practiced it, but I'm still nervous. I have no problem standing up in front of a room of investors trying to get them to give me money, but the thought of talking to this group of people is slightly terrifying."

"That's because you want to do right by Dan. Because you're a good friend. And a good man."

"Do you think so?" He asked the question in a way that made me think the answer was really important to him.

Despite not wanting to move, I lifted my head so that I could again meet his gaze. "I do. I think you're a good man. And I . . ."

I wanted to tell him. That I had feelings for him. That I most definitely wanted to see him again and date him and maybe adopt another cat with him and someday even more than that.

But Troy interrupted me before I could say too much. Apparently the camera crew wanted some specific footage of the bridal party toasting each other. He handed us flutes of champagne and we followed him to where everyone else was waiting.

"By the way," I told him as we walked, "you are a total wizard."

At my compliment Troy gave me an enigmatic smile and simply said, "I know."

The six of us stood in a circle and I was at a loss as to what we should be doing. I started to ask Hank, the director, but he made a cutting motion across his throat and I remembered that this was all being broadcast live.

Camden took the lead and said, "To the bride and groom!"

"To Dan and Sadie!" we said back, clinking our glasses and taking a drink. I mean, I didn't take a drink. The night wasn't over yet and I needed to keep my wits about me. But I did pretend.

I glanced around quickly and spotted Mandy and Brandy sitting together at their table eating. Brandy was actually smiling, so I figured that was a good thing. I felt myself relax. It seemed like everything was under control.

Dan and Sadie made their grand entrance a couple of minutes later, and we all applauded for them. The cheering got louder when Dan bent her back, kissing her soundly. They went out onto the dance floor to have their first dance as husband and wife.

Then it was time to cut the cake, where Dan very wisely did not smash cake in Sadie's face. I had never liked that tradition. Plus, that meant we were about to get cake soon, and that was good.

Camden and I were assigned to sit together and he got up to get food. He asked if I wanted anything, but I waved him off. I wanted to sit here for a second and take it all in. Sadie and Dan moved among the tables, talking to everyone. Troy was running around like a chipmunk on Ritalin. There were a lot more people dancing now and it was entertaining to watch how much fun they were having.

Krista came over to me and said, "We should go upstairs and get our luggage."

I'd totally forgotten that we needed to grab our stuff and leave it with the bell services so that we could make a quick exit when our taxi arrived. Camden was helping himself to a bunch of roast beef when I leaned in to tell him that I had to take care of something.

He winked at me. "Don't make me wait too long. I can't promise I'll be here when you get back."

That was the thing—I knew he would be. That he was reliable and that he was the kind of guy I could depend on.

It didn't take long to pack up my things because at this point I was basically a pro. I put an outfit into my carry-on bag so that I could change before I got on the plane.

I went back downstairs and left all of my stuff at the bellhop station, my keycard at the front desk to officially check out, and returned to the reception. The DJ had started playing "YMCA" and almost everybody was out on the dance floor, doing the arm movements along with the chorus. I felt a little like I should do a victory lap that it had all turned out okay.

Someone tugged on my arm, and to my surprise it was Sadie. "Would you come with me?" she asked.

"Of course."

She led me out of the reception, into the hallway just beyond. "I wanted to let you know that Dan and I are leaving."

"What? Now? But . . ." I looked toward the doors. "The toasts, throwing the bouquet, you're going to miss all of that."

"You were right today. All of this is just fluff. I didn't care about the wedding, I just wanted the marriage. Dan and I are headed back to New York because I don't want to wait another minute to start our lives together."

"But . . ."

"We cut the cake, we did our dance, we talked to everyone. The camera crews will keep streaming until they realize that we're gone, but they got what they needed from us."

"Okay," I said, realizing this was happening and was what she wanted. My job was to keep her happy, and this obviously made her very happy. "I'm guessing you didn't get a chance to say anything to Camden."

"No, I've been a little busy," she teased. "You can tell him. I officially waive my rights or give you permission to tell Camden the truth."

An uneasy pang settled in my gut. I had definitely been hoping for the cowardly way out. Now I was going to have to tell him. "I don't think what you just said would hold up in a court of law."

She shook her head. "It doesn't have to. You are officially off duty. The rest of the night is all yours. Dan's waiting for me out front. I have to get going." Then she took her bouquet, placing it in my hands. "If I had tossed the bouquet, there's only one person that I would have wanted to catch it. Now, go and get your man."

CHAPTER TWENTY-NINE

I went back into the ballroom, still carrying Sadie's flowers. Camden found me. "Isn't that the bridal bouquet?" he asked.

"Yep."

"What are you doing with it?" Another guy might have been panicked that I was carrying it, like I was trying to make some kind of declaration about my future plans, but he was just genuinely curious.

"Dan and Sadie left." I was still a bit in shock that they'd gone early. It made sense, but most brides I'd met wanted to soak up every single moment of their special day.

"Do you know what that means?" Camden asked. He took the bouquet and put it on the nearest table. Then he took me by both hands and began pulling me toward a darkened corner of the room.

"What?"

"It means we can spend the rest of the night doing whatever we want." The growly intent in his voice made my stomach flutter.

"Not the rest of the night," I told him. "I've got a plane to catch soon. But we can hang out until then." I knew leaving was necessary so that I could go help Desiree, but I was kind of kicking myself that I was going to miss out on spending more time with him.

"Good enough."

"What did you have in mind?" I asked as he got us away from prying eyes, behind a column of flowers on the edge of the ballroom.

He wrapped his arms around me. "You have amazingly soft and delicious lips and I'd like to explore them very carefully and very thoroughly."

My heart jumped up into my throat, pulsing hard. "I'm amenable to your plan," I managed to say.

I should tell him. Now. This was the perfect opportunity. We'd still have time to discuss everything before I got on a plane back to the mainland. I again found myself wishing that we hadn't changed our flights so that I'd have another night here in paradise with him. He was tracing the outline of my face with his fingers and I opened my mouth several times, intending to say the words I needed to say. The ones Sadie had given me permission to share.

"There's something you should know. About me," I told him.

Then his fingertips were running across my lips and I forgot how thinking worked.

"Are you secretly married?" he asked.

"What? No!"

"Then I can't think of anything else that we need to talk about right this second. I have other things in mind." His mouth followed the same path his fingers did, and burning shivers swept through me.

"Did you want to say something?" he teased, and I just shook my head. *Nope, not me. No, sir.*

Then his lips were on mine and I nearly groaned in relief at the contact I'd been dying for.

I didn't know how long we'd stood in that corner as Camden did exactly what he promised, a long and extensive exploration of my mouth while we were pressed desperately against each other, before I heard yelling.

Breaking off, my lips swollen and my head spinning, I tried to focus on what was happening.

"Dan! I'm here! Dan!"

"Lilith," Camden muttered in disbelief.

She was running through the ballroom in a wedding dress, being tailed by two security guards, yelling as she ran. "I want to have children with you! We can work things out! Dan! Where are you?"

I stood there in total disbelief, watching as the livestream cameras captured every moment. Oh, this was bad.

One of the guards caught up with her, picking her up by the waist and carrying her out of the room. I wondered what had gotten into her. While she'd seemed angry and determined before, nothing about her had said that she was unhinged.

"Well," I said, "I guess we were just part of something called making a scene. Sadie's not going to be happy."

"Neither is Dan. They're definitely going to have a conversation about this. I'm kind of glad they're gone." He looked around and said, "I'm going to go see what's happening. Make sure that she isn't let back in here."

"Okay." I nodded. He kissed me quickly and then went out the same doors as the guards.

I noticed Brandy off to my right. She tried to stand and swayed heavily to the left.

Uh-oh.

I made my way to her side and she threw one arm up when she saw me coming, like she was trying to fend me off. "Have you been drinking?" I asked.

"That's none of your beeswax!" she said. I wished Camden were still here. I needed to get her out of the room before anybody saw her wasted.

"They're not supposed to serve you."

"People leave these cute little glasses of champagne all over their tables," she informed me gleefully. Ew. She had been drinking people's leftover alcohol? That struck me as immeasurably sad.

"Come on, let's get you some coffee," I offered.

"Get your hands off me!" she demanded.

There was a loud slam and I heard Lilith yelling again. Brandy took advantage of the distraction to slip away from me.

She was headed straight for Geoff and Maybelle, who were standing near the dessert table.

There was nothing I could do to stop her. There had already been one major scene caught on film; I wasn't keen to add another. I tried to grab for her arm, to suggest that she come with me, but she just shrugged me off.

With every step we took the sense of impending doom grew stronger and stronger until I knew that everything was about to explode around me.

As if he'd sensed that I needed him, Camden joined me. "I think the Lilith situation is handled. What's going on here?"

"Sadie's mom is drunk. The good news is that I think things are finally about to get out of hand and will blow up in our faces soon, which means that it will all finally be over."

Sure enough, Brandy started screaming at Maybelle, who was quick to defend herself verbally. I didn't care for women calling other women names, so let's just say that Brandy called Maybelle something that rhymes with *foam-pecking boar*, and Maybelle screeched back that Brandy was a *bold trunk hitch* and things just went downhill from there.

Geoff was already trying to calm them both down and I was about ready to use all the curse words on everybody if they didn't stop immediately.

Instead, they escalated despite the three of us trying to intervene. Brandy actually took a swing at Maybelle and missed, but the momentum pushed her forward and she landed face-first in the cake. I watched in horror as the entire thing collapsed sideways, almost in slow motion, landing on Dan's elderly grandmother.

Who hadn't moved from her spot next to the table the entire evening. Until now. As all three tiers of the cake tumbled on top of her, Dan's grandma exploded out of her seat like someone had set her on fire, screaming at the top of her lungs like a banshee and flinging cake shrapnel everywhere she went.

Maybelle then jumped on top of Brandy, spreading more cake as she reached for her hair, yanking on it.

Initially I wasn't sure what to do first, but the two women had to be separated. I was aided by Geoff grabbing Maybelle by the waist and Camden picking up Brandy like she was a child.

"Where do you want her?" he asked, ignoring her struggles.

I glanced over my shoulder. All of the camera crews had their cameras pointed at us, capturing every moment live. Distress seeped into my skin as I registered the enormity of this. It was ruined. Everything.

Mandy ran up to us. "I just went upstairs to use the restroom. What happened?"

Her sister was shrieking at us as Geoff escorted Maybelle from the reception. Considering how drunk Brandy was, I wondered how long Mandy had left her alone for. But that was not the thing to concern myself with at the moment. I filled Mandy in quickly, and we decided that the best thing to do was to get Brandy up to her room. I had no idea how to do damage control here because there was no video that could be edited later. Everything was just out in the real world now and there was nothing I could do to stop it.

"I'm sorry," Mandy said with tears in her eyes. "The bartender said she wouldn't serve Brandy and I guess I just assumed it was safe. I never even considered this possibility."

Feeling ashamed that I'd judged her even for a moment, I said, "Me neither. Let's get her out of here."

Brandy went completely limp, like a rag doll, and I was terrified that she'd gotten alcohol poisoning or had lapsed into a coma and we were going to top off this house of horrors by calling for an ambulance. I ran over to her, wanting to help.

It had been a ruse designed to get Camden to let go of her, which he hadn't done. She kicked out her feet and one of them connected with my nose. There was a flash of darkness and then throbbing pain. I felt wetness on my face and looked down to see that I was bleeding all over my dress.

Huh. So much for being able to wear it again.

Camden let Brandy go, and she made a break for the doors leading outside with Mandy in hot pursuit.

"Are you okay?" he asked. He grabbed one of the napkins off a nearby table and handed it to me.

I nodded, pressing the napkin to my nose. "It's okay. I get nosebleeds all the time. You know, whenever the air is dry or when my face gets kicked." I pressed the napkin harder. "What part of the Old Testament do you think we're on now?"

"It's not that bad," he said, trying to placate me but it felt like there was no hope. "I'm going to go help with Brandy, but I'll be right back."

He kissed me on the forehead and I tried to remember whether I was supposed to lean my head back or forward. I settled for holding still and hoping that nothing was broken. I noted that Krista was busy helping Dan's grandma get cleaned up, Hank was yelling at the cameramen, and Troy was barking commands to his assistants, telling the DJ to play another song.

Sadie was going to be utterly humiliated. I had no idea what this was going to do to her online reputation. Would she lose sponsors? Followers? I tried calling her, but she didn't pick up. I told myself that it made sense that she'd turn off her phone, given that she and Dan were running away from the reception. They wouldn't want people to be able to get in touch with them.

That had to be it, right? It wasn't that Sadie had seen the live feed and was furious with me? I tried to ignore the rising sense of dread that this was only the beginning and things were about to get worse.

Although how they could possibly get worse than this, I wasn't sure.

I also had no idea how to fix any of this. The damage was done and online.

Camden joined me a few minutes later, sitting in a chair next to mine. "We got her up to her room. She was conscious and still had on most of her clothes, so I'm counting that as a win."

"Thank you."

"I'm here to help you in any way that I can. We make a pretty good team, don't we?"

I considered his words. It was so nice to have someone who was here for me. Of course he cared about Dan's wedding because they were close, but he made me feel like everything he'd done today had been because of me. It had been so long since anyone had made me feel that special.

There were smeared frosting and tiny chunks of cake stuck to his suit. "I hope that wasn't a rental," I told him, pointing at the food decorating his clothes. "I don't think you're going to get the deposit back."

"At least it isn't blood," he teased as I pulled the napkin away. It seemed like the bleeding had stopped. His smile faded when he saw my expression. "What is it?"

"I should have been out in front of this. It never should have happened."

He reached for my free hand and said, "You couldn't have predicted that any of this would happen."

"Sadie told me it might, that she was worried about it, and I should have prevented it."

Camden squeezed my hand gently and it was so reassuring, even though I didn't deserve it. "Rachel, this isn't your fault."

My throat felt heavy, thick. I blinked back tears. "It might not be my fault, but I definitely feel responsible. If I hadn't been busy with . . ." I let my voice trail off as I looked down at my feet.

"If you hadn't been busy with me." I heard the pain in his voice at my implication that he was responsible for this failure, too.

I met his gaze, feeling wounded by the upset I saw there. "Camden, no, that's not what I—"

"Rachel?" I heard a male voice ask.

I turned to see where it was coming from and my mouth opened in shock. *No.*

This was not happening.

No, no, no, no.

CHAPTER THIRTY

The man smiled at me, pointing at himself with both of his hands. "It's me. Vinnie Hemmings."

I had been a bridesmaid for Vinnie's wife, Theresa. I'd never even considered this possibility. We deliberately chose brides and weddings where there didn't seem to be any connections to our previous work. I stood up, still gaping in shock.

"Camden! How are you, man?" He shook hands with Camden. "Have a little trouble with the cake?"

"Something like that," Camden said as he got to his feet.

"How do you two know each other?" I asked—both because I was desperately curious and because I was trying to turn the conversation away from myself. Hoping I could somehow salvage this.

"Dan and I were in the same frat, and we all went to Ohio State," Vinnie said. "Theresa and I flew in this morning. I couldn't get the time off of work, but I definitely wanted to be here for Dan's big day! Our flight was delayed so we missed the wedding, but we got here for the reception. And this was certainly something, wasn't it? Nothing like my wedding! Right, Rachel?"

Camden gave me a questioning look. He was too smart to be put off for long. I ran through a hundred different scenarios in my head, but none of them were going to change what was about to happen. I just had to sit here, being flooded with dread and regret, and I couldn't stop it.

"Theresa! Look who's here!" Vinnie called out.

Theresa came over and as soon as she saw me, her face went slack. She was the bride who had put me in the yellow-feather-and-hot-pink getup. We'd never had any kind of crossover like this before. I had no plan B here.

This was so bad. Theresa had been awful from beginning to end. Apparently Vinnie had given her a budget that she'd gone wildly over. She'd asked me to refund my fees and I had a no-refund policy. Especially since we'd done every wild thing she'd asked us to. She just didn't want her new husband to find out that she'd spent so much money. I hadn't worried too much about it at the time, but now I was deeply regretting everything as I thought of a million different ways this could go.

Still oblivious, Vinnie said to me, "What are the odds of running into you? You must be friends with the bride."

"Rachel is the maid of honor," Camden said.

"That's a coincidence!" Vinnie again turned to Theresa, trying to get her to come over. "She was a bridesmaid at our wedding."

"Really?" Camden said, but there was something off in his voice. "Small world. How did you two meet?"

Theresa was still silent, probably every bit as freaked out as I was feeling. Vinnie didn't seem to notice, though. "They've been in a yoga class together for years."

Camden turned toward me, his expression serious. Accusing. "Vinnie lives in Vermont."

"Yeah." Vinnie finally seemed to be sensing that something might be off. "So does Rachel."

"Funny thing," Camden said, his eyes boring into me. "Vinnie and Theresa got married last year. I remember because Dan and I argued about going. We were busy and neither one of us could afford to miss work, so we compromised by sending a nice gift." Then he turned back toward Vinnie. "And Rachel told me she's been living in New York for the last four years. So unless that instructor in Vermont is worth interstate travel, I don't know how that's possible. Not to mention Rachel's deep-seated loathing for yoga."

Vinnie started asking questions, understandably confused. Theresa stepped in and tugged at his arm, dragging him off while he sputtered the whole way. He demanded to know what was going on. I saw the reluctant expression on her face, how she cast her eyes down, and then I heard my name. And the name of my company.

I wanted to glance up at Camden, to see how much he'd just overheard and if he'd worked things out yet. I couldn't meet his eyes. My whole life was falling down around me. Like every lie I'd told him had been part of an elaborate house of cards that was fluttering down so quickly there was no way that I could catch them and try to rebuild.

It was just gone.

My heart stopped and then restarted, but low and heavy so that I felt like I couldn't breathe. "I can explain. I couldn't before, but Sadie gave me permission and I can tell you what's going on."

"You lied to me." Camden's voice was so low that I nearly missed what he was saying. "You're not Sadie's friend. I took you at your word because of that friendship."

"If that's the only reason you trusted me and believed me when I said I wasn't some corporate spy, which I'm not, then I don't know . . ." What argument could I make? Yes, I wasn't a spy, but I had deceived him.

"None of this is about the spy thing. It's about the fact that you lied to me every day since we've met. What else have you lied about? Is anything you told me real?"

"Of course it was. Almost everything I told you was the truth. Or some version of the truth," I corrected myself. Like I wasn't an event coordinator. Not technically, but it was close.

"Oh, we're dealing with versions of the truth now?" He ran both of his hands through his hair and that sinking feeling in the pit of my stomach just got worse and worse. "I feel so stupid."

"This wasn't about you. I mean, what I said and what I did had nothing to do with you. It's between me and Sadie and was none of your business." It was like every possible wrong word that could fall out of my mouth did. I wished I could take it all back as soon as I'd said it.

His expression went flat. "Right. It is none of my business. You've made it abundantly clear from the beginning that you don't want me to be part of your life. You kept me at arm's length, even when I could tell you liked me, too. And I wanted to be with you so badly that I was willing to overlook it. I just ignored my instincts that something was going on."

Desperation began to build inside me. "Camden, wait. You haven't let me explain yet. There's a reason why I did what I did." I reached for his forearm, but he pulled it out of my reach.

"I don't need an explanation right now," Camden said, averting his gaze from me. His expression shattered me. He looked like he felt used, when that was so far from what had actually happened. Before I could tell him as much, he said, "What I need is to go for a walk."

Watching him walk away . . . it was like I recalled every bad thing that had ever happened to me. Every time my heart had been broken, my trust betrayed, the rug pulled out from under my feet, every time it seemed like things were never going to be okay again—this moment was a thousand times worse than all of those combined.

I'd known it. I'd known this would happen. That he would find out the truth and leave. He'd just proved me completely right. Krista had said I couldn't predict behavior, but I'd called this.

My chest physically hurt, as if someone had torn me open with their bare hands and pried out my heart. I had to cling to the back of my chair to stay upright. There was a stinging in my throat as anguish lanced through me, clawing at the pieces of me that were still functioning.

I realized that this incredible pain, one that threatened to drag me under and hold me there, wasn't because of regret or guilt or anything else.

I didn't just like Camden. I'd said I was starting to have feelings for him, but that wasn't it.

I'd fallen in love with him.

But I didn't cry. Even though my chest felt constricted and my eyes watered and my throat felt like someone was pressing against it, I held in those tears. Because it felt like I didn't deserve to cry. I had done this to myself.

I couldn't let myself drown in my pain. Time to focus on putting one foot in front of the other because I still had responsibilities. I got up and let Troy know that Dan and Sadie had left, so he was officially off duty. He looked relieved. I didn't have to say anything to Hank, given that all of the camera crews were already gone. Whether that was because they'd figured out that the newlyweds had left or because they'd inadvertently broadcast the ex-girlfriend / drunken mother / cake-toppling fiasco, I didn't know.

Then I noticed Vinnie had his phone out and that he repeatedly said my name, and the name of my company, Something Borrowed. He pointed his phone at me, his expression angry, and my heart was so devastated over what had just happened with Camden that it took me a minute to register what was going on.

He was telling the whole world about me. About my company. He turned his phone on Dan's cake-covered grandmother, and it wouldn't take much for somebody to connect everything that had just happened with me and my business.

This wasn't something my IT department could erase.

I was ruined. Anonymity was what I promised to all of my clients. I guessed Theresa had been right in her assumption that he would be furious about the money she'd spent and her lying to him, because Vinnie might have just single-handedly destroyed everything I'd created.

It was too much. All of this was too much for me to deal with. I had other issues to focus on. Like the wedding in New Jersey. My personal life was toast, but if I dwelled on that, I might never recover. I had to concentrate everything on my business.

Krista came over to me, looking alarmed at my expression. Even if I wasn't screaming and crying, obviously I looked like I wanted to. "What happened?" she asked.

I had to get out of there. The longer I stood there and let Vinnie show my face to the world, the worse this would be. "Long story. I think it's time we left for the airport."

She nodded, without asking for more information. Which was good, because I didn't think I had it in me to explain anything further without completely breaking down.

Krista and I collected our bags, and she asked one of the valets to grab us a taxi. We went into the bathroom to change into regular clothes and I debated what to do with my bridesmaid gown. I usually kept all of my bridesmaid dresses; I just wasn't sure I wanted to have the memories associated with this one.

I shoved it into my carry-on. I'd deal with it when I got home.

Camden's face flashed in my mind and I tried to shove it away. I couldn't think about him now. Especially when all of my instincts were screaming at me to find him, go after him so that he could understand why I'd done it and maybe we could work things out.

But hadn't he already given me his answer? He didn't want anything to do with me and I wasn't going to chase after him like some kind of pathetic puppy, begging for scraps of his attention.

What if I was wrong about that, though? Wasn't it worth finding out?

I headed out of the bathroom and joined Krista, who was waiting with the taxi. I hesitated.

Go after him, my mom's voice said. I couldn't. I had things to take care of. Plus, this was kind of her fault. She had such high expectations for me that I couldn't tolerate when relationships weren't perfect. I never left room for failure or to take risks or get my heart broken. And this was why. I'd taken that risk. I'd been willing to ask Sadie to break the NDA so that I could have a shot with Camden. And for what? To watch him walk away?

I couldn't chase after him because I couldn't bear him rejecting me a second time. I got into the taxi.

On the way to the airport I texted my attorney, knowing that he'd gone to bed hours earlier and that I might not hear from him when he woke up, given that it was still the weekend. I wasn't sure what would happen next. I also tried texting and calling Sadie several times to tell her the way things had blown up at the reception, but still no answer.

I felt so helpless, sitting in the back seat of this taxi. So very many things had gone wrong in such a short amount of time—Camden, the reception, and now possibly my business. I didn't know exactly what Vinnie had done. Or what he would do now. Would he tell Camden everything? Would any of this cause problems with Sadie? What if that video went viral? The one that had me standing helpless in the middle of all that chaos? Someone would see it. I'd been so dumb to assume that the NDAs and Taimani would keep me safe. I should have known this was a possibility.

For a second I couldn't catch my breath as I thought of all those women who depended on me, on the company that we'd built together. I'd let them down. Everything could be ruined. I leaned forward, bowing my head.

"It's okay," Krista said, rubbing my back. "Whatever it is, we can figure it out."

"Not this time," I told her.

I turned my phone off. If everything was going to be destroyed, I'd take a few hours of not knowing just how bad the fallout would be.

~

I wasn't able to sleep on the red-eye. I just kept running everything through my head over and over again. All of it was exceptionally bad, but probably the worst thing was realizing that whatever Camden had felt for me, it wasn't anywhere close to what I felt for him. If it had been, there was no way he would have been able to walk away from me.

It helped that Krista was on a different flight. She had tried to get me to open up at the airport, but I couldn't. I didn't want to be that woman sitting in the middle of the terminal sobbing her guts out. She did make me promise that I would talk to her later.

She probably should have defined *later*, because I had no intention of talking about this at all. I squashed it all down and threw it into an inner chest, intent on locking it up and never opening it again.

I arrived in New Jersey, grabbed my luggage, and went into the bathroom to change. I put up my hair, refusing to think about Camden carefully taking it down, pin by pin.

Once I finished my hair, I realized that I'd never turned my phone back on. When I did, it just kept dinging and buzzing like I had a thousand missed texts and phone calls. There was too much to try to sort out. I pulled up Desiree's last text to me with the address for the wedding venue, and headed out to grab a taxi.

We got on the road and I was glad that it was a morning wedding because if I'd had to wait until the evening with all my thoughts and doubts buzzing around me like a horde of angry bees, well, it wouldn't have been good.

When I arrived, Desiree was out on the front steps of the church waiting for me. She rushed over to hug me, her relief evident.

"How are you doing?" I asked, grabbing my luggage from the taxi.

"How are *you* doing?" she said. "You're the one who's internet famous. The Bloody Bridesmaid."

"What?" I asked. My heart slammed against my rib cage as she handed me her phone. It was a YouTube clip with Brandy flying into the cake and Dan's grandma running around, all of us trying to stop the fight, me getting kicked in the face. I scrolled through the links and somebody had even autotuned Brandy and Maybelle's fight.

I scanned some of the comments and there were haters who were using it as evidence that Sadie was a fake because she'd hired a bridesmaid and didn't have real friends, and some of her true-blue fans were upset that Sadie's life wasn't as perfect as they'd imagined it to be. Someone had nicknamed me "the Bloody Bridesmaid" and that was how they referred to me.

Then I saw my name. Rachel Vinson, the Bloody Bridesmaid. Owner of Something Borrowed. Over and over again.

The video already had over half a million views, and I watched as the numbers continued to climb every few seconds.

This was so, so bad.

It was like everything inside me just emptied out, leaving me cold and numb. I had to apologize to Sadie the first chance I got and see what I could do to try to make things right. I recognized that realistically there wasn't a whole lot, and despite my no-refund policy I could at least give back the fee she'd paid us as I'd failed so miserably in my duties.

But there was no time to deal with that right now, or how far it might have spread on social media. I gave Desiree back her phone. "We've got a wedding to fix. What's going on?"

She pointed back at the church. "Listen."

I could hear a woman screaming. "This is off-white when I very specifically said I wanted pure white bunting! Why is that so hard? You are literally ruining my wedding day!"

"It's been like this for the last couple of weeks," Desiree whispered to me. "Amber seemed so normal when we met her. But she's turned into this frothing, rabid nightmare and I don't even know what to do. No wonder none of her friends wanted to be a bridesmaid."

"Her husband sounds like a lucky guy," I murmured back, following her to the room where the bridal party was getting ready.

I was sorely lacking in my regular confidence but decided to do my best to fake it. My one hope was that muscle memory would take over and I'd find a way to soothe this bride.

We walked into the room where a very pretty redhead was still screaming about colors being wrong, but stopped short when she saw me. I waved to my employee Melissa, who was cowering in one of the corners and probably rethinking her decision in accepting employment with us.

"What are you doing here?" the bride asked.

Amber and I had never actually met; Desiree had set up this wedding. I was about to introduce myself when she held up one hand. "I don't need you to say anything. I know exactly who you are. The Bloody Bridesmaid. You promised that nobody would know that I had to hire professional bridesmaids."

I looked around at the wedding party, wanting to say that she was the one who had just revealed it. "Nobody did know."

She made a buzzer sound. "Wrong! The entire world knows. There are a thousand different memes about you and the wedding you just botched and how you overcharged that other couple. I can't believe you came here. Were you trying to humiliate me?"

"I'm sorry that—"

The bride stopped me. "I'm suing you for breach of contract. Take your bridesmaids and go. No one wants you here."

I nodded to my employees, Desiree and Melissa grabbed their purses, and we made a hasty exit. There was no point in trying to argue with the very upset bride. Maybe if all the stuff with Sadie and her reception going viral hadn't happened, I would have been able to find a way to talk Amber down. But I was doubting myself and my skills, and honestly, I didn't see the point.

Especially when I wasn't sure what was going to happen to my company and if I could fix things. My phone beeped again, with more texts. I glanced and saw that there were ten missed phone calls from my mother this morning alone. But I didn't call her back. I had no idea what I would even say. To her or to anyone else.

I didn't know how it was possible, but everything was so much worse than I'd initially imagined.

CHAPTER THIRTY-ONE

When I got home, I immediately started unpacking. The ritual of emptying out my bags, putting my stuff away, made me feel more like myself again.

Until I came across my bridesmaid dress. I sat down on the edge of my bed, half-heartedly wishing I'd tossed it in the trash when I'd had the chance. I ran my finger across the silky material, remembering why I hadn't been able to do it then and why I wouldn't do it now. I stuck it in my dry-cleaning bag, hoping they could get the bloodstains out.

I'd been operating at a no-feelings level, where I pushed everything aside and forged ahead with what I had to do, but that dress had made everything come rushing back and my sadness was like a weight crushing my chest, making it impossible for me to move or breathe.

Grabbing my purse, I reached for my happy box. And as I unfurled my little scrolls of paper, they weren't having their regular effect on me. I didn't feel better. Not even the one with the five gold stars on it. Instead, all I saw was Camden picking up the box off the ground, reading the words to me, and it was like I was back in front of that hotel, when he was taking care of me. I wanted him here so badly that my entire body ached from longing.

I made the mistake of getting on my phone, just to see the latest. There weren't any messages from my attorney, Gerald, but Desiree had forwarded me a link. It was a story from Amber's Instagram. I clicked on it.

"I hired Something Borrowed because my friends were all too selfish to stand up with me. And that company promised me discretion. That no one would know. Then the owner, Rachel Vinson, gets splashed all over the internet and shows up at my wedding! Everyone knew that I had to hire bridesmaids! I've never been so humiliated in my entire life. She ruined everything. I am going to sue her and shut her and her deceitful operation down."

That made me feel sick. All I ever tried to do was give women the weddings of their dreams and support them. And here was someone saying that I'd wrecked her day.

My doorbell buzzed, and for one heart-stopping moment, I hoped it was Camden. I let myself entertain a brief fantasy that somehow he'd shown up and would take me in his arms and make all of this okay. But that was stupid. He'd made it pretty clear things were over and hadn't rushed back to New York just to look me up.

I went over to the door and pushed the button. "Yeah?"

"It's me." Krista. "I have something you're going to want. Let me up."

I was tempted to tell her to go away but was too intrigued by what she might have. I pushed the buzzer to let her in the front entrance and unlocked my apartment door for her.

My faith was rewarded when she walked in with a pizza from Waldy's, one of my favorite places in the city.

"Pepperoni, extra sauce, and light cheese," she said. "Just the way you like it."

She set it down on my kitchen counter and I folded my arms. "I feel like this is an information pizza."

"It absolutely is an information pizza," she said, walking over to my couch and getting comfortable. "But in both receiving and giving info. Because I'm guessing you haven't been online recently and I think there's something you should see."

I got out two plates and grabbed slices for both of us and then joined her on the couch. "Oh, trust me, I've been online. I've seen all the carnage. I'm well aware of the fact that we're about to be sued into oblivion and that we may all be out of a job tomorrow."

She took her plate and set it down on her lap. "I'm talking about this." She showed me her phone, and there was a clip of Sadie talking. My heart pounded painfully in my chest, worried about how much more damage she could do.

"Sadie must be so mad at me," I said.

Krista ignored me and turned up the volume on her phone, and Sadie's voice filled the room.

"Hey, everyone. Well, I guess you've all seen my wedding footage by now. I left early so I think most of you saw it before I did. But there's two things you need to know. First, that my mother is an adult and made her own choices. She has personal issues that affect me and my family. I know I've hidden that part of my life from everyone, and I shouldn't have because I'm not the only person dealing with something like this and should have shared. Maybe I could have helped someone. Maybe you could have helped me. I don't know.

"And two, Rachel Vinson is a goddess. Because of my mom and her addiction, I've always kept people at arm's length. I don't have really close friends that I could ask to stand up with me on the most important day of my life. I heard about Rachel and her business, which is ingenious, by the way, and hiring her was one of the best things I've ever done. She and all of the women she works with are amazing and you guys would be lucky to hire her. I've talked to so many of you online about your weddings, about your bridesmaids getting wasted or being petty or just acting awful and making your wedding day harder. I didn't have any of that. I had the best support system in the world who did nothing but put me first. Rachel did everything in her power to make this the most unbelievable wedding ever. Even when things went wrong, and they so obviously did, she always had my back. I'm so thankful to her. I didn't just have an amazing maid of honor, I got a new friend."

Sadie was supposed to be on her modified honeymoon, enjoying her new husband. Instead she was online, defending me.

It was then that the tears finally broke free, like an overflowing river breaching a dam. I'd been holding them in for so long, I couldn't stop. My chest heaved and ached, my throat burning. Krista scooted over and put her arms around me, hugging me as I sobbed.

I had truly prepared for Sadie to throw me under the bus in order to protect herself and her brand. I should have known better. I should have given her the benefit of the doubt.

Once I'd turned myself into a soggy, snotty mess, Krista got up to grab me some paper towels so that I could clean up my now slightly swollen face. My eyes hurt. I wondered if they were puffy and bloodshot.

"I can't believe she did that," I said.

Krista replied, "I can. Everything she said was true. You twisted yourself into knots for her."

"But I didn't prevent all of that stuff from happening. I should have."

She frowned at me. "I love you, but that is so idiotic. You can't control other people and you can't control the world, either."

"I just really messed up." Because I had been distracted by falling in love with Camden Lewis, but there was no way I could speak his name, given my current state. I was only barely hanging on and was so close to another huge emotional outburst.

"What is the deeper thing going on here?" Krista asked. "Why do you always have to succeed? Is this about trying to please your unpleasable parents?"

"What makes you say that?"

"So many things in our life go back to our parents. My mom married an abusive man and I ended up following in her footsteps, reliving some of the same patterns. We can't let that kind of stuff have control over us."

I had to admit that she was right. I knew my parents adored me, but I often felt like I'd failed them in one aspect or another. Yes, I'd won a position in student government, but my mom had wanted to know why it was only for treasurer and not president. Yes, it was great that I'd been accepted to UCLA, but why didn't I get a full-ride scholarship? How nice for me that I'd started my own business and employed over a dozen people, but what about that whole grandchildren thing?

My mom was only human and probably had her own insecurities and issues that affected her and made her behave the way she did. Because I loved her, it was easy enough to forgive, but maybe Krista was right and I needed to examine and undo the ways that it had wormed into my life and made me feel panicked about failing.

About a potentially fantastic relationship failing before I had even given it a chance.

Krista handed me another paper towel. "You did the best you could and that's all anyone can ask of you."

"Maybe it's part of being an only child," I said.

"Maybe." She nodded. "But I don't know what that's like. I have four sisters and they're all pains in my butt."

That struck me as funny and I laughed. It was the first time I'd laughed in the last twenty-four hours and I was grateful for it. Then I remembered my situation and sobered up. "We don't know what's going to happen with the company."

"One thing at a time," she told me. Then she sat silently for a moment, as if carefully considering what to say next. "What about Camden?"

His name was like a knife being plunged into my gut. I actually scooted back on the couch, as if I could get away from the pain. "I don't want to talk about him."

Because I could think about Sadie and what had happened at the wedding and it was upsetting, but it wasn't world-ending. And when I thought about Camden . . . it was just more than I could bear.

I didn't want to think about moving forward with a life that didn't include him.

I couldn't let myself go down that path.

"Just tell me what happened. You should tell someone."

She was right. I'd already shed every tear that had been stored up inside me, so maybe I could get through this without completely breaking down. So I confided in her, telling her all the details of what had happened, what he'd said, how he was finished with me. With us.

"Where do you get that from?" she asked. "He didn't say he wanted to break up with you."

"I inferred it from him walking away from me. I'm pretty good at reading those kinds of obvious signals." He didn't stay and fight. That was the part that mattered.

She frowned at me. "Maybe he just needed a second."

"Well, he's had lots of those."

"Okay," she said in a tone that clearly said she didn't agree with me. "But you didn't stay and fight. You walked away, too."

Color rose in my cheeks. "I didn't. I had a job to do."

"You know you always do that, right? Make everything in your life about work. It was okay to like Camden. It was okay to feel hurt that he walked off. What's not okay is blaming him."

Despite my deep denial, even I could recognize the truth in her words. "He hasn't texted or called."

"Doesn't he have that big business deal he has to worry about? While dealing with a broken heart because you left him without a word? Plus, if I know you, and I do, you haven't texted or called him, either."

It was like her words had slapped me across the face. I actually put a hand up to my cheek, as if it were stinging with shock. I'd been so focused on myself I hadn't thought about what Camden might be going through. Even though I wanted to tell myself differently, he'd had real feelings for me. Was he feeling the same kind of heartbreak right now?

And I'd fled, like a thief in the night, trying to escape my crime scene and avoid paying for my mistakes.

I should have been braver. "He must be so mad." I whispered the words.

"You thought Sadie was mad at you, but look at what happened there."

"It's not like Camden can make a video where he tells the world he loves me. He doesn't have social media. Plus, I'm pretty sure cameras hadn't been invented yet when he bought his phone." Joking about his flip phone brought that stabbing feeling back. Was I ever going to feel like myself again? Or would there always be a part of me that missed him?

"You're the one who is always telling me to never give up," she reminded me. "Maybe you shouldn't give up with him, either."

All of this pain and heartache was happening because I couldn't stick to my boundaries. "I shouldn't have broken my rule." Everything could have been avoided. Well, the reception might still have gone up in flames, but my heart wouldn't be like a block of ice that had been dropped on the floor and shattered into a thousand pieces.

"Your rule is stupid," Krista told me for the thousandth time. "Do you know how much socializing goes on at weddings? How everywhere you look it's all love and romance? It's a fantastic place to meet men. I totally made out with that Rick guy."

My eyes went wide. "Dan's cousin, who you said was going to get back together with his girlfriend?"

"He probably did. Rachel, it was just kissing and it was fun. Technically I didn't break your rule," she said.

"My rule isn't supposed to have loopholes." Although that hadn't stopped me from throwing it out the window so that I could spend time with Camden. The pain pierced me again. I couldn't think about him.

So instead I asked her, "Do you want to watch a movie with me?" I needed the distraction. If she left me alone with my thoughts, not only was I going to eat an entire large Waldy's pizza by myself, but I would completely obsess over Camden. Reliving what had happened, thinking of all the ways I could have fixed it sooner but didn't. How if I'd forgotten all about my stupid rule and taken a chance with him earlier, I could have asked Sadie for her help and things would have been fine.

I guessed now I would never know and I had only myself to blame.

Krista said yes, so we watched a romantic comedy that didn't seem romantic or comedic to me, but it was better than sitting alone, overstuffed and super sad. Or thinking about how the last movie I'd watched had been with Camden.

My phone buzzed at me, but I reached over and turned it off without looking at it. Tonight I was going to forget about the rest of the world.

I would resume my workplace-drama, broken-heart, and existential-crisis issues in the morning.

CHAPTER THIRTY-TWO

The next morning when I woke up, I felt totally different. The throbbing pain and loss were still there, but I had messed up with Camden, too. I'd been afraid and let my fear of rejection and failure drive me away from him. I'd had all my excuses, but in the end they didn't add up to a whole lot other than what I'd so stupidly given up.

I was going to call him. After I did what I could to straighten out the rest of my life.

My first stop was Gerald's office. He'd received my messages over the weekend and was already hard at work on our defense if we were served. We talked about the possible repercussions, like what would happen if we had to go to court. Unfortunately at the moment we were in a holding position, waiting for the Vinnie- and Amber-type clients to file suits against us.

I told him about my fear that my business would fold, as we'd relied on discretion. I couldn't see anyone wanting to hire us again. Gerald, ever the realist, agreed with me that it might be a possibility and said he'd work on next steps.

It was depressing news, but at least I had a game plan. As Krista had kept reminding me, I wasn't in control. But if I made plans the best I could and kept moving forward, things would be okay.

On my way to the office, my mom called me. I felt a twinge of guilt that I hadn't been returning her calls. Before I could even say hello or acknowledge her, she said, "You're one of those internet means."

"It's *meme*, Mom."

"Mememom?" she repeated.

"No, it's just *meme*. I was—" I stepped off the curb to cross the street and decided that I didn't have it in me to explain what I meant. I already felt emotionally spent and it was only ten o'clock in the morning. "Don't worry about it. Some celebrity will get pregnant or go to rehab or reveal that they're a secret cannibal and then people will forget all about me."

"You've worked so hard to be successful and keep things secret and now it's everywhere. People are making fun of you and that wedding. I'm upset for you."

That made two of us, but I didn't need her to get riled up in my defense. "I promise that everything is going to be okay." It probably wasn't something I should be promising, but she wasn't the only one who needed to hear it.

"We just worry about you."

"I know you do." And I understood that her worry and wanting me to be the best were another way for her to say that she loved me.

"I hope you know that all Dad and I want is for you to be happy."

Stopping in front of my favorite bakery, I smiled, even though she couldn't see me. "I do know that, Mom. I'll call you later."

I ordered two dozen doughnuts and waited while they boxed them up for me. I found my mind drifting and I wondered what Camden was doing right then. He still had his company going public this week. He had to be really busy, especially considering all the phone calls he'd ignored while we'd been together. He might have a ton of fires to put out.

Had any of these videos blown back on their company? He had been very concerned about how investors perceived their reputation. I hoped none of this had affected them.

Maybe I should wait to call him until after his deal went through. He already had so much on his plate.

I paid for my order and the clerk handed me my boxes and then I walked the two blocks to my office. When I got to my floor I didn't go through the front doors, preferring to sneak in through the back entrance that was directly next to my office. I'd emailed the receptionist, Brinley, early this morning to have her call everyone and tell them to come in for a staff meeting. The doughnuts were my feeble attempt to make sugary amends for everything that had gone down.

After making my way to the conference room, I found to my surprise that everyone had already arrived. They seemed like they'd been talking for a while.

I stood in the doorway for a second and heard my most recent hire, Heather, say, "He was the cutest guy ever and wanted to take me out. I said no because of Rachel's rule but I really wanted to go."

Her words struck me. That rule, based on something that had happened to me years ago, was stupid. I was so shut off from relationships and the possibility of meeting someone new that I'd clung to it in order to deny my growing feelings for Camden.

Dan had given Camden a dumb rule, and Camden had totally ignored it. I was Dan, trying to stop my employees and friends from living their lives and flirting with people they met at weddings. As if I could control any of that. I hadn't even been able to control it for myself.

I'd been at fault for more than one thing.

Someone noticed me and shushed the other women. I had anticipated getting here before all of them, but Krista's knowing grin made me think she was responsible for everyone gathering early.

I put the doughnuts on the table and it seemed like such a small gesture in light of what was going on. There was no way for me to make this better for them.

"Thanks, everybody, for coming," I said as I walked to the head of the table. I didn't sit down; I had too much nervous energy to do anything but pace back and forth.

"You don't need to say anything," Krista told me. "We are all a hundred percent on your side and will do whatever you need us to do."

"I don't know that it will be that easy. I promise that I'm going to be transparent in every decision I make and get your input. This is your company, too. We are all in this together."

Desiree raised her hand, like we were in a classroom, and then spoke. "What's going to happen?"

"Gerald doesn't have any answers yet. Unfortunately I think we're going to have to wait and see. We'll reach out to the brides who have already hired us and see how they're feeling about going forward. If we're able to stay in business, things are going to change."

It was time to let things go. I couldn't be in control of everything. I continued, "Our rule about secrecy will most likely change. That and the no-dating-guests rule."

There were a couple of gasps and some little cheers.

"I know how you guys feel about it. I was just afraid that if you got involved with someone from a wedding we'd get caught if we slipped up. Which happened anyways. I just wanted to, I don't know, protect you guys."

Desiree said with a patient smile, "We don't need your protection. We are grown women who can take care of ourselves."

"I know that. I wasn't trying to imply otherwise." I took a deep breath, willing myself not to get emotional. Did they know how important they were to me?

"And we appreciate it," Krista interjected. "We know how much you care." There was a murmur of agreement from the rest of the group.

"Thanks," I said. "And we are where we are. We made our bed, and I guess now we have to lie in it."

Krista said, "At least we did a really good job of it. There's a fancy comforter and a bed skirt and pillows no one's allowed to sleep on."

"Thanks, guys," I said with a smile. "Get in touch with the brides you're currently working with and I'll meet with you individually later to see where things stand." People got up, some left the room, others grabbed doughnuts. Krista came over and hugged me, correctly sensing that I needed it.

She walked back to my office with me. "Can I get you anything? A coffee? Crumbs from the doughnuts that haven't been devoured yet?"

"I'm good. Thank you." I had some damage control to do. Gerald had advised against me contacting Bridezilla Amber or Angry Vinnie. He wanted me to do all my communication with them through him and I didn't pay the man hundreds of dollars an hour to ignore his advice. But there were other clients, both current and former, that I could reach out to.

Brinley burst into my office, carrying a stack of pink notes. "Rachel! You're here! I didn't know you were here!"

"I came in the back," I said, pointing over my shoulder. "What's up?"

"What is up?" she repeated, pushing her glasses back up her nose. "Do you see this? There is a pile of voice mails and messages that I've taken this morning."

My stomach sank. "From clients who are upset?"

"What? No. This is from people who want to hire us." She shoved the pink messages into my hands. "People are clamoring for our services. And we've had at least thirty different phone calls from media outlets—newspapers, magazines, online sites—who want to talk to us about what we do. They're calling you a genius for 'filling an obvious need in the market.' This has blown up in the best way possible!"

I sat down in my chair, ready to put my head between my knees. This was such good news. Such. Good. News. I'd thought I'd ruined everything and to find out that I hadn't? I couldn't remember the last time I'd felt so relieved.

"I'm going to tell everyone," Krista said.

I got her inclination. I sort of wanted to do that, too.

Brinley handed me another message. "This woman said you have to call her first, right away. That it's very important. She made me swear."

My first thought was that my mom had gotten impatient, but then I saw the name. Sadie.

I dialed her number immediately and Brinley left my office, closing the door behind her.

Sadie answered on the first ring. "Hello?"

"It's Rachel! How are you?"

"I'm great. It's you I'm worried about. I left you a couple of voice mails. How are you?"

I got that throat-thickening sensation, but I wasn't going to cry. "I've been better. I saw your video. Thank you for that. I was so worried that my entire company would immediately fold, but our phone has apparently been ringing off the hook with people who want to hire us."

"You should see my DMs and email! So many people want to talk to me about this. They're saying I'm a trendsetter. I've added like, a hundred thousand new followers since the reception."

"That is fantastic!" I was thrilled that something good had come out of all this mess.

"Not only that, but my mom was able to see how she was acting and she's been talking about going to rehab. I don't know if she actually will, but I'm really hopeful that this time things might be different."

"Sadie, that makes me so happy for you."

"Thank you." She paused, as if waiting for me to say something in return, but then went on. "Anyway, I was just calling to check on you. To see how you were doing and if anything's changed. You know, in your life."

I'd just told her how much better things were. That was kind of a weird thing to say.

She kept on in that sort of rambling tone. "So . . . I'm going to get back to Dan. Let's keep in touch, okay?"

I promised I would and hung up my phone. I started thumbing through the messages, excited that even if we were sued we might still be able to find a way to stay in business.

Brinley buzzed my phone and I pushed the intercom button. "Yes?"

"There's someone here in the conference room that wants to talk to you about an event on Friday."

"Thank you!" It was kind of last minute, but we'd certainly done it before. I stood up and my office phone buzzed again from Krista's extension.

When I pushed the button she said, "Sadie and Krista ex machina for the win!" and hung up.

What was that supposed to mean? I nearly called her back for an explanation but I wasn't in a position to keep a potential client waiting. I walked into the conference room and my heart came to a complete and total stop when I saw who was standing there.

Camden.

CHAPTER THIRTY-THREE

This was what Krista had meant and why Sadie had been strange. They'd set this up.

He stood there in a slate-gray suit that looked like it had been tailored specifically for him. He was impossibly handsome and I was having a hard time breathing.

"Hello, Rachel."

For a second I thought maybe I was hallucinating from lack of sleep but when he spoke his voice had that melting effect on my knees and I knew that it was him. He was here.

"Why?" I asked, and then modified it because he couldn't hear what I was thinking in my head. "Why are you here?"

He smiled mysteriously. I'd missed him so much that I was aching from it. I wanted nothing more than to run across the room and launch myself at him.

"I thought you never wanted to see me again," I said, unable to keep the hurt tone out of my voice.

"I never said that, Rachel."

"But . . ." How could I explain everything in just a few words? "You walked away."

"I said I needed a walk, not that I never wanted to speak to you again."

Oh. That was true but . . . "You didn't call me." I left out the part where I hadn't called him, either, even though I'd really wanted to.

"You're right. I didn't. Because what I have to say has to be said in person." He undid the button on his coat and then put his hands into his pants pockets, like he was preparing for something. "I talked with Sadie. She told me everything."

"Okay." I wrapped my arms around my chest, not knowing where this was going.

"I wish you'd stayed so that we could have talked things through." I wished that, too. I was so afraid of being that vulnerable that I'd flown thousands of miles away from him. He went on, "And I wish that I hadn't gone for that walk. That I'd given you a chance to explain. It was just sort of like all of my worst fears were being confirmed and that you'd been using me and I was too stupid to figure it out."

"I know how afraid you've been for this deal. I get it. It's one of the reasons I was scared to tell you. Given your past and what you were going through I thought you wouldn't be able to forgive me."

"Rachel." He shook his head and there was so much tenderness in his gaze that I let my arms drop and only just refrained from going over to hug him. "You were lying about something that you were legally obligated to lie about. I'm not angry about that. I just wish that you hadn't made up your mind as to how I'd react without even giving me a chance."

"You're right," I agreed. "I shouldn't have done that."

"I promise from now on that I will always stay and listen. I'm also sorry that I hurt you. That is the absolute last thing I would ever want to do. Can you forgive me?"

I had a hard enough time resisting him when I wasn't allowed to be with him. Now that all those restrictions were gone? How could I say no? "Of course I can. But only if you forgive me, too."

"There's nothing to forgive," he said as he started to slowly walk toward me. "It seems like we both run away from things that make us uncomfortable. I promise to stop, if you will, too. At least with each other."

He got so close to me that it took every bit of strength I possessed not to wrap myself around him. "I kind of want to run away right now," I confessed.

Camden reached up and put his hand on the side of my face, and I leaned into his touch. "That's fine. Whenever you feel like you need to run, know that I'll always understand. And that I'll come and find you."

I breathed his name, so thankful to have him here. "You're really not mad that I lied?"

"Rachel, the things I know about you, the things I can't live without, not one of those has anything to do with you being Sadie's friend. I would still feel this way even if there hadn't been any wedding. No Sadie and no Dan, if we'd met at a party or in a bar this thing between us still would have happened. I liked you from the first time we met and used my suspicions as an excuse to get close to you."

"I used the NDA as my excuse to keep my distance," I told him. "That and the whole not-dating-wedding-guests thing, which isn't a rule anymore."

"Good. But I think we didn't finish up our truth game. There are some things about me you should know." He put his hands on my waist, pulling me closer, and I breathed him in, happily. "I snore. I'm kind of a slob. I work too much."

"Me? I sleep like the dead. I find cleaning therapeutic. And I work too much, too."

"Maybe we can remind each other to slow down." He touched my hair. "When we're not in your office, maybe you can take this down for me."

Anticipatory tingles shot through me. "Or you could do it."

He kissed me on my nose. "Looking forward to it. Is there anything else you think we should say right now?"

"Maybe we should promise that we won't lie to each other again."

"Who wants a relationship based on honesty and actual communication? Ick," he teased.

My heart beat so hard in my chest I worried I might pass out. He had gone for a walk, but I was the one who had abandoned him more. I'd flown across an ocean and an entire continent to avoid my feelings for him. Maybe it was because of my parents' expectations, but I'd never been very good with failing or self-forgiveness. I held everything in my life to an unrealistic standard of perfection.

Maybe it was time to change that. To let myself be vulnerable with him. To take that terrifying risk. Even if he didn't feel the same and ran off screaming. "Honesty is important. I always want to be honest with you." I took a deep breath and then said, "I love you."

And whatever I feared or hoped for, he surprised me, leaving me on that ledge alone, not saying anything. His eyes softened, his arms tightened around me, but for a nerve-destroying moment he didn't speak.

Until he did. "I have something for you." Then he reached inside his coat pocket and took out a tiny scroll of rolled-up paper and handed it to me. "Here. For your happy box."

I was still so scared, so unsure, and my hands trembled as I opened it and read it out loud. "You make me laugh."

What? Then he gave me another one. "You are so talented and brilliant."

And another. "The happiest I've ever been is with you."

"I admire you."

"You are beautiful."

Then there was one more scroll. "This is the most important one," he said.

I pushed the edges apart and my voice caught as I read, "I'm in love with you."

He smirked, like he'd made me say something I hadn't already confessed to. "You love me."

"You love me, too," I retorted.

"Potato, tomato."

At that I laughed and threw my arms around his neck, holding tightly to his messages. I was going to keep those notes for forever.

Him, too, if he'd let me.

"I really do love you," I said, experiencing such relief at finally being able to express what I'd been feeling for him.

"I know."

"So I guess this means I like mildew."

He knit his eyebrows together. "What?"

"You said you'd grow on me like mildew."

Recognition flooded his features. "I did. And I was right. Like always."

"Let's not get ahead of ourselves," I said. We didn't need to start this relationship off with Camden thinking he was always right.

"Your receptionist said you had this Friday free. I'm going to assume that's true for every Friday for the rest of our lives."

Happiness spread through me like a warm honey, filling every crevice until there was nothing inside me but love and light. "I'll have to check my calendar."

His arms tightened around me. "You do that. But I think if I don't kiss you soon, our audience is going to riot."

"What?" I turned my head to see every single one of my employees lined up, watching us through the glass windows like we were their own personal soap opera. Krista was eating the last Bavarian cream and she gave me a big thumbs-up with her free hand.

Camden turned my chin back toward him and captured my mouth with his. I melted against him. Why was it so much more powerful and amazing now that there was a declared emotion behind it? If even a tiny part of me had questioned whether he really was in love with me, that kiss erased all doubt.

He broke away when everybody outside started cheering and chanting my name. He laughed and I traced the outline of the dimple in his left cheek.

Then he said, "So I know you hate it when I ask you questions, but I have this really big one that I'm going to ask you in the not-so-distant future, if that's okay with you. Just so you know."

I couldn't help myself. I absolutely beamed at him.

"What are you grinning about?" he asked, teasing.

"My mom is going to be so happy."

EPILOGUE

One year later . . .

I sat on the couch, impatiently waiting for Camden to come home. We'd made each other a promise that we'd always be home by seven o'clock at night, no matter what. Even if we had to bring work home with us, we'd decided to make spending time together a priority.

I was supposed to be doing work right now, but I was way too distracted. I nudged the large stack of résumés sitting on my coffee table with my toe, wishing they would disappear.

Things had been going so well for me. Bridezilla Amber never filed suit when Gerald pointed out that, unlike Sadie's NDA, Amber's non-disclosure agreement prevented her from speaking about our arrangement. (Each NDA was customized differently with each bride.) She had publicly outed me and he had been excited at the idea of suing for breach of contract. I'd told him no, that I wanted to focus on the positive. I did make her submit an apology and had gotten more than my fair share of pleasure from that.

At Gerald's direction I still hadn't broken any of my NDAs, so there was no fear of a lawsuit. I turned down all the media requests, but they found other people who were willing and able to talk about my services and my business had continued to grow. We'd hired a dozen new employees in the last six months and the résumés I had were so that we could hire at least five more.

Camden had also been talking to me about franchising, a possibility that excited me. I was going to have my own little empire.

Instead of getting the résumés, I reached for our wedding photo album. I was feeling particularly nostalgic today, and I flipped through the pages slowly. I'd hired Troy to be my wedding planner and had done my best to keep it simple. Which hadn't been easy with fifteen bridesmaids. Krista had been my maid of honor and all of my other employees had insisted they be part of my big day. Sadie had served as a bridesmaid, too, given how close she and I had become. Her baby bump was adorably small in each of the pictures.

Camden looked perfect in every shot, and I ran my hand across a photo of us kissing right after the minister had declared us husband and wife. I also loved the one just after that, where Camden stopped to hug Irene as we walked back down the aisle. She jokingly called the peach fuzz on her head her "Chia Pet hair," but we were all just beyond relieved that she'd gone into remission and had come to the wedding happy and healthy.

My mom had spent most of the day crying with joy. I didn't think there was a single picture where she wasn't crying. The questions about grandchildren had tapered off because she'd gone back to school to get her master's degree in special education and her days were currently filled with precious kids. "Have to get my fix somehow," she was fond of saying.

Belle, Camden's cat, who now loved me the most, jumped into my lap, purring. It was as if she knew something had changed with me.

I stroked her head and glanced up at the clock. It was 7:02. Somebody was going to be in trouble. I lived for this time of day. Today, especially. We were both so busy, Camden even more so after his successful IPO. But we always had dinner together and discussed our wins and losses, our hopes and our fears. In the quiet part of our evening we talked, laughed, and loved. No one understood me like he did.

Which he proved when he walked in the door. "Sorry I'm a little late! But in my defense I brought you pizza."

"If I wasn't married to you already, I'd marry you again," I told him. I put Belle on the couch and came over to greet him, kissing him hello and then following him into our kitchen.

He got out plates and set them on the table, finally noticing what I'd put there for him. "What's this?" he asked.

It was a line of rolled-up pieces of paper. "Open them and find out."

Camden picked up the first one. "You."

Then the second. "Are."

"Going," he read, then got another. "To."

"Be," he said. "This is taking a really long time."

"It's how you asked me to marry you," I reminded him.

"Right. But *will you marry me* is only four words. This is like a novel."

"Keep reading," I said.

He unrolled the sixth one. "A. Okay, I feel like you could have added another word to this one and used less paper."

I pointed to the seventh rolled-up piece of paper. "Just open it, wise guy."

"Father," he read, and it was like it didn't register at first.

To be honest, I was more than a little bit nervous as to how he'd react. We both definitely wanted kids, but we had decided to wait. Until things calmed down a bit for us professionally. We'd been married for only a month and this didn't figure into any of our plans.

But I'd already learned long ago that I had to let go of trying to stick to a plan and let life happen, and I was beyond thrilled to be having a baby. It was one of the best things that had ever happened to me, and I hoped he would share in my joy.

The timing wasn't great, but I knew we could get through anything because we were a fantastic team.

"I'm going to be a dad?" he asked, sounding bewildered.

I nodded, both worried and excited, all at the same time.

Then he came over to me and picked me up, holding me against him. "Are you serious? You're pregnant?"

"Yes. Are you okay with it?"

He kissed me. Then he kissed me again. And again. "Okay with it? I'm deliriously happy! You're having my baby! You are going to be the best mother ever."

I was so relieved and so happy. "And you will be a great dad."

It was like I got a little glimpse into our future and in my mind I could see Camden running and laughing with a toddler, lifting her up into the air while she giggled. He was going to be such a fun and loving father.

He put me down and looked around, and then dived onto the couch. It took me a second to figure out what he was doing. He had grabbed my phone.

"Ha!" he said. "I get to call your mom."

"She's my mom," I reminded him, but he didn't seem to hear me. That was probably due in part to the fact that my parents had basically become his parents, too. I suspected they might like him better than me. The dogs certainly did.

"I want to be her favorite son-in-law."

"You're her only son-in-law."

"Which means I can be her least favorite, too." He had such a pleading look in his eyes that there was no way I could tell him no.

"Fine. You can tell her." It honestly didn't matter which one of us it came from. She was probably going to have a heart attack when she heard.

He grinned and turned on my phone, dialing the number. "Mom? Hi! Guess what?"

AUTHOR'S NOTE

Thank you for reading my story! I hope you liked getting to know Camden and Rachel and enjoyed them falling in love as much as I did. If you'd like to find out when I've written something new, make sure you sign up for my newsletter at www.sariahwilson.com, where I most definitely will not spam you. (I'm happy when I send out a newsletter once a month!)

And if you feel so inclined, I'd love for you to leave a review on Amazon, on Goodreads, with your hairdresser's cousin's roommate's blog, via a skywriter, in graffiti on the side of a bookstore, on the back of your electric bill, or any other place you want. I would be so grateful. Thanks!

ACKNOWLEDGMENTS

For everyone who is reading this—thank you. I can't tell you how much your support means to me—it is often quite literally the thing that keeps me going when the writing is hard. Hoping that you will enjoy and laugh and swoon and that for a short, brief amount of time, I maybe made your burdens a little easier to bear.

A huge thank-you to Alison Dasho—I'm so grateful for all of your support and input and the way you always guide me in the best possible direction. I'm beyond thankful that I get to work with you and the entire phenomenal Montlake team (Anh Schluep, Lauren Grange, Kris Beecroft, Leonard Sampson, Jillian Cline, Andrew George, Erin Calligan Mooney, and Jessica Preeg). As always, thank you to Charlotte Herscher, whom I wish was sitting next to me when I was writing this manuscript the first time so that I could have added your and Alison's brilliant suggestions.

Thank you to the copyeditors and proofreaders who find all my mistakes and continuity errors and gently guide me in the right direction (Kellie Osborne, Sarah Vostok, and Tara Whitaker). A special shout-out to Philip Pascuzzo for this absolutely delightful cover. It captures the book perfectly!

For my agent, Sarah Younger—you are simply the best and make everything in my professional life better. Thank you for letting me complain and fret and always cheering me on. Every author should be so lucky to have an agent like you!

Thank you to Dana, Julia, and Hailey of Dana Kaye Publicity for everything you guys do and the way that you keep me on track and for all the great advice.

My Facebook readers' group—I'm so grateful for the support and kind words and all the reviews you leave for me. You guys help me out so much when I'm doubting myself!

For my kids—you are the light in my life and I'm so grateful that I get to be your mom.

And Kevin, you're still the best thing that's ever happened to me.

ABOUT THE AUTHOR

Photo © 2020 Jordan Batt

Sariah Wilson is the *USA Today* bestselling author of *The Seat Filler*, *Roommaid*, *Just a Boyfriend*, the Royals of Monterra series, and the #Lovestruck novels. She has never jumped out of an airplane, has never climbed Mount Everest, and is not a former CIA operative. She has, however, been madly, passionately in love with her soul mate and is a fervent believer in happily ever afters—which is why she writes romance. She grew up in Southern California, graduated from Brigham Young University (go Cougars!) with a semi-useless degree in history, and is the oldest of nine (yes, nine). She currently lives with the aforementioned soul mate and their children in Utah, along with three cats named Pixel, Callie, and Belle, who do not get along (the cats, not the kids—although the kids sometimes have their issues, too). For more information, visit her website at www.sariahwilson.com.